The Drowning of Innocence

Pádraig O'Gorman

Icon O'Clast Press

REVIEWS OF "THE DROWNING OF INNOCENCE

"This novel accompanied me beautifully through my summer travels and holidays. I absolutely ATE it! The tenderness and passion with which it has been written. I enjoyed meandering with the lives of the characters, and learning more about this difficult history through their eyes. I loved the aliveness in the environment and its creatures, which was so rich and often felt as though it were another person witnessing and absorbing all that was happening."
Tara, London

"Riveting. Caught up with the characters and story from the beginning. The intimacy and loss experienced in Michael and Eileen's relationship was, for me, quite emotional, I did cry. Very moving and beautifully written. I was placed there alongside them, almost embarrassingly so at times. I loved the character of Father Paul. I thought it would be nice to have someone like that in my life. I very much liked the way the story was laid out. Couldn't wait to find out how things were going to turn out for each of the characters. Also, for me, there was a lot more to the history of Ireland and it's troubles than I had known. Sorry about the English, what can I say."
Mick, New Jersey

"Just finished The Drowning of Innocence. Absolutely excellent, couldn't put it down. I could relate well to the historic background of the story as I have done a little research myself. I had an uncle who was involved with Michael Collins, but this novel added so much more detail and the story-line right along the way was gripping."
Liam, Brussels

"An absorbing novel, sensitively written. The book pulled me in and I found it hard to put it down. The lovers accept their fate as sacrifices have to be made for an independent Ireland. The mood of the time comes across beautifully, with sorrow but no regrets, capturing a mysticism which appears to wrap up the heart, body and soul of Irish people. A very good read."
Julie, Nottingham

"This story is multi-layered and the characters multifaceted. I laughed with them and I cried with them. Their spirituality shines through in lines that are sublime.
'A day replete with intrinsic immanence to capture the heart and soul',
'the essence of the mystery of the eternal in the now'.
But the tragedy of the history recounted is almost too sad for words:
'a division of bitterness that would wound immeasurably and hopelessly all their desires and dreams'.
I thought Gerard Manley Hopkins' God's Grandeur was a perfect expression of the hope we have, and The Pogues "And The Band Played Waltzing Matilda" (actually written by an Aussie, Eric Bogle,) perfectly expressed the despair we share."
Dave, Brisbane

"So, I took this novel down to the river today to finish it. I really liked the second half. I had guessed very early on how the characters linked together so it was interesting to see how the plot slowly unravelled to reach a satisfying conclusion. The emotion of finding a birth family after the search was very poignant and realistically written. I also liked the fact that one single action determines our fate for the rest of our lives and often once the die is cast there is no turning back, reconciliation and often no forgiveness of self."
Sue London

"I loved this novel. I got it last Saturday and could not put it down. I loved the characters and the flowers. Way back on my mother's side were Huguenots who left France because of religious persecution, stopped in Holland and sailed to Virginia in the 1650's. My ex-husband's grandparents were Irish Catholic and came to NYC in the 1920's. His grandfather has been a signal person on a ship in WWI. I wonder what more of their story was. They met over here. Anyway, I had lots of connections with the story. So glad I could read it."
Barbara, Michigan

"I have loved this novel. It really has stayed with me since I finished it and I've been thinking about it a lot. I love the way scenes are described from different angles, like a Picasso painting, and emotions are gradually drawn to a pinpoint. The ending made me cry too, in a good way, it was very powerful."
Caroline, Loughborough

"I have just finished this novel. I started it as soon as I bought it, got half way through & decided "No this is a book I wanted to read whilst totally relaxed with no interruptions" so I brought it along on the cruise and finished it within 2 days. What can I say, wow, I was there in that book, what an amazing piece of writing. Not only did it open my eyes to the troubles all those years ago in Ireland (which I am ashamed to say I wasn't too familiar with to the extent of detail in this story) but also the entwinement & coming together of the families at the end, it was so heart warming that I wanted it to carry on (although I don't know how!)"
Linda, Nottingham

"I bought this novel this week and managed to read it on Friday, sitting in my car in the middle of town. I found it very moving in many places and would like to thank you for writing it."
Michael, Bantry

"What a feat! The novelist shows incredible narrative skill, taking on so many pillars of 20th century Irish and World history and life and weaving a sweeping plot so tightly together. Equally, I really do admire all that incredible research which underlies the whole historical backdrop. A great feel for language into the bargain. And of course the music references – they very adroitly aid and abet the plot and the characters themselves as well of course of underlining precise moments in time. In short: the author is some artist.
Michael, Madrid

"The Drowning of Innocence weaves the dark history of The Irish War of Independence with all it's facts and realities, with a softer story of love and resilience. This book is cleverly written as it provides the reader with a multi-dimensional view to war, and is told with emotion, imagination and balance."
Julie, Cork

First Published 2017

by Icon O'Clast Press,

29, Bamba Street,

Clonakilty,

Cork, P85FP60

Ireland

Content copyright © Pádraig O'Gorman 2017

Illustrations copyright © Emily Catherine 2017

The events covered by this work of fiction were and remain controversial. The depiction of these events and the historical characters are the result of the author's imagination applied to detailed research and study. The main characters of the story are fictional and any resemblance to persons, living or dead, are purely coincidental.

All rights reserved. No portion of this book may be reproduced, stored in a retrieval system or transmitted at any time or by any means, mechanical, electronic, photocopying, recording or otherwise, without the prior, written permission of the publisher.

ISBN 978-0-9957843-9-0

Book cover and other illustrations by Emily Catherine.

www.emilycatherineillustration.com

Doodles by Sue Kohler.

First print June 2017

2nd print 2024

Thank you for supporting independent publishing

For Ezra

"Turning and turning in the widening gyre
The falcon cannot hear the falconer;
Things fall apart; the centre cannot hold;
Mere anarchy is loosed upon the world,
The blood-dimmed tide is loosed, and everywhere
The ceremony of innocence is drowned;
The best lack all conviction, while the worst
Are full of passionate intensity.
Surely some revelation is at hand;
Surely the Second Coming is at hand.
The Second Coming! Hardly are those words out
When a vast image out of Spiritus Mundi
Troubles my sight: somewhere in sands of the desert
A shape with lion body and the head of a man,
A gaze blank and pitiless as the sun,
Is moving its slow thighs, while all about it
Reel shadows of the indignant desert birds.
The darkness drops again; but now I know
That twenty centuries of stony sleep
Were vexed to nightmare by a rocking cradle,
And what rough beast, its hour come round at last,
Slouches towards Bethlehem to be born?

The Second Coming

W.B. Yeats

Prologue

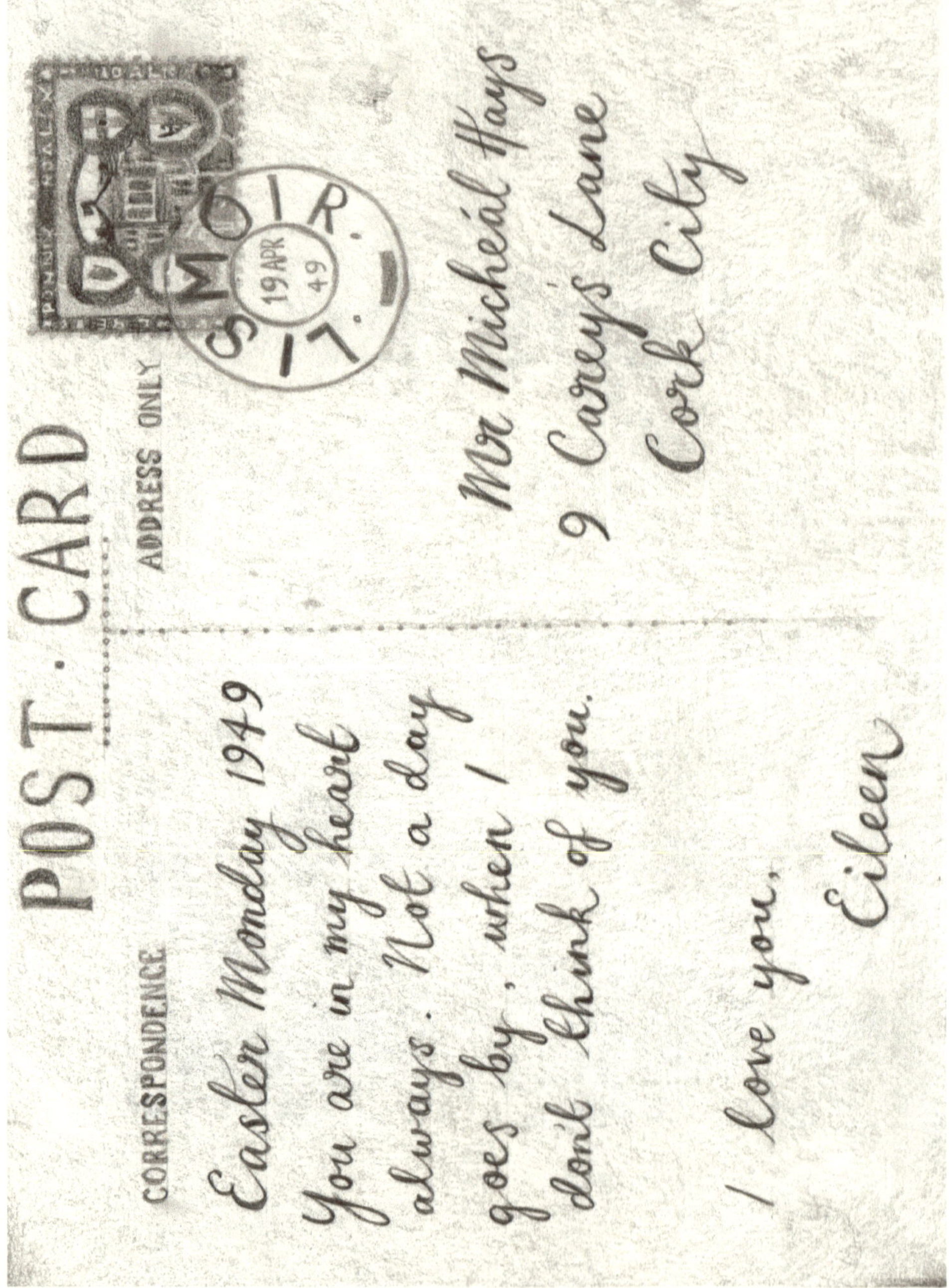

Three things will last forever —faith, hope, and love —and the greatest of these is love.

Lismore, County Waterford

Easter Monday, 1949

Eileen woke early. "Oh my God, this is it," she thought. "We have all suffered so much for today." She tried to keep her thoughts at bay. She knew it would paralyse her if she harboured them, as it had done many times before, certainly in the early years. But of course it was hopeless. Not a moment passed that she did not think of Rosaleen; Of that adorable, sweet, vulnerable face looking up at her for the last time, no more than a few hours old, as she handed her to the midwife; Twenty six long years ago; The stone the only part of her to go with her baby.

Then and many times since, she had pined for Micheál, Mattie or Da, but all were gone, taken from her by that terrible visitation of conflict and death. The dream of a life and children with Micheál undone in a few catastrophic weeks.

The previous evening she had heard the call of the corncrake across the fields, the first of the year. Calling, calling for a mate throughout the night; It had well nigh broken her heart.

Today, Ireland would become a republic, but not in the way they had dreamed of together all those years before. Those dreams had been recomposed as a nightmare. British imperialism banished, but not that of Rome. The politicians equating "Republic" as "Roman Catholic" and the country had become pinched, narrow, bigoted, judgemental, an oppressive state, replete with all its poisonous secrets and entanglements.

Today was the day when all of Eileen's unsustainable losses would come to an end. She took the simple card she had painted these last few days. Tears flowed as she wrote, "You are in my heart always. Not a day goes by when I don't think of you. I love you, Eileen." She addressed the card familiarly to Micheál at his Carey's Lane address choking back a sob at its evocation.

Closing the door of her tiny, quaint cottage, she walked up the secluded boreen, crossed the bridge into the old town for the last time and posted it. Then she returned home, without goodbyes, not even to Méabh, to end it all.

Simply, and with as much dignity as she could muster.

Cork Harbour,

27th August, 1922

As the hawsers were released and RMS Laconia left Queenstown, the morning sun sparkled on the expansive bay and headland. It was a beautiful and captivating sight. The irony was not lost on Micheál. He clambered up to the deck, his whole being conflicted, his thoughts a scramble, beating in his head and filling his stomach with a nauseating fear. He passed people on the stairwell and was oblivious of them. He was leaving Ireland. He was leaving Cork. He was leaving Eileen. At the end of himself, he was standing at the edge of memory. The bristling and gnawing foreboding that he would never see Carey's Lane, Crosshaven or Guagán Barra ever again. The life he knew and adored, gone forever. The corroding fear which had gripped him during the previous week convulsed his stomach. He retched and reached for the rail of the deck. His young, vibrant twenty-two year old self dissolved.

Three years before when he joined the Volunteers, he knew he was taking a risk with an indeterminate future. He did not know then how it would end. But Oh God, not this. This far worse than his own martyrdom.

He had been smuggled on board the ship through the kindness of Brother Paul. Paul, always there in their lives as a light, comforting presence. The big bear of a man, there for Micheál, there for Eileen, there for Mattie. This time, however, Micheál saw that even Paul had been reduced by the unfolded tragedy. As they bid one another goodbye, it was all that Paul could muster not to collapse. His last words "I will look out for her as best I can."

No matter how he tried, Micheál could not eliminate the recurring image in his head. The cataclysmic moment, his finger pulling gently on the trigger, accurate as ever, felling his target. Afterwards it was confirmed what he already knew. Mattie was dead.

The week had been a blur after that. Fleeing Cork after the invasion of Free State troops. Moving like an automaton, to the safety of the countryside, following orders. The fateful ambush at Béal na Bláth. Mick Collins killed. Rumours abounding that it could only have been Micheál. He was known everywhere as the sharpshooter, the sniper. He had to be rescued fast. In consummate rage, the Free Staters were closing in on him, Collin's "Squad" desperate for revenge. He was on the run, Brother Paul his only refuge.

Now on the deck of the Laconia, with only the expanse of ocean between

The Drowning of Innocence

him and New York, he was enveloped by time and emptiness. Nothing to distract him, to occupy his mind, abandoned to his thoughts and their consequences. He knew, irrevocably, that he would never see Eileen again. Their love obliterated by the bitterness of what had taken place. "Mattie, Oh Mattie," he wailed inwardly. Eileen could now only see her dead brother's face in his. He had lost everything; Eileen, their shared love, their common dream, their future together.

The war and its blood sacrifice had stripped him of this and everything. And for what?

The country had been duped by Lloyd George and Churchill into a dreadful compromise of a treaty; Was left beleaguered by the power and machinations of the Orange Order; The Roman church hierarchy had already flexed its muscles; The genie of bloodletting that had escaped into their lives was holding full sway. His comrades and fellow insurgents had metamorphosed unrecognisably. He suspected he had too. The nascent idealism that had consumed Micheál's soul and had driven him on, extinguished. He had nothing left; No dream for Ireland; No longer able to touch its soil. Memories had now telescoped into that one gut-wrenching moment of finality. No Mattie. No Eileen. No life.

What he did not know, what he could not know, was that at that very instant, growing inside Eileen, his daughter quickened for the very first time.

Perhaps sensing this was also a moment for her.

The Ha'penny Flea Market, Dublin

28th August, 2010

Alannah loved her Saturdays. On this particular morning the sun shone delightfully on the city streets, embellishing even its grime with incandescent splendour. It seemed as if everyone was skipping along, an effervescent joy wreathing people's faces. There was something evocative about the mood, Dublin of old, the streets and quays exhibiting their shabby, even dingy charm. Dirty Dublin.

Walking over the Ha'penny Bridge, she was struck with nostalgia remembering the many happy days she had spent here in the 70's. Days of unlimited freedom, unbounded optimism, uproarious laughter; Carefree days when the city had captivated her and won her heart. She had loved her time at UCD, its ramshackle campus on Earlsfield Terrace; Escapes from lectures to the Green and 'Mulligans' and 'Toners', for all the world like naughty schoolchildren.

Music was alive then, conversation rich, dialogue intense. The first time she heard The Bothy Band, a moment that put her in touch with deep resonances in her soul, a sense of being Irish for the first time in her life, proud, strong. It was an awakening, a throwing off of shackles, the city rising from sleep like a 'Rip Van Winkle' to look anew at life and possibility, their time together as students spent questioning, searching, questioning. They had rejected exhaustively the narrow pathways of the previous generation, which like a toxin was seeking to envelop their souls. Her mother, Rose, did not understand her in those days but thankfully she was gracious and did not get in her way.

When she thought of her Ma, a poignant gasp caught her unawares. She stopped on the middle of the wrought iron bridge to recover her breath and equilibrium. 'Ma, how I miss you' she thought. And as was often her practice, reached for the stone in her bag and drew it out. She marvelled once again at its beauty, recalling the times as a child when it had enchanted her with its vibrant colours; 'Shaped and etched by the wild Atlantic', she had been told. Her birth stone, the thing that kept alive the memory of her mother. She said a short prayer of gratitude as she reflected a while, gazing at the river coursing below, transfixed by powerful recollections like a visitation, the sense of her mother graciously touching her. She held the stone gently and then returned it to her bag.

Ah the stone! Nobody knew or could recall where it had come from. Ma

  The Drowning of Innocence

had told her it was something she had always possessed; Its mystery shrouded like her own origin. Her Ma had discovered she had been adopted when she was thirteen. Her adoptive mother quietly informing Ma in the bedroom of their Waterford home, all those years ago. Ma had been stunned by the news and so taken aback that questions evaded her, too unbalanced by the revelation to articulate any response. She had been left bewildered for some time afterwards and by the time she felt ready to enquire more, she felt restrained by the pain she may cause her mother in raising the subject. It became a soft taboo. 'Better to let things lie,' she had told Alannah.

Out of respect Alannah had thought the same. It was not that important really, was it? Who her grandparents were? That was the past, wasn't it?. And goodness knows Ireland had enough of a past. Lately though, with her Ma gone, the matter had raised itself again. Quietly, softly, like a recollection whose substance had disappeared but still left behind a residual thrill of familiarity. Ireland had changed and the secrecy and taboos which had dominated its recent past were being lifted. Things were being revisited and a different narrative was emerging. So much harm had been caused through the blanket of forgetfulness that had enveloped the country for well nigh a century, that now there appeared a common resolve never to surrender to such amnesia again.

Then, for Alannah, there was the birth of her first grandchild, Ezra, just last year. What inexpressible joy, eclipsing, if that were possible, the feelings, she recalled that accompanied her own children's' births. She could not explain it. Was it that she had reached the stage in her life where consciousness of beauty, of the transience and preciousness of time and life had opened up for her the door to the present moment? She had cleared her life of striving, of that she was sure and so able to be mindful of this adorable 'little man', drinking him in, in all his innocence, his unfettered exploration, hugely infected by his wide-eyed wonder at the world. She had become enchanted, was more in love than she had ever been or thought possible, was in awe of her own daughter, carrying and giving birth, of the wild mysticism of such a thing. And Ezra, dear sweet Ezra, growing from day to day, becoming more himself each time she saw him.

It had caused her to think of other births, her own of course, and then Ma's. The relief, joy, wonder of such moments arrested as she reflected achingly of her birth Grandma and of Ma herself 'given away' and the circumstances that had conspired to produce such a devastating event. It had eaten away at her for weeks now. To find out why, to understand this, had become an obsession, producing a gnawing restlessness that dominated her free moments.

The sun shining brightly on the Liffey roused her from her thoughts. The tide was in and the old river looked grand this morning. She headed for Lower Liffey Street and the Ha'penny Flea Market.

Alannah had always been considered an extremely attractive woman by her friends, although disarmingly oblivious of that fact herself. Her face often described as pretty, which even in her sixties, held on to its bright cheerfulness. Her almond-shaped, deep blue eyes, cerulean blue, were the most striking thing about her appearance. Her eyes and fine cheekbones evoked timelessness. Her long hair swept up in a French twist framed these exquisite features. Her body, lithe and graceful, defied her years and she moved with an unassuming grace that captured attention. She usually dressed in an understated but contemporary manner from clothes she had sought with great guile and perspicacity in second-hand shops and flea markets and carried herself always with unique flair and dignity.

She loved wandering around flea markets. There she became immersed, absorbed, looking for inspiration and 'finds'. She knew she had an eye for things and could always be relied upon to discover a treasure. In the beginning, she had to overcome her self-consciousness when she stopped at stalls. She wanted to scan, select, touch without being pounced on for a sale. Then, slowly she had understood that stall holders often enjoyed others admiring their collection. She hadn't been to the Ha'penny before and was excited by its possibility.

The market inside the Grand Social was vibrant with colour and laughter and was, surprisingly and deliciously, cool in the shade. Alannah was in her element. Moving slowly, scanning as she went, she felt inexorably drawn to one stall full of curio's and memorabilia. Touching such objects was always reverential for her, acknowledging their intimacy and innate history.

Placed on one side was a shoe box full of postcards of bygone days. These were always a special treat, the colours hand painted, often faded, the detail full of imperfections, reminding her, as many things did, of Leonard Cohen's splendid lyric, "There's a crack, a crack in everything, it's how the light gets in."

Halfway through her perusal, she drew out a postcard depicting Guagán Barra's church and lake. She could see immediately it was hand-painted with vibrant, exultant colours, like a travelogue poster of the 1930's, yet betraying

          The Drowning of Innocence

the rich talent of the artist. Deep, sombre, earthy greens, effulgent, spirited
mustards, bright orange-reds flaming from the image with an extravagant
exuberance. The card was quite old. As she touched it, a quiver ran through
her whole being, a sense of excitement, anticipation, even recognition. The
image captured perfectly the impressions of her visit to Guagán a few years
back when on holiday in Killarney. Its calm, ethereal serenity. Painted in
coruscating colours, the reflection of the trees and oratory in the lake was
vividly real and provided subtlety, profundity to the scene. She was taken
aback. "Gosh this is a find," she thought.

Turning the card in her hand, she saw it was already used, written-on in
elegant copperplate script - the kind of attention to detail that people gave to
their communication in years gone by. Her heart skipped a beat as she read,

"You are in my heart always. Not a day goes by, when I don't think of you.
I love you, Eileen"

The sentiments took Alannah's breath away. "My goodness, how sweet."
Her wild imaginings took flight as she considered what could be the story
behind this declaration of love and devotion. Extraordinary. The post mark
was clear enough and added to the exquisite appeal of the thing. The charming
circle of the date stamp with LÍSMÓIR on the circumference, and inset with 19
APR 1949. Again in that elegant copperplate it was addressed to 'Mr. Micheál
Hays, 9, Carey's Lane, Cork City.'

"Hi, I'm Alannah. Can you tell me anything about this card," she said to
the stall owner.

"Conas tá tú, Alannah, mo Chroí, I'm Séamus. Well, I tell you, its been with
me for years that box and I hardly sell anything out of it. Let me think. All I
can remember is picking it up from a character who used to do house
clearances in Cork. An original rag and bone man, you know. Long gone now
I imagine. He was fairly long in the tooth when I bought stuff from him. Why,
what have you found there?"

"It's a postcard. It's swept my heart away."

"Ah, Holy Mary Mother of God, but that's gorgeous," Seamus couldn't
restrain a smile. "Well in all my years serving time here, I have never seen that
in the box before. There you go Alannah. It belongs to you. I can't take any
money for that. What was it the Beatles sang 'Can't buy me love, yeah'. But
don't let me be seeing you on the Antiques Roadshow and it worth 5000 Euros.

Off you go with it and may it bring you joy, inspiration and comfort. For it's a holy thing indeed. Don't you think?"

"I do indeed Séamus. I'll tell you what. I'll try and find out the story. That will keep me out of mischief. And when I do, I'll come back and buy you a Guinness."

"If you find out that story, Alannah, it's me who'll be standing the round and it'll be more than Guinness we'll be drinking. Off you go now before I change my mind."

Séamus gave his hand a flick and with a twinkle in his eye sent her on her way.

Alannah left the market on a high. A profound, transcendent, luminous sense of this moment in time enveloping her. She felt exhilarated but could not fully explain it. She thought she would always remember how she felt at that precise instant. Was it the simply exquisite, hand-painted image of Guagán? Or the brief words that encapsulated the passion of a lifetime? She didn't know, but somehow, incongruously it gave impetus to her own recent obsession of discovering the story of her unknown grandmother; The loss and giving away of her child, her dear mother Rose.

"If the story behind the postcard has captured me so much, how much more should the discovery of my own hidden past compel me?"

In the late afternoon, as she boarded the train at Heuston station bound for Waterford, Alannah travelled home with a deep and firm conviction that she must now discover her story. She owed this to herself and she knew also that, down along the line, she would want to be able to tell it to her beloved Ezra.

     The Drowning of Innocence

Halcyon Day

Cork City,

June 1914

It was when he was in the middle of it that Michael knew this would be a day he would never forget. Flowing from Joan, an early June day, pregnant with the sap of life, a gentle breeze and the warmth of the sun urgently beckoning all outside. "We'll go to Crosshaven, together," Joan had said, "All of us, for a picnic and a day out. Won't it be grand."

Surprisingly for Michael, Claude and Charlie agreed and greeted the idea enthusiastically. He was not used to being included in his brothers' plans. Somehow, he always felt different to them. There was a strangeness in them and his father that had caused him to feel an outsider in his own family. The way Michael saw things had always appeared strange to them and he was continually ridiculed at the dinner table when he voiced his opinion. It did not help that Michael was reduced to stuttering by this treatment. But today was different. It seemed as if they were caught up in another, separate incarnation. Today, they were laughing, joking with him, Claude had even given him a playful clip on the ear as he mounted his bicycle.

What's more, on Joan's insistence, they said it was okay to pick up Mattie at Blackrock. Most of the time, Michael felt that his Dad and brothers did not approve of Mattie. Joan was adamant however. She knew that Michael needed Mattie along so that the day could work its magic. Claude and Charlie just shrugged.

How Michael loved Joan. Without her, he knew he would not have been able to surmount the trial of his mother's passing. Even though she was only in her teens, there was a maturity and depth in his sister that had comforted him and gave him hope in the darkest of days. He had watched her as she cared for their mother during the long painful months as the disease took over, as she struggled for breath, coughing uncontrollably; Joan always there.

His older brothers were trapped then. Contained by the same stoical spirit that had encircled their Dad. Michael saw all three retire into themselves during that terrible time. Even though they were young men, just touching twenty, they seemed old to Michael, a resignation emerging to a path of life facing them. Inseparably bound in their convictions, they were to follow their father's footsteps and join the Munster Fusiliers in a few weeks, "The Dirty

Shirts", Percy Hays' pride and joy. As second generation regulars, they would be trained at the Curragh and then embark for Rangoon to join their father's old battalion. The excitement of this dominated their lives.

Maybe it was their impending departure which imbued in his brothers the spirit of generosity which had coloured this moment. There was no doubting their gaiety as they exited Carey's Lane, leaving the Huguenot quarter behind. Charlie was particularly buoyant as he headed over Parnell bridge. He burst into 'Phil the Fluter's Ball'. The singing was infectious and pedestrians grinned when they saw this peculiar procession. All the family joined him in the chorus, singing skittishly,

> *"With the toot of the flute, and the twiddle of the fiddle-O!*
> *Hopping in the middle, like a herrin' on the griddle-O!*
> *Up! down, hands around, crossing to the wall-O!*
> *Hadn't we the gaiety at Phil the Fluter's Ball."*

Michael felt alive. The strange, fearful foreboding that had overwhelmed him as they buried their mother was evaporating. It was incongruous. In one way, he felt it was somehow wrong to be this happy, but it was almost as if he could see his mother in his mind's eye, that beautiful, graceful face, dispensing her rich blessing as a sacrament, even enjoying this moment with them. Her sons and daughter together, heading for a day out, laughter in their eyes.

Marie Hays was from proud, Huguenot stock. Her deep blue eyes, finely chiselled face and sandy hair usually caught up in a braid, a savoir-faire always about her. A fierce attention to detail and a sensitivity captured and enriched by the beauty and skill with which she applied herself to draughting and making lace. She was the centre of her family, the quiet, strong presence. By example and simple charm, she had enriched their world, making them better people. Michael felt his Dad would be lost without her.

The ride to Blackrock took half an hour and Mattie was waiting for them at Riverview under the shadow of the castle, with a bike he had borrowed from neighbours. Good old Mattie. Michael had first met him when he joined the under thirteen hurling team at Blackrock, two years previously. The two were inseparable since, like twins. They had a symbiotic relationship on the hurling pitch, could always find one another with a pass and with one deft flick of the hurley escape their markers. Michael's brothers had never understood his fascination with the game, for them it was uncultured and unsophisticated, almost barbaric. Claude was opening bat and wicket keeper for the county cricket club and poured scorn on the Fenian game. But Michael loved the passion, skill and virtuosity that it fostered and the exhilaration and fervour for the game in the city. He followed the county side's progress every year as an obsession. He never felt more alive than when he held his hurley in his hand. In anticipation of the strand at Crosshaven, he had brought it with him.

Mattie jumped on his bike when they approached but quickly flew off again, landing in a painful huddle on the rough ground. The chain had broken.

"Oh dear, Mattie. That's a shame," said Joan, feeling sorry for him.

Mattie picked himself up off the ground, a little embarrassed, stoutly refusing to surrender to tears at his grazed knee and disappointment. The day seemed doomed for him.

Joan saw out of the corner of her eye his Da, Con Barry, appear at the front door with Mattie's younger sister Eileen.

"What do we have here," chirruped this small, gentle-faced smiling man. He walked through the gate holding his daughter's hand.

"The chain's broken, Da, What can I do? I won't be able to go now."

"Yerra, sure that's easy fixed, boy," replied Con is his sing-song Cork accent. "Just give me a couple of minutes."

Joan found it deeply affecting to watch this man move with purpose under the adoring gaze of his 12 year old daughter. The economy and skill with which the chain was fixed was admirable, the gentle mocking humour infectious, adding a generous warmth to the day. Eileen, meanwhile, stood alongside him. She looked at Joan with eager, entreating eyes. Joan interpreted the obvious, silent request.

"Do you want to come too, Eileen?"

"Oh yes, please." and turning to her Da pleaded, "Da, is that alright?"

"I don't see why not, girl. Seeing as your favourite fellow is in the party." Con roared with gleeful mischief.

Eileen's face immediately flushed a beautiful, soft, pink in both embarrassment and mortification. Con looked at Joan, giving her a knowing wink.

"Gosh," he thought, as he looked at her, "Such beautiful blue eyes. She'll be a catch for someone."

Joan was further amused that poor Michael remained oblivious of the interaction, as he busily caught up with Mattie. With Mattie's bicycle fixed and in working order, Eileen was adamant she wanted Michael to give her a crossbar. She ran over to him in full confidence of her lift. When everyone was ready they took the road again, all taking their lead from Charlie as he regaled them with his full repertoire of songs.

They followed the river road through Passage. Eileen was fulfilling her wildest imaginings, here, nestled in Michael's warm and protective frame, she inhaled the sweetness of his breath as he belted out the tunes initiated by Charlie. Joan watched both of them and was deeply amused and charmed as she saw the intoxicated and gleeful expression on Eileen's face. It beguiled her immensely to observe how unaware Michael was of this infatuation. What fun!

They passed the seventeen mile journey delirious with the beauty of the day. At times, Mattie, Michael, Eileen and Joan stopped for a break and at Monkstown, they had an ice-cream. The mouth of the river opening up in front of them to reveal the extraordinary expanse of the harbour stretched out as far as the eye could see. On this June day, it was a jewel. Captivating and punctuated by islands and inlets, Michael not for the first time, felt glad to be born and live in this part of the world. Something inside him, deep inside, had always reverberated with the juxtaposition of land and water which had been richly carved out by the wild Atlantic. His heart was full.

Claude and Charlie had sped on ahead, eager to get on with the day and full of the adventure that awaited them. They had now become engrossed in discussing the coming war. They felt proud and glad to be alive at this time, thrilled with the opportunity to travel and join comrades in seeking glory. From Carrigaline, they set one another a race to Crosshaven. Their energy expended, immersed in the competition, momentarily usurping their preoccupation with enlisting and the more momentous adventures ahead. Cycling along the length of the Owenabue river estuary, its ten-mile stretch; The vibrant green copses on either side enhancing the serene beauty of the water as it gently flowed towards the Atlantic. Here and there, fishermen drew up nets in anticipation, birdsong filled their ears, the day a joyous celebration of being alive.

On arriving at Crosshaven before the others, they found the strand deserted. The strong, warm summer breeze whipped up Atlantic waves which crashed

     The Drowning of Innocence

on the bay. The two lads quickly togged out and jumped in the water. Their strong, muscular frames cutting an easy path through the waves; alternatively riding or crashing through the rolling surf. They were revelling in this perfect summer's day, full of energy, life, and optimism. They were the chosen pair, good-looking, strong, secure in their position, they felt masters of all that they surveyed.

When the others arrived over an hour later, they found Claude and Charlie stretched out on a corner of the strand, chatting. Michael and Mattie, as a matter of course, spread out and with hurley in hands pucked the sliothar to one another high into the sky, practicing their ability to pluck it out of the air or the difficult skill of double-pulling on the ball over their heads. They were in their element. In their imagination, on the field for the Munster semi-final against Waterford the following Sunday - stroke for stroke, urging their beloved county to victory.

Joan and Eileen clambered out onto the rocks to explore the pools. They were searching for treasure, stones honed by the tide into motley colours and shapes. They crept over rocks as silently and diligently as they could, seeking undisturbed wildlife. Joan's eye for detail, shape, colour, carefully tutored over the years by her mother, their guide. There were moments when Joan held her breath as she remembered times like this with her mother. She caught herself, knew she could not afford such indulgence. She must be strong now. She knew her mother would expect it of her, strong for her father and particularly for her older brothers. Their impending departure filled her with dread. Although proud of them, she also feared for their naivety and enthusiasm and knew they would not hold back. They had been shaped by duty and obligation and could be relied upon to be loyal and devoted. But she had her questions. She did not know or care too much about the world of politics, Europe now far too messy for her to understand. She had a deep foreboding.

Her thoughts were interrupted by a squeal of delight from Eileen.

"Look Joan," She exclaimed. In her hand was a small stone. "Its like a heart. So romantic. I love the way I can see waves in it."

Eileen was pointing to the layered rows of thin, wavy lines which mimicked the action of the sea.

"I love the browns, greys, greens, orange colours. Oh its my best find ever."

The joy in the little girl's face was so all-encompassing. It brought Joan back from her reverie. This was truly the trophy of the day, a lovely moment.

Her two brothers were still stretched out on the strand but in their minds, they were a long way from Cork.

"Can you imagine, in a couple of months we will be in Rangoon," Charlie said. "I wonder what that will be like. I am so excited by it all, travelling across the world."

"Yes" said Claude, "but I am sure the war is going to come. That will change everything. It will be our chance to show what we are made of, that we are brave, don't you think? The Germans need to be stopped. We can't let them get away with what they are up to."

It was evident they both looked forward to the adventure as a growing up, a cleansing, a release of their pent-up emotions, a chance to show their worth, their loyalty, their patriotism.

"The Balkans are going to flare up again and that will bring things to a head and the sooner the better," said Charlie.

"And we will be there. We will be part of it," said Claude, "Whoopee!!"

As they explored these thoughts, lying on their backs on the sand on this beautiful early summers day in Crosshaven, county Cork, they felt the world opening up in front of them with its endless possibilities. They would go to war. They could be counted on. Claude knew from facing down fast bowlers what it meant to stand strong. He had understood and practiced for years the forcefulness, strength of will, self-assertion and standing firm against an enemy which had become integral to his code of behaviour, as a cricketer, as a man. They knew through being steeped in the traditions of the Munster Fusiliers that they would win and that the victory would be quick, decisive and sweet.

All their activities were interrupted by a scream from Joan. Mattie and Michael looked up from their game to see Eileen in the sea; Joan at the edge of the rock, prostrate, in desperation, reaching outwards towards Eileen as she was swept away. The boys became transfixed with horror as the Atlantic, which prior to that moment had been a glorious spectacle; Translucent, green waves crashing on the rocks, had now metamorphosed into a violent maelstrom, a fierce enemy gathering Eileen up and away and tossing her like a helpless rag doll, its formidable power reducing the two small boys to utter helplessness. Mattie sank to his knees in a kind of prayer; Michael's heart in his mouth, forlorn.

          The Drowning of Innocence

Then he saw Charlie already in the water, his strong, muscular frame cutting a path through the waves. His big brother to the rescue, all his hopes pinned on him. It seemed to take an age before he reached her but eventually they saw him grab hold of her and raise her aloft, her small, sweet face consumed by the fearful drama of it all. Charlie gently cradled her in his muscular frame and back stroked slowly to the shore; Then carried her to the strand and towels. They all surrounded her and after a moment of gathering themselves, made jokes to help her relax. The crisis was over and Charlie's action their major celebration.

Claude grinned with quiet satisfaction and looked over at his brother. Their eyes met and Claude saw his brother, his soul mate, as if for the first time. He was in awe of him, his beauty and manliness and wondered at what kind of life lay before this charismatic figure. He would go on to accomplish great things, of that Claude was sure. And he would be there beside him to support him and urge him on. He drew a deep breath of satisfaction, glad to be alive, glad he had the companionship of such a man, as a brother.

While Eileen's clothes dried, they ate their picnic lunch, sandwiches and lemonade. She remembered the stone and was glad to discover it still in her pocket. In an extraordinary way, the day had been further sanctified by the drama. The unspoken 'what if's' filling the recesses of their mind, as they gloried in the fact that everything was perfect.

At the end of the day they walked up to the railway station. When the train pulled into Crosshaven, they stored their bikes in the goods carriage. They travelled home, exhausted from their day, in a cabin they had commandeered for themselves. The late sun was shining on the estuary as the train hugged the shoreline. The golden hue lapped on the water and rivulets of waves created sparkling diamonds, richer and more true than the real thing. Flocks of birds carved their way across the sun, in search of a haven. The land beyond at Aghada, translucent in the setting sun, windows of gold lighting up the vista with its promise of riches ahead. Their journey was idyllic, peaceful. They were together, happy, even joyful as a group. A simple, rich, generous, grace-filled life awaited them.

For all of them, in one way or another, this day, this perfect Crosshaven day, would serve as a portend. Many, many times in later years, they would remember this moment and wish with all their hearts that they could return to it and start again.

Forgotten Men

"I know that I shall meet my fate
Somewhere among the clouds above;
Those that I fight I do not hate
Those that I guard I do not love;
My country is Kiltartan Cross,
My countrymen Kiltartan's poor,
No likely end could bring them loss
Or leave them happier than before.
Nor law, nor duty bade me fight,
Nor public man, nor cheering crowds,
A lonely impulse of delight
Drove to this tumult in the clouds;
I balanced all, brought all to mind,
The years to come seemed waste of breath,
A waste of breath the years behind
In balance with this life, this death."

An Irish Airman Foretells his death
W.B. Yeats

"We live so much under the shadow of sudden death. One sees things very differently to ordinary times. Life is normally complicated. Here it is savagely simple. Eat while you can. Help all you can. Sleep when and where you can. And above all grin, and keep a stiff upper lip. Even a mechanical smile is better than an anxious look. Worrying is not good for the men.

Percival Fenwick, Gallipoli April 1915

And some there be, which have no memorial; who are perished, as though they had never been; and are become as though they had never been born; and their children after them

Ecclesiasticus 44:9

Alexandria, Egypt
Easter Monday, 1915

Miss Joan Hays,
9, Carey's Lane,
Cork

Dear Joan,

I am writing to let you know that Charlie and I are both well. Can you imagine? We have just arrived in Alexandria. Charlie is in the best of form and is by far the most popular man in his platoon. He is a great source of humour and fun. Everybody loves him. He has been a great hit with the girls in Coventry. On the way over he had his platoon doubled up with his jokes and of course Percy French songs. He had some of the men reduced to tears with his rendition of "The Mountains of Mourne".

We are finally on the move and I am sure we will see action in the next few weeks. This is exciting for us as the training had become really boring. I hope you will not worry about us. Although knowing you I am sure you will.

Its great that both of us are together, Charlie and I. We keep one another's spirits up. And I know if anything happened to him, I am always there. We will never leave one another wounded on the field of battle. My brother as you know is also my dearest friend and I feel so proud to be going into battle alongside him. Its a great day for us and our family. Dad is surely proud.

All my love

Claude   XXX

Mudros, Greece,
22nd April 1915

Miss Joan Hays,
9, Carey's Lane,
Cork

Dear Little Sis,

Its "good-time Charlie" here sending you my love from across the sea. I'm having the time of my life. I love the whole experience of travelling. Of course you know from Claude that we have just passed through Alexandria, the capital of the ancient world. I am sorry I don't write much, but at least you have Claude to give you the news and the scandal. You can imagine me, wandering in and out of the souks. Great fun!!!! Somehow, I managed to connect with the traders and we made one another laugh.

We are now ready for battle and I have found that I am among the first troops to go. This is most thrilling and I am looking forward to the time when we are ashore. You never know what's going to happen, of course. But if anything does happen to Claude or me, don't let it upset you too much. Because, dear Sis, you must remember that thousands are losing their brothers daily.

Don't get gloomy over this letter. We are not dead yet by a long way. In fact, I have never felt better in all my life. And there was never a German or Turk born or a bullet made that could kill a dirty shirt.

Your loving brother,

Charlie   XXX

Helles Bay, The Dardanelles, Turkey

25th April 1915,

Claude didn't get much sleep. The invasion had been postponed because of
the weather, but now they were underway. He had been excited after the
Commander had outlined that they were part of a pincer movement to overrun
the Turkish defences on the Dardanelles peninsula and open the way to
Constantinople, link up with Russian troops and eventually open an eastern
front in the war. There were to be a series of landings on the southern tip of the
peninsula of which they were a part. French troops would act as a
diversionary measure on the Turkish mainland. The ANZAC troops would
land further up the peninsula and cut off the Turkish retreat. He was slightly
worried, as were others, that they did not know too much about the lie of the
land but knew their job was to capture the higher ground as quickly as
possible.

His fears were allayed by assurances from Command that the shelling
would decimate the Turkish defences. There was a general feeling that the
Turkish army would be overwhelmed by the barrage and roll over. This made
sense to him and he was confident in their ability to get the job done.

When told that they would land on an old Collier 'the Clyde', all of them
hidden inside as it ran aground on the shore, he was amused by the plan. So
close geographically to Ancient Troy, they had come up with a twentieth
century 'Trojan Horse'. How he loved that story as a child. Now they were
writing their own version. They would make history.

The Munster fusiliers had transferred from their vessel 'Caledonia' to the
'The Clyde' during the night. 'The Clyde' had four holes cut in the hull on the
port and starboard sides. When it would run aground, an attached motor
hopper would swing round in front of 'The Clyde' and fill the gap between the
grounded steam collier and the shore. This would form a bridge over which
the troops would leave through the holes onto a gangway, jump onto the
hopper and run to the shore.

The Dublin Fusiliers would travel ahead in rowing boats to establish a
beachhead.

Before dawn, 'The Albion' bombarded the coastline and the Turkish
defences. Claude was astounded at the severity and thought no troops could
withstand it. He had never heard such noise, the thunderous roar the very

embodiment of death and destruction. The screeching noise of shells, reminiscent of an accelerating steam train and the rocking, deafening explosions that followed the very apparition of destruction. As if the sound was an entity in itself, he felt encompassed by it, that this was all that was left in the world. The acrid smell of exploding shells mixed with the sweat building in the men waiting, waiting for their own move. "So this is war," he thought and grimaced.

The men had been abnormally quiet. This from fellows he had come to know as light hearted, divil-may-care characters from Cork, Kerry, Limerick and beyond. They and he were filled with a sense of something impending which was way beyond their knowledge or imagination. He looked at their faces and for the most part saw young features stare back at him. Simple men, farmers, porters, railway workers from the small towns around the province, at home in the making of hay but not here, in the cramped confines of the vessel, waiting, waiting. He could not help reflect on their vulnerability against the barrage of noise cascading outside, deafening all their senses. He sought out Charlie but could not find him among the sea of anxious faces awaiting their tryst with destiny.

As part of the vanguard, Claude was stationed near one of the sallyports and could see everything taking shape. Dawn had arrived to greet a beautiful day, with not a breath of wind and just a slight haze which was rapidly disappearing. It was strangely and eerily quiet as they neared the shore. He was confident the Turks had retreated from the shelling. How could anyone have survived that? Yet he sensed an oppressive air of tension mounting beside him among the fusiliers.

Out of the sallyport, Claude could see the advance party of Dublin fusiliers, in rowing boats, forty men aboard each, travelling alongside. Two hundred yards from the shore, the boats were set adrift from their steam pinnaces. They began to pull ashore with their own oars, men from the pinnaces giving professional backing to the unskilled efforts of the loaded-up soldiers. It was slow progress.

Everything seemed to be going to plan and Claude began to fill up with a quiet optimism.

Suddenly all hell broke loose. Enfilading fire strafed across the water. Claude could see the 'Dubs' like sitting ducks. The fire incessant, picking off the oarsmen. The boats started to drift. Man after man was hit, many falling overboard and immediately sinking under their heavy packs. Claude was

                The Drowning of Innocence

dumbstruck by the suddenness and unreality of what was taking place in front of him. He could not pull his eyes away from the unfolding horror. Men being hit, screaming, screaming, in pain and terror, their cries of "Mammeeee, Mammeeee, Maam, Maaaam" reducing everything to an excruciating vulnerability. He was hypnotised by what he was seeing, left with a picture and vision that would haunt him forever.

Many of the boats were peppered, pierced and percolated with holes. Claude could see it was a massacre. So many of his countrymen mown down and disappearing without a trace. Like rats in a trap. Their bodies tipped grotesquely over the sides, like mechanical acrobats. Their boats, unhelmed and powerless, drifting away from the shore and sinking as they became further pierced with bullet holes. Claude could see that of the first boat of forty men, only three reached the shore.

'The Clyde' ran aground imperceptibly and there was no jar. The ground was shallower than thought, however, and it beached eighty yards from the shore. The hopper which was supposed to form the bridge between 'The Clyde' and the shore sheared away and left the old collier marooned that distance from the beach. They were cut off and helpless. It was a fiasco. Claude saw two men jump from the deck into the water and, under heavy fire, bring small lighters around as the alternative. Goodness knows how they managed it but after thirty minutes, they had secured a makeshift bridge of boats from the edge of the gangway to the land.

The order was given to go. The men piled out onto the gangway and immediately came under intense fire. Many did not even make it beyond their first steps, but were hit and fell on the spot. Shrieks of agony came from the lips of the wounded, rendering those waiting inside helpless and panic-stricken. The fear was all consuming. Wrestling with the dread of it each man gathered himself and ran out to certain death as if to a firing squad.

Those that made it past the gangway, clambered over the lighters to the shore, but presented an easy target to the three platoons of Turks, no more than sixty four men, armed with rifles and one Pom Pom. They were encamped in trenches less than three hundred yards away. So well embedded were they, that the early morning barrage, although terrifying, had not altered their strength or conviction. They were ready, they were waiting, they were determined and the carnage that followed was inevitable.

Claude did not know what drove him on when it was his turn to run down the gangway and onto the lighters. He was acting on pure instinct, his legs felt like jelly but with a supreme effort he forced them to move. In his mind he felt that it was essential that the 'Munsters' got a run on the Turks' guns and overwhelm them. Otherwise they would all be finished.

With supreme strength of will he forced his strong, athletic body, fuelled by rage and adrenalin, and catapulted himself down the gangway. He hid his fear and blind panic by screaming at others to follow and join him. When he skipped and ran across the lighters he was vaguely aware that he was running over his comrades, lying where they had fallen at the bottom of the boats. The sacrilege of it all further violating his being. For a moment, he saw their faces; Young men, no more than children, their countenance shaped by horror and fear. In the end, he could not bear their unseeing eyes and he instinctively leapt overboard. Immediately out of his depth and dragged under by the weight of his pack, he was engulfed by the sea. Strangely away from the horror of the screaming sounds of death, he began to relax. He felt himself drift. Something deep inside however, maybe it was his need to be there for Charlie arrested his descent. Adrenaline coursed through him and with a supreme effort he resurfaced. He scrabbled about desperately for his knife. Freeing it, he cut the straps of his pack and it slipped from him. With strong, desperate strokes, he made for the shoreline.

On reaching the ground he lay in the shallow water, catching his breath, summoning his energy. He was an easy target, but somehow the Turk fire was concentrated on the fusiliers exiting 'The Clyde'. Exiting to near certain death.

Claude raised his head slightly and could see a small escarpment, no more than three feet high, just ahead of him. He summoned all his energy and sprang to his feet. Through a hail of bullets, miraculously missing him, he covered the ground and dived to safety under the embankment. Five others, from other platoons, there already. He knew them well. McEvoy, Dunne, Fitzgerald, Murphy and Cronin. Good blokes. At least here they would not draw fire. They could take a break and plan.

After he was rested, Claude's eyes were sucked back to the scene behind him. In either madness or desperation, the dead fusiliers which had clogged up the gangway were flung into the sea, to make way so that more men could pour out of the collier, wade ashore and be killed in turn. It was as if the men themselves had found the whole situation unimaginable and had entered a netherworld. Did they think that by storming ashore, hour after hour, they could change what faced them, and vanquish the defenders? Just by the sheer weight of their numbers if nothing else?

          The Drowning of Innocence

Out of the corner of his eye, Claude saw Charlie disembark. Fear gripped him as he watched on, helplessly, at Charlie's passage down the gangway. He was open for all the world to see as he ran down the makeshift platform and sprang onto a lighter. From the lighters, he made his way through the water to a small rocky spit jutting out into the sea from the land, seeking cover and respite there. Claude could see from his angle that it was a trap. He looked hopelessly on as Charlie made his way towards the rock, the trap, the tryst with death. The Turks had that area taped and Claude watched in horror as Charlie was hit three or four times, the impact sending him backwards, his arms flailing, the weight of his pack pulling him under, his young life disappearing without a trace. Gone. Gone.

Claude was on his feet. In an instant. By instinct. Bizarrely, the image of the Crosshaven rescue in his mind, an intense desire to save his brother, to reciprocate his bravery and generosity of spirit. Before he could move forward, McEvoy had taken him down with a fierce tackle. Claude hit the ground hard and was dragged back under cover by the others. They held him fast as he wailed and screamed, flailing his arms in an effort to get free. "Charlie, Charlie" He screamed. For ten minutes he was uncontrollable until eventually the expended energy of it all overtook him and his despairing efforts were replaced and subsumed by an extraordinary lethargy.

He heard his own screams as if that of a stranger, resounding over the bleak and bloody landscape and mixing with the cacophony of wails and caterwauling of the men dying, slowly on the beach. Charlie was gone. Here, miles from home in this God-forsaken place.

The next few hours were a blur. He could see that the company commanders had finally seen sense and issued orders to stop the disembarkation. Silence reigned and all along the water's edge and especially near the remaining boats the sea was crimson with blood, as it lapped its gruesome baggage towards the shore. "I am in hell," Claude thought in the semi-conscious world into which he had slumped.

Day past into night. As evening fell, the remainder of the fusiliers left 'The Clyde' under cover of darkness, largely unscathed. They spent the first part of the night digging themselves in. During the night, Claude's dreams were full of the turmoil of the previous day, his despair at his helplessness, the men in the lighters staring up at him, his wonder at still being alive in the middle of this madness, the sounds and smells and sights filling his subconscious as a vision full of dread and trepidation. As he slipped between wakefulness and sleep, he was conscious of McEvoy and Cronin, their strength loaned to him.

With morning, came no respite. They knew they had to press on and capture the fort and village of Sedd-el-Bahr. The Munster and Dublin Fusilier officers and ranks had been so decimated that they were reformed into a new regiment and quickly nicknamed 'The Dubsters'.

Claude had now bonded with McEvoy and Cronin and together they moved over the ground towards the village. There were huge wire entanglements blocking the way. The issued wire cutters useless in breaching them.

Away to his left, Claude saw Willie Cosgrove run out. He was a big bruiser of a man from Aghada. "What the fuck is he doing," Claude thought, "Has he gone mad altogether?" He then saw Willie, with his bare hands, grab the post which held the wire and with a great heave pull it out of the ground and continue to do this, running along from post to post, until he had opened up a way through. Claude cheered along with the rest of the men at his achievement and piled through the gap he had made.

Although the village was in ruins from the shelling, it provided perfect cover for snipers. They moved carefully and together. The chattering fear they experienced as they moved forward, overcome only by the presence of others alongside. Claude saw two Turks on a wall of a small house oblivious of his progress on their flank. He took aim and shot one of the them, the other diving for safety. Killing for the first time left him empty inside, a nausea he was soon to overcome. It seemed strange to him, almost a game that to kill or be killed was determined merely by the accident of who saw whom first. It certainly did not give him any satisfaction for the loss of either his brother or the carnage he had witnessed the day before. By the end of the morning, after fierce fighting, some of it hand-to-hand, the fort and village had been taken and held.

On the third day, the three of them were detailed to go back to the beach to help clear and bury the dead. There they faced the chilling spectacle of hundreds of bodies still lying perfectly preserved in the water, with unseeing eyes, staring glassily at nothing. In his vulnerable state, Claude reached out to the other men and they were not found wanting. At that moment, he knew he loved them and would not desert them. They had become his family, replacing his brother who was gone from his life.

Boat hooks were used to drag the sunken bodies to the shore. Claude knew where Charlie would be and at about three o' clock could see one of the hooks dragging him to where he stood, each yard offering a jarring finality to his loss. McEvoy and Cronin helped him take Charlie to the mass grave that had been dug and with the greatest tenderness, laid him to rest among the other men. Their Cork accents nurturing and holding him in his overwhelming loss. "He was a good man, your brother. Great gas. A grand man. You should be proud of him, boy. We will give him the send-off he deserves." Claude's last view of his brother totally eclipsed the image he had held of him since Crosshaven. Many of the bodies were mangled and unrecognisable.

The twenty strong detail of men carefully shovelled the sand and clay over their dead, a stillness enveloping them in the midst of the noise of battle in the hills above. When they were finished, Seán McEvoy quietly intoned "The Minstrel Boy" on his mouth organ. The other men joined in with a reverence that belied their context. Claude was overcome by the intimacy, the fellowship, the magnanimous gallantry shown by them. Their common voices joined in an imperceptibly soft cadence as they sang together a ballad they had known since their childhood, growing up in the fields of Munster and Leinster, miles and an epoch away from where they stood. Their baritone voices transformed the air to a lullaby.

Claude was magnetised by a remembrance of his mother holding both his and Charlie's hands, just six years old, as they walked down the Mardyke, underneath the stately elm trees, leaves drifting gently in the breeze, the morning light glistening on the river Lee. This vision comforted him that they were both together now but also reduced him to the edge of tears as he fought to hold himself together and sing along with the others. He broke when he sang "his father's sword",

"The Minstrel Boy to the war is gone
In the ranks of death you will find him;
His father's sword he hath girded on,
And his wild harp slung behind him
"Land of Song!" said the warrior bard,
"Tho' all the world betrays thee,
One sword, at least, thy rights shall guard,
One faithful harp shall praise thee!"

As they sang, the horror of what had taken place enveloped the men. Over one thousand bodies, twisted, torn and unrecognisable had been interred in the ground beneath where they stood, lain together in geometric disarray and in incomprehensible intimacy, to be left there, forlorn, abandoned, in remote foreign soil when they moved on.

It was all they could do to continue with the refrain. It was to be their last tribute to brave young men, no more than boys, companions with whom they had shared so much. They dug deep for the courage to continue, to honour, to falteringly say goodbye. Their legs were about to give way but they held fast, filled their lungs and roared in defiance at the heavens:

> *The Minstrel fell! But the foeman's chain*
> *Could not bring his proud soul under;*
> *The harp he lov'd ne'er spoke again,*
> *For he tore its chords asunder;*
> *And said "No chains shall sully thee,*
> *Thou soul of love and brav'ry!*
> *Thy songs were made for the pure and free,*
> *They shall never sound in slavery!"*

When they had finished, Claude and the others knew they had to be strong, dignified, together now as they faced the remainder of the campaign. They owed this to their faithful fellow soldiers who had fallen. They had honoured the slain in song and now they felt girded to go on and through their deeds ensure their sacrifice would not be in vain.

Later in the week, Claude, McEvoy and Cronin, along with others in the "Dubsters" came to understand that only five officers and three hundred and seventy two soldiers remained of the twenty one officers and one thousand Munster Fusiliers that left Coventry one month before. The Dublin Fusiliers lost twenty one officers and five hundred and sixty men in those fifteen, terrible minutes on the morning of 25th April 1915; a day to be etched in memory. Over the months that followed the number of Irishmen killed would exceed three thousand.

Claude hoped with all his heart that he would be able to forget the day he landed on Gallipoli and the day he buried Charlie. Years later, his desire, however, was obliterated by a paradox. Those terrible, terrible days remained forever fixed in his mind as an ever present reality, as "just yesterday". They had, however, been extirpated without a trace from the memory of his fledgling nation state, eclipsed by other events that would take place the following Easter. The men who died miles from home were on the wrong side of history. There would be no nurture from the community for their grieving families. By that time, Gallipoli had even become an object of scorn in song. *"It was better to die neath an Irish sky than in Suvla or Sedd-El-Bahr"* deeply wounding him, adding insult to the hundreds of deaths he had witnessed.

By then, Claude thought, to be forgotten was the ultimate desolation. To be

     The Drowning of Innocence

edited out of life and memory, given no place in the recollection of family and community, that for him became the unsustainable burden. In those days, years later, he began to wonder if they had all been a dream, all those men; Just imaginary boyhood companions, the rich thrill of their company and faces merely a phantom? Certainly he could never share their name, their story, their deeds with anyone else. The shame they bore for being part of the 'British' war was too great for that.

So he would pass his days at work in Kelleher wholesale confectionery in Maylor Street, diligently completing order and bookkeeping records under the kindly and compassionate eye of Seán Kelleher, Joan's Husband. At night-time, every evening, he would find solace in the Hi-B pub on his favourite stool in the corner. There he would be quiet mostly, and listen and watch the merriment around him, occasionally chipping in with a Percy French chorus.

At times when the pain of memory visited and brought with it a nauseating and fearful tremor, he would ask for as many double 'Paddy' whiskeys as was necessary to sail through such episodes intact. It was the knowing that he had come home and Charlie hadn't that he couldn't get beyond.

To survive or capitulate had morphed into the dominant theme of his existence, a daily choice which he mostly waived, as the flame and wick so brutally and effectively damaged on the Dardanelles peninsula desperately flickered seeking some redeeming light but was mostly engulfed by the acrid trail of suffocating smoke.

Gallipoli,
12th May 1915,

Miss Joan Hays,
9, Carey's Lane,
Cork

Dear Joan,

You may know by now that Charlie is no longer with us. I hope you know he died bravely here as we landed. We were able to retrieve his body and give him a decent burial. The lads were great to me, supporting me, even keeping me alive. I know this will be a big blow to you, Dad and Michael. I hope I can soften it by saying we have the bravest of brothers, much loved by all. The other men have been visibly shaken by his loss.

I hope you can help Dad see that he should be enormously proud. Nothing went to plan when we landed here and we lost many, many good men. The Turks fought with determination and still continue to do so. There will be many homes throughout Ireland grieving these days and I am so sad that ours is one.

I could not save or rescue him. I know that now. But I felt terrible for days blaming myself for not doing more. I owe my life to Dan Cronin and Séamus McEvoy. They stopped me running futilely to help Charlie. We have changed now as men here. Something has happened to us. We know that without one another we would be lost. It has drawn us close. There is a dependence and camaraderie that I would not have expected to happen. We literally would die for one another.

I know that may seem strange to you. But dear Joan, it is now all I can cling onto. This bond between us. This band of brothers in arms.

I send you, Dad and Michael all my love. I will promise to keep myself as safe as possible and will not take stupid risks.

For now, Your loving brother,

Claude XXX

The Drowning of Innocence

Alexandria,
9th January 1916,

Miss Joan Hays,
9, Carey's Lane,
Cork

Dear Joan,

We have left Gallipoli and have arrived in Egypt. I know you will be relieved by this. It was a horrible experience leaving Charlie behind. I miss him so much. Its a dull ache I live with. I felt a bleak loneliness evacuating the place.

In the last nine months we have seen the waste of war in front of our eyes and we are changed. I will never be able to fully explain to you what we have been through. But dear Joan, I want to try or else I will go mad. I know I can get into trouble for writing this but I am taking a chance and smuggled the letter out. Anyway I am past caring. The only important thing for me now is to be faithful to my fellow soldiers of Munster.

So all those letters I sent in the last few months were just to keep your spirits up, to let you know I am alive and kicking. This letter is different. We have left the Dardanelles after a fruitless nine months and left thousands of good men behind.

My mind is dominated by two things, anger and horror. I am so angry at the incompetence of the campaign. After the landings, we spent four months trying to capture the main town in the area, Krithia. Time and time again we tried to mount an assault. This cost thousands of men as we tried many times to overrun the Turks. Over the months, you could measure our progress in hundreds of yards.

You can imagine my fury when I discovered months later, when talking to a Scottish Borderer, that on the very first day of the campaign, when we lost Charlie, they were within a stones throw of Krithia, arriving there without opposition from the other side of the peninsula and seeing no Turks. Then they sat down. "What," I said. "You sat down?" "Yes," he said. "The commander didn't know what to do. After that we retreated." I was apoplectic with rage when I heard this and was visibly shaken. Can you imagine, Joan, this town we have spent months trying to capture? Losing thousands of good men trying! Day after day, waves of assault, all coming to nothing. The commanders not varying tactics much, we were just urged to run at them. It was hopeless. And they could have captured it on the very first day!!!!? Madness. Most of us are now fatalistic. I still don't understand why I am alive. I feel so guilty about that.

A big consolation during the months was meeting up with the Australians. They are very brave. What I love most about them is their irreverence. They have a different view on all this to us. So many of them from Ireland and although now speaking with a broad Australian twang, they're still very Irish. They are much more questioning than

Forgotten Men   45

I am and I have had many discussions with them. We all joined up for glory, hoping to make a statement that small nations have a right to exist and the attack on Belgium was our rallying cry. After this, I fail to see what happened in Gallipoli as anything to do with that sentiment. I also, along with the other men, developed a begrudging admiration for the Turks.

The Aussies tell me how in May, after we were here three weeks, they met them face-to-face. Because there were so many dead men between the ANZAC lines and the Turks, lying rotting, the stench awful, the Turks asked for an armistice, to bury the dead. Can you imagine, former enemies spent a day, side-by-side, carrying the bodies and giving them a decent burial? The Aussies tell me it changed them. After that, they were no longer able to dismiss the Turks as 'devils'. I also admire how they fought to protect their homeland.

Our days here have been like hell. Bodies decomposing for weeks in no man's land. The stench horrible and flies were everywhere. We were unable to eat without swallowing the blighters. All of us have been very sick, regularly. "The Turkey Trots" we called it to make light of the discomfort. But it was horrible. We found ourselves going fifteen, sixteen times a day into rotten latrines. Just a wooden plank over a pit, pulsating with a foul stench.

One night, one of the men who was on guard disappeared for three hours. When he reappeared he was courtmartialed. He said he had been caught short by the trots and had been in the latrines the whole time. He wasn't believed and was executed. I'm glad I didn't have to make that decision. Many of us hanker for some excuse to get away even for a few hours, so all of us could have been in his position. We live on the edge.

The greatest horrors have been the shelling - shrapnel bursting over our heads - harbingers of death. It is impossible to imagine it. When the shelling begins, often at night, we huddle and tremble together in sheer tension and frayed nerves. There is a faraway moan which turns into a scream, then a roar like a runaway train followed by a ground shaking crash and a diabolical red light. They reduced many of the men to shrivelling wrecks. The uncertainty of it all and the destruction. To see a friend blown apart by these devils of death demolishes morale. It was all we could do to keep sane and keep our spirits up.

The weather changed through the whole time from hot, fetid summer with beating sun when water became like gold to in the end, a perilously cold winter. In the early days when I was drinking, I found it difficult to swallow because of the foul taste. Later on that day, when I crept above the creek from where I got the water and I could see blood seeping into it from the men lying lifeless by its side. I had become a ghoul, literally drinking the blood of my enemy.

     The Drowning of Innocence

When the monsoon came, rain poured down and we lived in mud and filth. The ravines filled with gushing water making the land impassible. We wished then for the summer back. The last couple of months as winter set in filled us with dread. The cold was biting. When they called it quits and we were told to retreat to the beach for evacuation, we were so relieved.

We were among the last to leave. Miraculously, we escaped without any casualties.

We kept on the whole time and of that we can at least be proud. Trying always to support one another and be loyal to our values. Ready to do anything to help our brothers. It was what kept us going. Soon we learnt not to get too close, though, as losing someone in battle became too upsetting. Séamus McEvoy, who became a close companion after Charlie's burial, was killed during our assault on Krithia. It left me weak for days.

I know this will be hard for you to read. Don't show it to Dad. I am enclosing another letter that you can show him. I want you to know, Joan, as I do not want to keep it from you. I hope you will be strong enough to bear it. I am asking a lot of my little sister. I am out of there now and heading for France. Who knows what faces us then.

I send you my love as always. Now you mean everything to me.

Your loving brother,

Claude XXX

<table>
<tr><td>

Passchendaele,
26th November 1917,

</td><td>

Miss Joan Hays,
9, Carey's Lane,
Cork

</td></tr>
</table>

Dear Joan,

I hope this finds you well. Things continue to be tough for us here. As you already know the uprising in Dublin last year has changed how we are seen by everyone. After all that, we are not trusted here anymore. The Germans are even pouring scorn on us from their trenches, hoisting placards abusing us.

I can't myself understand what is happening at home. It feels like a betrayal of what we are doing. Who were those people anyway? Connolly, Pearse, the others? Where did they spring from? Some of the men are for it though, feeling aggrieved at the waste of life we have seen here. We fight on though as we always have done, for one another and the dirty shirts. We will not leave our honour because of these taunts. Even men in other regiments have come to cat-call at us saying "Here come the Shinners."

We feel as well that the officers are not giving us our due. They have all come to the conclusion that we are the weak front, not to be trusted, and if anything fails it is because we have not shown the bravery of others. There is a terrible arrogance about the British which I have not seen before. Good Irishmen are treated as if they were plebs and imbeciles, nothing but cannon fodder. I have seen it myself at close quarters and it was all I could do to stop myself reacting, grabbing some of the officers by the throat. It could almost turn one into a Fenian the way they behave. It is all very depressing.

Nevertheless, we give our all and have been very much part of the last victory at Passchendaele. One of the Dubs, Tom Kettle, the politician was killed at Ginchy last year and wrote this beautiful thing. Its a heartbreaking piece, written for his baby daughter, but in many, many ways, it sums up how I feel about it all after three long years.

"You'll ask why I abandoned you, my own,
And the dear heart that was your baby throne,
To dice with death. And oh! they'll give you rhyme
And reason: some will call the thing sublime,
And some decry it in a knowing tone.
So here, while the mad guns curse overhead,
And tired men sigh with mud for couch and floor,
Know that we fools, now with the foolish dead,
Died not for flag, nor King, nor Emperor,
But for a dream, born in a herdsman's shed,
And for the secret Scripture of the poor."

                    The Drowning of Innocence

In the midst of it all, all this madness, I think of our mother and her simple faith. It gave her a grace and dignity to bear everything. Although I cannot match her, I also cannot forget her and in all I do I feel her here beside me. And poor Charlie. Oh, how I miss my brother. I hope things will change soon and that we will bring this thing to an end. Then we will be home in Cork again. I hope I can adjust. Although I am fearful for the new thing that has hit the country.

I send my love to you and especially to Dad and I hope he is bearing up. I imagine things must continue to be hard for him.

How is Michael? He must be a grown man now, fully seventeen years of age. I am so glad he missed all this. It is one of the things that keeps me going. That my little brother can live his life outside of and after this madness.

Your loving brother

Claude XXX

Sergeant Claude Hays,
1st Munster Fusiliers,
Army Postal Service,
France
10th January, 1918

My Dear Claude,

I am sorry to have to give you sad news. Dad passed away yesterday. He caught the 'flu and was too weak to fight it. They say it came to Cork from an American troop ship which had docked at Queenstown. All on board were hit with it and it spread to the city. So he became another casualty in this great war.

As you can imagine Dad was never the same after the news about Charlie. It broke his heart and without Mam he had struggled to cope. I tried to keep everything from him, but I suspect, because he knew about war, he suffered with you in silence.

He died peacefully. He just gave up I think. Michael and I and others from the family were there at the end, which was a blessing. In one strange way I am relieved as I think that the world had gone too crazy and he could not make sense of it. He certainly did not understand the rise of Republicanism here. I think he was convinced that Home Rule would come and that it would be enough. I also feel he was heartbroken about the fighting between Catholics and Protestants in the north. Belfast has gone crazy and he hated it.

He, bless him, never saw religion as a mechanism for division and always had so many good Catholic friends to convince him of the rightness of that. None of that enveloping bitterness has been present as his passing. Its gratifying to see Catholics and Protestants filing through the door, happily reminiscing together about the "good auld days". Their Cork accents singing the stories. Now he is no longer with us and has gone ahead to be with Mam and Charlie. I think he will be happy there. So I can't be sad.

Michael is OK. But there is a bewilderment in his eyes which I know he tries to keep from me. He has his own life now. You know, he went to Ballingeary the last two summers to the Irish college. He loved it and has become an accomplished musician. He and Mattie are in a small band. Michael plays the bodhrán and Mattie the fiddle. They are very good. I am glad he has this to take him away from all the disease, death and destruction coursing the world.

So don't be sad. I think we were given the gift of our parents for a while. They taught us so much. And we owe it to them to be strong now.

                    The Drowning of Innocence

I am proud of you, my dear brother. I see you holding onto your sensitivity in the midst of all you have been part of. That is the true heritage of our parents.

I will write again when I have more time, but am now caught up in all the arrangements.

Much love to you, dear Brother

Joan XXX

Becoming a Gael

"As our language wanes and dies, the golden legends of the far-off centuries fade and pass away. No one sees their influence upon culture; no one sees their educational power."
"Every craggy and gnarled tree has its own strange and graceful legend attached to it."
Douglás de hÍde

Irish College,Ballingeary, County Cork,

June 1919

You could see just by watching him that Michael loved these times. His face shone beatifically, emphasising his strong, masculine features, the energy of his youth. It was as if the music came from deep within him. Adeptly, with his hands and fingers, he drew a sound from the bodhrán that was both haunting and energetic. Mattie and he were one, enmeshed in what they were doing. Mattie coaxing soaring and exhilarating notes from the fiddle that set the floor alight. Michael generating the rhythm to which the dancers were skilfully in step, adding a syncopation to his beat, percussively rapping the wooden floor of the hall, sean-nós style, with their toes. The first Céilidh of that year's Summer College.

At that moment, Michael had the confidence to sneak a glance at her. Across the room he could see she was transported by the music, skipping, tripping and gliding gracefully, at one with the tune. His breath was arrested temporarily as he saw her beauty, the joy, the laughter in her face, captivating all around. "Eileen," he whispered the name under his breath, practising its utterance, gaining a feel for it. "Eileen," wondering how that one name, that simple name, could encapsulate all he longed for, all he wanted in life.

For days now, there had been a pain in his heart as he knew that he would never have the resolve to approach her. He knew that such resolve was required at the same moment, the very same instant, he realised he lacked it. She seemed to him as dew in the field in the morning, adding a glistening luminosity to the day, but ephemeral nonetheless. Or like the clay he threw on the wheel everyday, knowing that unless he grasped it and coaxed out of it the shape it wanted to be, it would descend into chaos. He felt he should grasp the moment with Eileen in the same way, with the same sense of abandonment, urging what could be between them into life.

He had seen other boys, particularly Mattie, adept and successful at this during the summer months of '17 and '18, here in Ballingeary. Chatting to the girls, walking out, creating their romances, he had gazed on them in wonderment. From one day to the next a new love appeared, like cobwebs woven through branches, glistening in the sun, like transcending apparitions lacing their lives.

How did it happen? How did the boys have the nerve? What did they say first? What did they say second!!!? In his shyness, he felt they were like

The Drowning of Innocence

another species. He witnessed the evident jubilation of new flames and how it changed both the boys and the girls. He envied their lightness and their walks, hand in hand, in the beautiful countryside around Guagán Barra, transforming their individual summers, creating memories to last.

The boys had even succumbed to making posies of wildflowers; Montbrecia, Foxglove, Wood Anemone and Cuckoo Flower, the clever ones lacing the display with Honeysuckle for fragrance. The road from Ballingeary to Gougán was lined with Fuchsia, wild, maddeningly wild in its abandon; pinks, purples and reds sprawling onto the boreen, sometimes overreaching the span, piggy-backing on overhanging branches and creating a cathedral-like effect, a tunnel of darkness where couples could be alone together and sneak a long, passionate kiss. He had also watched their sad farewells at the end of the summer, as they embraced falteringly for one last time. The whole adventure seemed to him exquisite, faultless, desired like nothing else had been in his life so far and yet, so unattainable.

Eileen had appeared this summer for the first time when they had boarded the train, with the others, in Cork city on the opening day. He was taken aback by her as they made the journey across the county. She was there in front of him for the first time in years. He had not seen her when he visited Riverview on the odd occasion since Charlie was killed. Mattie and he usually met at the hurling club and then on to music lessons with Brother Paul at the Franciscan Friary in Liberty Street.

There were ten of them seated in the compartment all squashed together, Eileen on the opposite seat near the door to the corridor, he by the window. During the two-hour train journey, he was transfixed by her, casting furtive glances when he thought no-one was looking. He loved how unselfconscious she was, a natural ease about her, at peace with her very being. He took her in, the breadth of her. Her raven-black hair framing her perfectly proportioned face, her emerald green eyes enhanced and outlined by long slender, deep black lashes, her lips, delicate and slightly parted, full and inviting, mesmerising. She had metamorphosed from the little girl he remembered into this tall, slender, beautiful woman. She had long, long beautiful legs which set off the perfection of her body; Her shapely curves thrilling, her breasts pressing against her blouse with the unspeakable promise of their shape beneath as he sneaked a glance at them. Her perfect figure throwing Michael into a disarray he had never before encountered.

He had noticed beautiful women of course and been taken aback by the wonder of them, the unsettling bewilderment it generated in his being. The

questions they had raised in him "Why have I never noticed this before?"
"What has changed in me?" But this was different. This was Eileen, Mattie's
sister, someone touchable, reachable, present. How was he going to cope? To
him she exuded indeed radiated sensuality and sexuality. He wondered what
it would be like to touch her, there or there? He caught himself thinking that
and blushed in confusion. He immediately looked across at Mattie to see if he
had noticed but saw his friend was totally engaged in chatting to a girl he had
been sweet on last year, at least one of the girls, it being Mattie.

Michael breathed a sigh of relief and stared out the window. The train had
left Bandon behind heading for Macroom. Through the smoke Michael
observed the tranquil Cork countryside. He took comfort in the familiar musty
smell of the fabric on the head rest as he leaned against it. The smell of smoke
and grit from the engine chugging up ahead somehow beguiling. He thought
of Brother Paul and knew that he would find this situation very funny. He told
Brother Paul everything.

Brother Paul had become his mentor and friend. He was the only one able
to hold him, keep him from dissolving when Charlie was killed. With grace
and simple wisdom he had helped Michael grow strong, tutored him and
Mattie in Gaelic music, poetry and the arts. Under his coaching, they had both
become excellent musicians. He had provided them with a deep, easy
appreciation of their culture and heritage.

A charming man, with a sagacious wit and repartee, Paul was totally at
peace with himself as only a man entering his sixty fifth year can be. Someone
who dealt with things as they came along in life, not seeking to control or
shape, simply greeting each moment and circumstance as a guest. He had long
since let go the tyranny of seeking to prove himself. All the things he had
achieved were forgotten as simply moments in time. He understood that what
was important was who he had become, not what he had achieved. Simply
dressed in his Franciscan robes, he had 'no airs or graces' about him.

He spent most of the year unobtrusively wandering around Cork city,
providing a compassionate ear to his own informal flock. How they became
his, no-one could guess, but it seemed to many who appreciated him and had
benefited from his simple understanding that his congregation was extensive.
Everyone knew him. For a Dubliner he achieved a unique accolade. He was
welcome in Cork. Indeed by this time he had probably become an honorary
Corkonian. Not that he would accept that, of course. His love for the boys in
blue 'The Dubs' and Bohemians football club 'The Bohs' prohibited any
altering of allegiance. So he remained a Dubliner adrift in Cork, an anomaly,

          The Drowning of Innocence

but finding his way into people's homes, lives and confidence.

Brother Paul brought many of the boys and girls of the city together. They admired him. He was open, free, he never judged, all felt welcome. For Michael he was an incarnation in male form of his dearly missed mother. He was like no priest or vicar Mattie or Michael had ever known.

Paul had introduced Michael to a local potter. Perhaps he recognised in him the rich artistic genes he inherited from his mother. Michael immediately took to clay, loved its touch, was absorbed by the skill and delicacy required to shape and mould. When at the wheel, he became his own king and master, sure and certain in all he set out to accomplish, with the determination and passion of the young.

In 1916, a year after Charlie's death, Brother Paul supported Mattie and Michael to go to the summer college. Times were changing and the war had delivered a foment of division, pain and grief. He hated the inheritance passed on by his generation with its Victorian certitudes, its posturing for glory. He had no respect for his own church with its imperialist vision and was deeply suspicious of the vast seminary of Maynooth, churning out foot-soldiers to propagate a narrow, fundamentalist and oppressive reading of the sacred and mystical. The bigotry it fostered as silencing as any penal law.

He thought of his church and the ruling classes as predators, seeking to ensnare and trap young lives, fearful of the challenge to the status quo which came from young people who sought a fresh vision for the world and for Ireland. For Paul, the future for these young Irish men and women lay in their heritage, rich tradition and identity through exposure to their language, arts and culture at the summer college. This, along with the deep friendships formed would see them through.

In 1919, it was Eileen's turn to join the boys. She had been excited at the thought as the summer approached. Her love for Michael had not dimmed over the years and she was looking forward to spending time in his company.

Things did not work out like she expected however. From the first day Eileen was conscious of Michael shunning her and whenever she joined a company of which Michael was a part; at the dinner table or whiling time away in the long evenings in the balming sun, Michael always rose and left very soon afterwards. This had cut Eileen to the quick and she did not understand it.

After ten days, it was unbearable and she was becoming miserable. She knew that if she was to get any joy out of the summer, out of these precious days in this extraordinary countryside, she would have to resolve in her mind what was happening. "Why is Michael deliberately avoiding me?" "Am I making myself too vulnerable?" "Am I being immature?" "Obsessed?" These thoughts and others railed around her head, often preventing sleep and were particularly acute when she woke in the middle of the night. Then, cringing in embarrassment at her predicament, she saw herself, a woman fully seventeen years old but behaving like an infatuated schoolgirl.

After one particularly turbulent night, her thoughts madly out of control, she resolved with determination to 'catch the bull by the horns.' The first free time of the day was early evening at six o'clock. It was a particularly beautiful, midsummer's day and the lateral light from the sun brought an iridescent hue to the grass, trees and bushes. Eileen quickly approached Michael after tea lest her courage fail her.

"Michael, I would like to go for a walk with you. I need desperately to talk to you about something."

She had practiced these words time and again in her mind during the day, visualising their execution. When she spoke them to Michael, however, they tumbled out of her in a rush, one word jumping over the other, like sheep out of a pen. She saw straight away the alarm in Michael's face. "Oh gosh" she thought, "What have I done? Can I take it back?"

Of all the things that Michael could have dreamed of happening, this was the most unlikely. His heart skipped a beat, his face became flushed and confused, but he managed to stumble out a "Yes."

As they fell in together, step by step, leaving the grounds of the Summer School behind, his confidence grew, and with a beating heart, he suggested he show her somewhere special. After three years at the college, he had found his way around this northwestern corner of the county. He had discovered a secret place for himself during previous summers, a place he often retired to, to think and absorb the things he was learning. He knew immediately that this was a place to show Eileen. It was his place of formation, where he had slowly come to terms with the losses that life had laid before him, his Mum, Charlie, his Dad last year. "I will take her there."

They took the boreen to Guagán. Michael's shyness began to disappear and he began to feel at home with her. The nervousness that he had lived with began to diffuse.

      The Drowning of Innocence

"Michael, I have been really looking forward to seeing you, but I can't help feeling that you are avoiding me. I am sorry, so sorry. I really, really like you, Michael, always have but now I feel I am in the way, getting on your nerves. What have I done wrong?"

Michael's heart skipped a beat when he heard her say "I really, really like you". He was struck by her maturity, her openness, her vulnerability. A thrilling sensation leapt inside him and her words opened a way for him.

"Gosh, Eileen. Nothing, not at all, the opposite. When I saw you again after all these years, something happened to me. I had such overwhelming feelings for you and I didn't know what to do with them."

He stopped suddenly, blushing fiercely as this unexpected outburst. "There I go again," he thought, "blurting out too much, too soon". Eileen reached for his hand and held it, her eyes beseeching him to continue.

Her touch, her sweet gentle touch thrilled him. Her eyes, her beautiful face, smiling earnestly at him, took his breath away. "This is how it is," he thought. "After all those years of yearning. But, my goodness, it's so much more."

"I felt there was no way that you could feel the same about me and so to avoid the hurt of disappointment and to avoid getting in your way, I have been keeping myself to myself. Every time you came into a room, my heart would pound so much. I honestly could not take my eyes from you and looked for you everywhere. Sorry Eileen, I couldn't bear it. And I'm sorry I hurt you."

She laughed. "Its alright Michael. One thing though. Don't tell your sister what you have been through. She would find that hysterically funny. She knows I have been crazy about you for years."

An exhilarating peace and joy overtook them both as their words met, joined and wove a safe place between them. The evening opened up. The iridescent light, the perfume of the hedgerows along the road seemed to gather in an even greater intensity, transforming this little part of north west Cork with its translucent loch, the Shehy mountains, the woods and hedgerows into a kind of paradise for them both.

As they approached Guagán, he took her by the hand and led her through the woods, through his secret pathway. The bond between them already magically complete. After a few minutes, the dense wood opened into a clearing, a tiny amphitheatre. A deep and dry moss carpeted the ground, vividly green with a hue of purple at the edges. The bank formed natural steps towards a tall and old Stone Pine tree. The thick branches of the tree shaped like a stairway up to its crown, fifty feet above them in the air. At the base of the tree was a small spring that fed the River Lee, like a rivulet, coursing alongside. They stopped and cupped water from a duct that he had carved from wood the year before. Eileen was silent as he showed her the intricate celtic knotwork and spirals decorating the sides of the duct, carved from Elder wood. She was charmed by its delicate, exquisite beauty.

"I want to show you my secret place. Are you ready for adventure?"

She smiled with excitement as he led the way up the tree, giving her help when she needed it but also marvelling at her agility. When he reached the top, he urged her to put her head through the crown.   In total amazement, she saw a carpet of branches displayed in front of her like the best laid lawn. He climbed out onto the crown and lay down.

"Its perfectly safe. I discovered it two years ago and have bounced on it and it has held me easily. No-one knows about it. This is where I come to be on my own."

Intoxicated by this intimacy and shared experience, she climbed through the crown and lay beside him.

The evening was perfect. He talked freely as he had never done before in his life. They conversed in Irish together, delighting in the rich lilt of the language and the mellifluous nature of its cadence, structure and tone. He spoke about his loss and confusion when his mother and Charlie died. He talked about his father and the lack of understanding that had existed between them and how painful that had been in the weeks before he had passed away the previous winter. They laughed together with the relief of one another's companionship, the two of them on top of a tree, away from everything, gazing at the sky as it changed colour, the light lingered with the setting sun, intertwining shades of rose-pink, crimson, lavender and violet.

At one point, Eileen reached into her pocket and through force of habit, drew out her stone. She loved the feel of it and lying on the crown of the tree, between heaven and earth, seemed the perfect place to draw from its strength.

"What have you got there?"

She handed it to him carefully.

"Gosh, its beautiful. Where did you get it from?"

                          The Drowning of Innocence

She roared with laughter. "Oh Michael, you don't know? Don't tell Joan about this either." She smiled as she reminded him sweetly about the day in Crosshaven, all those years before.

They reminisced about many things. Their beings drawing closer, now enmeshed, a kind of osmosis taking place where the point of their joining became imperceptible, like the most natural thing in the world, a coalescence, a knitting together, a fastening, a mingling of souls. They had discovered each other as 'Anam Cara.'

"Even the birds are jealous of us, Michael," she laughed, gazing at the furious evening activity in the branches all around them.

As the sun set, they climbed down and made their way home, the long June dusk providing an ethereal light for their journey. They heard the corncrake call its lonely plaintiff cry. They stopped for a moment, utterly transfixed by this rasping, mechanical, metallic echo; A beckoning of longing for its mate. The sound, beautiful here as it traversed over the meadow towards them both, would come back to haunt Eileen in years to come.

"Do you know, my Granny used to say that it's corncrakes lying on their backs all over the world that hold up the sky. 'Don't disturb them,' she would say. 'It's the very strain of all that work that has them worn out, their voices gone, poor things.'"

The sweet simplicity of this story from her lips overwhelmed him and he spun her around, grasped both her hands and looked deeply in her eyes. "God," he thought, "I don't ever want to be separated from this beautiful woman."

"What's the matter?" She looked at him, perplexed.

"It's nothing." Overcome with embarrassment at his impetuosity.

They walked on, hand in hand. From across the lake and above the cry of the curlew and the sharp warning of the redshank, stridently saying 'stay away, stay away', they could hear the sound of children playing outside a farmhouse on the far side of the Coomroe valley, their delighted melody skipping over the water towards them. As dusk grew in the sky, turning the vista towards muted monochrome colours, flocks and flocks of starlings coalesced and diffused creating elaborate, shifting, amoeba-like patterns in the evening sky, an effervescent charcoal painting; Waves on waves of beauty, the sound of their wings evoking the coast thirty miles away. This natural sonata provided the perfect denouement to their tryst.

That evening flowed into many that the two of them clandestinely sought. They spent hours over the next fortnight together, sharing their dreams. Michael explained how affected he was by his brother's commitment to the 'British' war. He explained his growing sense of consciousness, that he had no truck with the vanities of the Protestant Ascendancy and that was why he had found himself painfully at odds with his father.

He became quiet as rebukes from his father were played out in his mind.

"Why are you on the side of these troublemakers?"

"Don't you see that they are disturbing the security of rule?"

"Look what being part of Empire has given us here in Cork, its architecture, its commerce. Its place in the scheme of things."

"When did you become so ungrateful, so contrary?"

"How in heaven's name did I get it so wrong with you?"

"When I think of Charlie's great sacrifice and Claude's continuing dedication and devotion, you are a real disappointment to me and your mother's memory."

Every word and phrase a dagger in the heart, driving them further from one another.

These and other arguments had burnt a deep hole in his consciousness and had saddened him but in all his reflections he remained steadfast with the unshakeable conviction that he was 'Irish'.

She, recognising his need for silence as these remembrances gripped his consciousness, held his hand as he came back to himself.

"You know, Eileen, at first I thought I was being a real amadán. Of course I am Irish. But then I realised that in reality none of us really are, don't you think? It's been knocked out of us. We have lost touch with our roots and now see ourselves as second class. I was very angry at the beginning when I realised what had happened to us as a people but as I began to understand more and more of our poetry and storytelling, our heritage, I relaxed into a discovery of who I really am. I have loved that part of it all. Its opening up through music and song. It's my real life now and it makes sense of everything

    The Drowning of Innocence

I do here and in Cork. As I work throwing pots, playing hurling, making music with the band. It has brought me home to myself in a way I could not have dreamed of. Of course it put me at odds with Da and that was really hard. But I can't help it. I am a Gael and there's nothing can change that. Its the most natural thing in the world."

"Gosh, I didn't know any of that about you. I thought being a Protestant 'n all, these things wouldn't occur to you. I'm sorry, I guess we are so ignorant of one another's lives."

"So normal, Eileen. It's the way most people see us. Most people don't know we are a mixed bag, us Prods. Different churches - All at odds with one another. We couldn't be more different. What do you think of Wolfe Tone's words? I love them so much I learnt them by heart. *'To unite Protestant, Catholic and Dissenter under the common name of Irishmen in order to break the connection with England, the never failing source of all our political evils."*

"That's amazing." She thought these words, which she had heard before, never sounded so fresh, so alive, coming from him.

"The United Irishmen were a threat, don't you think? Westminster mightily afraid of the French revolution 'n all. And losing America. Don't you think they could see that an alliance between Catholics and Protestants would spell ruin for them?"

"You're probably right, Michael. Protestants and Catholics as near neighbours, fellow countrymen and we know next to nothing about one another."

"I think they spent decades dividing us, separating us. "Divide et Impera' that's their mantra, isn't it? They do it everywhere. In India, with Muslims and Hindus. It's vicious, clever stuff. Carson and the Orange Order didn't spring from nowhere. They were carefully nurtured through scaremongering tactics by the Tories."

On other days they talked about British rule, the idealism of the 1916 martyrs and the growing sense of insurrection abroad, particularly in Cork. Michael was giddy with excitement.

"I don't want to miss out, Eileen. I want to be ready. When I heard Tomás McCurtain speak, I was so excited. What do you think?"

"I worry for you both, you and Mattie. You're too enthusiastic. You need to stop and think. War is not some great and glorious adventure. You of all people should know that.

Hearing this, he stopped for a minute to catch himself, stifling a quiet sob.

"Oh sorry," she said, reaching out in compassion for the lost soul of him.

"Charlie, oh Charlie," He wailed. "With all that eagerness to go off and fight the British war. It still hurts. I can't get away from it. The terrible waste of his life. Gallipoli. So many Irish families in deep pain and loss because of Churchill's cynical opportunism."

He looked over at her as tears streamed down her face.

"What, Eileen?"

"I owe my life to your brother. I think of him often. And I miss him too. So much. This is the first time I have been able to tell someone, anyone, what I feel."

He put his arm around her as they comforted one another. In a short while Michael picked up on his rage, his anger not being fully exorcised.

"Oh how I hate the British establishment with their cruelty, blindness and arrogance and particularly the Churchills. All that 'Ulster will fight and Ulster will be right' madness. Father and son together, wreaking havoc on our people. They make my blood boil. I would do anything to rid this country of their dominant influence."

She was taken aback by his forcefulness.

"I don't think hatred is a good place to start, Michael. It does not serve Charlie's memory well."

In her mind came flashes of Charlie cycling away in front of them all, belting out 'Whistling Phil McHugh' on the road to Crosshaven.

After a long silence she said.

"I agree, though, that we have the chance now to find something else for ourselves. A different country, a different way of doing things. Something that includes all of us and is more honest. But Michael, you can't create all this beauty in your work and hate at the same time. We have to find another way."

     The Drowning of Innocence

On that particular day they had not taken refuge in their intimate tree-top retreat. They had found a space by the lake looking out onto the island which held the small chapel of Guagán Barra, with its old monastic ruins beyond. Eileen was struck by the silence and tranquillity and drew Michael's attention to it.

"I love this place. The old ruins speak to me. Honestly it's as if I can hear the monks chanting as they did in the fifth century. That's something to aspire to, isn't it, Michael? Can you imagine, this country of ours rising again to become a force in Europe like it was all those centuries ago. That's our real heritage, isn't it? A land of scholarship and beauty, a place from which the deep wisdom of the soil and landscape can be passed on to the rest of Europe. Goodness knows, these last few years show Europe really needs it. We could become modern-day Finbarrs!"

She laughed pointing to the small oratory dedicated to St Finbarr. He joined in the laughter, his mood lifting with hers.

"OK, provided I don't have to become celibate and do without you." And at that moment as if to emphasise the point, he drew her tenderly towards him and kissed her lips with a mixture of abandon and intimacy. Her stomach did somersaults with the thrill of it. The first time they had kissed. She floated home that evening to the college, alive with dreams of their future together.

There was an intensity about their life at the college which formed their relationship. Ballingeary had become a counterculture, a place shaped in opposition to the indignity and preposterous nature of Empire. The very existence of this alternative caused them to argue, discuss the nature of British intent towards Ireland.

"Surely, Michael, at Versailles, they have to see the inconsistency in their rallying cry for Belgium and other small nations at the beginning of the war and the now denial of our equal right for self-determination. They can't have their cake and eat it?"

"I don't trust them, Eileen. Sure, if they let go of Ireland, then the rest of their Empire would collapse, as night follows day. They are too in love with their own power and pomp."

"But won't the Americans put pressure on them?"

"Well I'm not so sure. They aren't giving DeValera much of their time now he's over there. All these big nations just prop one another up, don't you think? In any case, the British want to keep our harbours. They would never give up Queenstown. They like to rule the waves."

"Perhaps you're right. But it breaks my heart to see our country divided. The Orange Order and the Tories. Home Rule was never going to happen with them around. They are cute boyos. They knew exactly how to work the whole thing. They're going to get their six counties now. We were naive. Redmond was naive. We lost badly."

"Absolutely, Eileen, the die is cast. Home Rule is dead. We need more in any case. And we'll have to fight them for it. I'm nervous of what's coming. More so now because of what you've said. But I don't want to be found wanting either. There's no turning back now. The mood in Cork has changed forever."

There, at that moment, with storm clouds sweeping over the valley, as they made their way back to the college, Eileen's mood plunged to mirror the sky's darkening, visited by a premonition of the time that was almost upon them. A time that would transform both of them, the city and county that was their home, forever.

Michael was oblivious. To him the conversations delighted him. Somehow, strengthening him in his resolve. Their attraction to one another, deep, innocent and charming was amplified by the shared conviction they had for a new Ireland. A dream to pursue together. It was beyond his imagination that he could talk so easily and effortlessly and truly to this beautiful woman. A deep bond of friendship and knowingness was growing between them. They had become like peas in a pod.

The landscape around Gougán captured and framed these days and enveloped them in beauty; Moments when the rain beat softly on the lake evoking in them a strong sense of nostalgia; Soft days, the sun chasing the clouds across the fields, accentuating a panoply of colours and shapes; the juxtaposition of land and water carving a deep sense of belonging, on occasion moving Michael to tears with the majestic quality of it all. These represented the happiest days of their lives. His confidence visibly grew. He felt powerful, even immortal, during those heady weeks.

The county hurling championship was taking place during the summer. In the second round, Blackrock were up against Carrigtwohill who had beaten them in the '18 final. Mattie and Michael were determined to avenge that and spent a lot of time in training. Over the previous year, they had graduated into

The Drowning of Innocence

the senior team and developed a telepathic centrefield partnership which had been instrumental in guiding Blackrock to return to their place of dominance after four years. The city was gripped with excitement as these two rivals prepared for the game. A large crowd gathered at the Athletic Grounds. The RIC were out in force, spying on those attending and threatening to stop the game. They had lifted many Republicans at previous games and there was an additional air of tension because hidden among the crowd alongside Tomás McCurtain appeared the 'Big Fella', Mick Collins himself, who had gained a fierce reputation as a veteran of the 1916 Rising and was now the most wanted man in Ireland.

Both of the lads had travelled for the game. Waiting for it to begin, Michael composed himself. These were moments of sheer bliss for him. He loved the smell of the newly mown grass and carefully turned the sliothar in the palm of his hand, nurturing it, coaxing it as a friend. He loved the shape of it, the stitching raised and the two skins, enveloping the ball, cupped as in an embrace. The adrenaline raced in his stomach and he was eager to begin.

The game itself was fast and furious, close and skilful. It was difficult for both teams to escape their markers but Carrigtwohill had sneaked into the lead with two points to spare and minutes left on the clock. The Rockies needed a goal as a point would surely mean they would run out of time.

The Carrig goalkeeper took a long puckout. In the centre of the pitch Michael kept his eye on the ball as it dropped from the sky. His timing immaculate, he soared above his Carrig marker and caught the sliothar perfectly. Surrounded by defenders he slipped the ball to Mattie, free on the wing. Mattie took the ball without breaking stride and began soloing towards the Carrig goal, the sliothar balanced perfectly on his hurley, with defenders trailing in his wake. As he neared the goal, the Carrig corner back cut off his route. With a deft flick, Mattie hooked the ball over the defender and watched it soar high, dropping just outside the parallelogram. Michael had tracked the run and sprung with flawless timing towards the angle of the sliothar, pulling with his hurley over his head and burying the ball in the back of the net. For a moment the crowd were silent but then erupted into a tumultuous roar to greet the score. They had done it. They had their revenge on the humiliation of last year's final and would march on to the next round.

After the game, Mattie and Michael, flushed with excitement from the contest, were introduced to Michael Collins.

"We need men like you," Collins quipped as he looked deeply into their eyes.

Mattie was too quick to respond, overawed by the man himself.

"We're ready, Sir," he said.

Collins held Michael's stare. It seemed to Michael as if he wanted to exert his will over him. Michael resisted. Chastened by the experience of both his brothers, he was not ready to bend his will to any man, no matter how famous or charismatic. Collins turned to a man standing next to him.

"This is Tom Hales, Lads," He said "He will look after you."

Then to Hales he pointed towards the lads.

"These are Cork diamonds you got here, Tom, I want you to fucking well send me progress reports on them. Two fucking diamonds."

Hales spoke to them quietly and in confidence about the seriousness of joining the Volunteers. He agreed a swearing-in ceremony with them in the city at the end of Summer.

In the early evening, Michael and Mattie took the train back to Macroom and the Summer College. Mattie was animated through meeting Collins. He had immediately fallen under the man's spell and was in awe. Michael remained reticent.

When school finished at the end of summer, both were sworn in together as Volunteers in the Irish Republican Army, soldiers for Irish freedom. That day, they came of age. Michael saw the day as a kind of baptism, his fulfilment and true anointing as a Gael.

As an acknowledgement of the internal transformation, a recognition of the transmutation that had reshaped his life, he changed his name and from that moment on was known to all as Micheál not Michael.

The Drowning of Innocence

The Price of Freedom

"Judged by English standards the Irish are a difficult and unsatisfactory people. Their civilisation is different and in many ways lower than that of the English. They are entirely lacking in the Englishman's distinctive respect for the truth . . . many were of a degenerate type and their methods of waging war were in most cases barbarous, influenced by hatred and devoid of courage"

Record of the rebellion in Ireland, 1920–21 (Jeudwine Papers, Imperial War Museum)

"If the persons approaching (a patrol) carry their hands in their pockets, or are in any way suspicious-looking, shoot them down. You may make mistakes occasionally and innocent persons may be shot, but that cannot be helped, and you are bound to get the right parties some time. The more you shoot, the better I will like you, and I assure you no policeman will get into trouble for shooting any man.

Lt. Colonel Gerald Brice Ferguson Smyth, June, 1920

"It is not those who can inflict the most but those that can suffer the most who will conquer."
Terence McSwiney, Lord Mayor of Cork Inaugural Speech
March, 1920

"Our freedom must be had at all hazards. If the men of property will not help us they must fall; we will free ourselves by the aid of that large and respectable class of the community - the men of no property."
Theobald Wolfe Tone - 1798

"..........................our part
To murmur name upon name, As a mother names her child
When sleep at last has come on limbs that had run wild.
What is it but nightfall? No, no, not night but death;
Was it needless death after all?
For England may keep faith for all that is done and said.
We know their dream; enough to know they dreamed and are dead;
And what if excess of love bewildered them till they died?
I write it out in a verse -
MacDonagh and MacBride And Connolly and Pearse
Now and in time to be, wherever green is worn,
Are changed, changed utterly:
A terrible beauty is born."
From Easter 1916, W.B. YEATS

Cork City,

Early June 1920

Cornelius Barry or Con as he was known to his workmates and friends was a strongly built man, short in stature, handsome features with a receding hairline he accepted with amusement and equanimity. "Good men always come out on top," he would joke with those who teased him. He was a quiet man, a man who minded his own business, kept himself to himself, not really needing the affirmation of friendship. Yet he was well liked and indeed well known in the Blackrock parish.

Without doubt it was his daughter, Eileen, who was his pride and joy. Over the years there had evolved a deep, blossoming friendship between the two, full of mutual admiration and respect. From an early age, he had seen in her something of himself, an undemonstrative intelligence, a reflective train of thought, a way of looking at the world and wanting to alter it to a shape they both recognised within themselves. Her beauty, gained from her mother, was something that charmed and delighted him. He watched her growth, saw in her an instinctive capacity to build close companionship with her school pals. She possessed a sensitive empathy that made all her friends feel safe in her company.

Con from early on had made a vow to himself that all her abundant talents would be nurtured and fostered, if he could help it. It was through hard work, taking three jobs on a day, that he had shepherded her through the 'Ursulines' and then on to study Art at University College Cork. For Con the hardships and difficulties he endured to make this possible were borne lightly. His reward those moments in the day when he could sit with his daughter as she explained excitedly to him what she had discovered.

Mattie, his son, took care of himself. He was always an active boy and rarely about the house. Any time Con saw him he had either a hurley or a fiddle in his hands and was heading off on his bike to the training pitch or the Franciscans. Con felt that Mattie was raising himself and saw the deep influence on him of his boyhood friendship with Michael Hays, now calling himself Micheál. Con reflected on this with a grin, a mixture of pride and amusement.

He remembered with delight Eileen's return from the Irish College last summer a woman, no longer a girl. She had started a romance with Micheál and it was captivating to see them with one another since. Con was thrilled for

The Drowning of Innocence

Eileen. He had seen for years the crush she had on Micheál and it was gratifying to see it come to fruition. They were childhood sweethearts, really, like himself and Mary. Con saw the signs.

He was slightly concerned that Mary would find Micheál's faith a problem, him not being a Catholic, but that could wait for later. He liked Micheál and had seen for years that he was a good lad and now had become a fine young man. He also saw the sadness in his eyes. There was no doubt Micheál had it very tough, losing his Ma, brother and Da all in such a short space of time. And in such terrible ways. Tough for anyone and so to his credit that Micheál was turning out to be such a good young man.

Con liked that he and his son Mattie were best of friends. Whenever he could find the time, he would turn up at a Rockies game and watch quietly from the sidelines as they played their hearts out. He was proud of his son at those moments. Mattie was Mattie, he thought and would be alright.

Because of all this, Con was largely a contented man, still in love with the woman he married all those years before. Mary and he were an undemonstrative couple. Those who knew them well could easily see the devotion which they lavished on their children. Mary had developed a deep piety after the children were born. She regularly attended mass at the Poor Clares convent on College Road. Con didn't mind that at all. He saw her contentment, even if occasionally he worried about her scruples; That she may not be able to cope with the ambiguities that certainly would come their way through their children's more liberal and open development, a product of the changes which had enveloped the city.

Con's work gave him immense satisfaction. He had learned carpentry from his Da and was supremely gifted around wood and possessed a deftness to create functional yet aesthetic pieces in the smallest of spaces. Because of this, he was always in demand for extra work to complement his employment at Passage dockyard.

He had been employed at Passage for the past twenty years and had seen and survived its many changes. In the early years he worked in the saw mill and suffered as a consequence, the noise of the heavy machinery damaging his hearing and leaving him partially deaf. It was an affliction which he had learned to live with and had afforded him a kind of peace and protection from the world. Happily he had been transferred to the relative peace of the joinery five years previously and this had suited his creative talents well.

Con loved the early morning and evening journeys on the train from Blackrock to Passage and as a Corkman had a fierce pride in the beauty of the line which skirted the river estuary all along its route. Those moments in the day were a time for reflection, for himself, as he gazed out the window of the carriage and took in the passing landscape and the changing seasons.

He had tried to shut out the growing tension that had overtaken the city in the last few years. Earlier this year, he had, along with others, been horrified by the murder of Tomás McCurtain, the popular Lord Mayor of the city. People said it was the RIC that did it, as a reprisal, bursting into his house in the early hours of the morning with blackened faces and shooting him dead in front of his wife and children.

He had seen photos of the children since. He could not take in fully the measure of this outrage and hid it carefully in the back of his mind. Terence McSwiney was elected to replace McCurtain as Mayor but the growing tension remained, unabated. Con feared for his children in the middle of all of this. He could see they were becoming politicised, their time in the Irish College, which he had supported wholeheartedly, had turned them, at a very young age, into ardent idealists. He suspected that Mattie had already joined the Volunteers and knew there was little he could do to dissuade him.

Cork was alive. There was a vehemence about the people that had transformed everything. They were charged now, beginning with the execution of the 1916 leaders and certainly after the murder of their own Lord Mayor. It was almost as if the city had become a republic, all in its own right, ungovernable, certainly to the British. It was not in Con's nature to rise to such provocation though. In his heart he dreamed of a different Ireland and this was why he was investing so much effort in his daughter. He felt that was contribution enough.

In the last month, things had taken a turn for the worst. Platoons of British soldiers had arrived in the city, a dishevelled lot, and had begun to throw their weight around. They had been assembled from the four corners of Scotland, England and Wales. People were avoiding them and there were stories of beatings and cruelty not heard before. They were getting a nickname for themselves; 'Black and Tans' on account that they didn't seem to have regular uniforms but strode about in a mixture of army khaki and police navy blue.

Whatever their name, Con was aware that they were dangerous, that they took on anyone wherever they found them and there was no telling what would happen after that. Because his various jobs took him all around the city

     The Drowning of Innocence

at all times of the day and night, Mary had become afraid. He had to promise her he would be careful.

It was early evening when he got off the train at Blackrock station. The sky was murky with a light mist covering everything. His plan was to make a quick detour to a big house on the Marina on his way home to price a job which he had heard about that day at the joinery. At the top of Blackrock Road, he heard the bells of Shandon calling out six o'clock. He stopped where he was for the Angelus. Con was not a religious man, but neither was he one to upset tradition and that everything stopped for the Angelus had been deeply ingrained in him since his childhood. He now used that time to think of Mary, just small moments when he remembered her kindness and devotion to himself and their children over the years. The comfortable home she had made for the three of them. It had become the punctuation in his daily routine. Having forgotten the words of the Angelus over the years, he replaced them with 'Hail Marys' the words quietly and repetitively intoned in his head. The Shandon bells were tapering off the sixth tone as he finished the final Hail Mary "Holy Mary, Mother of God, pray for us sinners now and at the hour of our death, Amen."

On opening his eyes, he saw the dreaded 'Black and Tans' ahead, standing by their Crossley tender, smoking, just waiting. He couldn't tell whether they had seen him or not. He felt a menacing atmosphere in the air and didn't want to hang about. He changed tack and set to double back where he had come to find another way home. He shoved his hands into his pockets, trying for all the world to affect a 'divil-may-care' mood. The last thing he wanted to do was to run into these fellows. It was for Con a fateful decision.

The 'Tans' had seen him. Not liking the way he turned around, they shouted to him to "get your fucking hands out of your pockets and put them in the air." Con didn't hear and oblivious to the drama behind him walked slowly on, continuing to act as nonchalantly as possible. Within seconds, the 'Tans' opened fire and brought him down. They sprinted the hundred yards towards him, guns at the ready and when they reached him found him dead, blood rippling from his prostrate body, seeping out over the pavement and roadside.

The evening had closed in around the scene. It was as if a sudden and eerie darkness had descended, one of those summer days which through an abrupt freak in the weather turns everything to Autumn. Neighbours heard the gunshots and ran out onto the street. Seeing Con's prostrate body lying on the ground, the crowd was overcome with rage.

The Price of Freedom

"Fuck you, you bastards."

"Go back to where you fecking came from."

"Leave him alone, you Gobshites."

"You fucking murderers."

Recognising the danger, the 'Tans' ran back up the road to their tender and sped towards the city, deserting the scene, with a dawning realisation that from now on everywhere, everywhere in Cork, was enemy territory to them. It was a cataclysmic moment. They had brought the war to Blackrock, to Cork city. They had left behind them, slain like a dog, a true son of the parish and the city, a simple, honest, unassuming, good man. The people would never forget this. The people would not forgive this. By that one arrogant, stupid act, they had sewn to the wind. In the months to come, they would reap the whirlwind.

Maureen O'Sullivan was broken in two when she saw Con. Good, kindhearted Con, who wouldn't hurt a fly, lying there, prone, his lifeblood oozing out onto the pavement. "Mary will be in bits," she thought.

"Go up to Riverview, boy, and tell the family," she told her son Séamus.

The young lad, although overcome by the dread of what he had seen, ran fiercely up the road to the Barry household. His heart was pounding inside him as he tried to focus, everything he did done out of simple repetition, one thing after the other, one leg driving another, away from the bleak scene of devastation, but knowing he was the harbinger of a terrible revelation. When he reached Riverview he ran up to and pounded on the front door, trying to get his dreadful task over with as quickly as he could.

He screamed "Mary, Eileen, Mattie, come quickly, Con's been shot."

Eileen opened the door to the ashen-faced young lad and like a punch in her gut immediately knew that her life had changed irrevocably and irredeemably. Her mother came out of the kitchen and seeing the boy and Eileen let out a deep wail and collapsed to the floor. Chaos followed for Eileen. All she wanted was to run as fast as she could to be at her father's side but here before her was her mother, crumpled on the floor, deep, deep, soundless sobs racking her body. Cleft in two, Eileen reached down to hold her mother and Mary's body dissolved in her arms. She held her there for what seemed like hours, all the time trying to wake up from this terrible nightmare into which she had been plunged. She knew this is where she had to be. She could not leave this

     The Drowning of Innocence

broken woman's side, now, not at this moment, perhaps not ever again.

Eileen did not remember when Mattie came home. She saw the disbelief in his eyes when he heard what had happened and the speed with which he turned round to head out and up the Blackrock Road. She only remembered his return hours later, an utterly changed man. Then there was a deep darkness in his eyes which Eileen had never seen before. As he entered the house, a rage and anger coursed through his body and his very being. Eileen could not look at him. She became very afraid of the transfiguration taking shape before her eyes. It was a moment that would come back to haunt her.

Mattie did not look at her, nor his mother nor the gathered neighbours and family in the kitchen; gathered there to comfort Mary. He rushed past Eileen and up the stairs to his room. He emerged minutes later with a revolver. A revolver!!!! Eileen was stunned. How did Mattie have a revolver?

"No Mattie, No. No. No Nooooo!!!!!" She screamed and held onto him as he wrestled to get her away.

"I have to get them," he screamed. "I can't let these bastards get away with this."

As he forced her away and reached the open doorway of the house, Tom Hales appeared before him, Micheál by his side. Hales grabbed Mattie and took him outside as Micheál saw Eileen and rushed towards her, held her in a deep, long comforting embrace. For the first time, she let it all out, the anguish, the pain, the bewilderment, the awful nightmare of a night, the descent into hell, the terrifying thing that had befallen them. Sobs coursed through her frame, tears streaming down her face, her life and being macerated by the unfolded horror. Micheál was helpless, could say nothing, he just held her and murmured over and over again "Mo Stóir, Mo Stóir."

At the front of the house, Mattie was engaged in a fierce argument with Tom Hales.

"I have to find them, I can't let them get away with this. What did my Da ever do to anyone. I got to kill these bastards."

"You are a soldier now, Mattie. You have to think strategically. You have to think of the cause."

"Fuck the cause if they can get away with killing my Da."

"Mattie, Mattie, you know what we have to do. You know what Collins is saying. We have to create mayhem for the fuckers. But, Mattie, to create mayhem means we have to be disciplined. We can't go off half-cocked. Those fuckers are experienced, they have better weapons. We will catch them, don't you worry. But not now."

"You promise."

"Yes Mattie, I promise. Look, I have been on the phone to Collins himself already. He knows about the situation. Don't worry, we will take care of everything, you, your family and them."

Mattie began to calm down but his face was set in stone.

"But I don't want you to lose how you are feeling, Mattie. We will use that. Don't you worry."

The night passed. Somehow, with the help of neighbours, they managed to get Con back from the morgue and laid him out in the front room. He looked peaceful, somehow and that helped Eileen and Mary to say their goodbyes.

That night, the night before the removal and funeral, Eileen sat up with her Da, after her Mam had gone to bed. She felt an intimacy with him as she knelt beside the bed where he was laid out, in that small front room where they had spent so much time together, each little ornament and framed picture evoking in her a remembrance of things that had passed and would be no more.

A certain light had gone out of her life, this strong man, this simple man. She knew she had the privilege of knowing him like no other, the deep genetic bond that was carved out in both of them, granting them, during the now too short a time they had together, a symbiosis, a recognition sometimes spoken, sometimes felt, of a shared and desired world totally at odds with the one which was being conceived by the machinations of powerful men. With tears flowing, she thanked this wonderful man for bequeathing to her that insight and determination.

Dawn arrived and the funeral took place at St Michaels. The family and parishioners wanted it to be small, a local community saying goodbye to this good man. They resisted the cry to make Con a hero or symbol and for that Eileen was deeply grateful. After mass and the burial in the small church cemetery, family and neighbours came back to the house.

True to his word, Tom Hales had laid on the Guinness barrels, sandwiches,

The Drowning of Innocence

crúibíns and bottles of Paddy. Con was given a rare old send-off. Mattie was restrained, organised and acting with dignity took the lead in honouring his Da. There was a coldness in him that Eileen and Micheál found shocking. They had not seen him shed a tear and after the display of wrath which had overtaken him as he left the house on that fateful night, he had since seemed measured, calm, an ethereal distance consuming him. Gone was the winsome, effervescent Mattie that charmed. This current and very present incarnation was cold, calculating, seemingly indifferent to all around him.

They set up with musical instruments in the kitchen and the dancing spread out into the backyard overlooking the River Lee. It was the last time Mattie and Micheál played with one another. They dug deep into their reservoir of tunes and one after another without a break in between, they kept the dancers dancing and moving, generating an evening to remember, a sign, a monument, a shrine, a memorial, a cromlech in melody to a good, simple man gone from this earth to receive his reward.

During the course of the evening, Eileen remained strong, greeting the neighbours and listening to their many stories, reminiscences, reflections about her Da. Their kind words like a balm as she was carried along by a wave of love and affection. Towards the evening's end, she knew what was required of her. She felt compelled to give back, to send family, friends, neighbours out into the night abounding with reflection of the man who had shaped her. He had always loved "The Bantry Girl's Lament" and could be found whistling it while he worked. Now, she stepped forward to sing it, sweetly, falteringly to those who had come to mourn; As a gift to them,

> *"Ah who will plough the fields now and who will sow the corn,*
> *And who will watch the sheep now and keep them neatly shorn,*
> *The stack that's in the haggard unthreshed it may remain,*
> *Since Johnny, lovely Johnny went to fight the king of Spain"*

Family and friends gathered around, shaken, moved by the courage of this young woman, seeing her as if for the very first time. Most were found weeping silently, touched and cleansed as the words of the song rolled over them, their spirits inexplicably lifting as Eileen, without faltering, continued,

> *"At wakes and hurling matches your likes we'll never see,*
> *Until you return again to us a stóirín óg mo chroí,*
> *And won't you trod the buckeens who show us much disdain*
> *Because our eyes are not so bright as those you'll meet in Spain"*

Micheál could see the immense effort this was taking from her and made to move forward. Then he saw Mary Barry rise from her seat and join her daughter. With their arms around one another, bolstering one another, they continued their homage to their man. Eileen could feel her Ma's heartbeat, fast, a woman unused to garnering such attention. The symmetry in their voices couching the words in an embrace of love and tenderness, Ma's eyes closed, her heart open for the first time since that fateful night as she came home to herself,

"If cruel fate will not permit our Johnny to return
This awful loss we Bantry girls will never cease to mourn
We'll resign ourselves to our sad lot and die in grief and pain
Since Johnny died for Ireland's plight in the foreign land of Spain"

The Drowning of Innocence

Dublin City,

Late June 1920

During the following week, Mattie was summoned to Dublin to meet the Big Fella. He walked into his command room overlooking the Castle, the epicentre of British rule.

"I'm sorry for your trouble, Mattie," Collins said when he greeted him.

"Thank you and thank you for all your help, sir."

"Listen, boy, we want to do more. We will take care of your mother and sister. I don't want you to be worrying about them. I know your Da is gone but things can go on the same. They won't go short. Eileen, that's her name, isn't it, she can continue studying. We will take care of it all. Sure what else could we do. Your Uncle Tadgh is a great man and good friend."

Mattie, lost for words, looked at him with gratitude.

"But its you we want to talk to. I know from Tom you are very upset, and rightly so, boy. They are right fucking bastards those Tans. I want you to have a chance to get back at them. Is that OK with you?"

Mattie could hardly contain himself. "Absolutely, sir, Yes sir." He gesticulated with his whole being.

"Well, I thought so. I saw it in you the first time at the hurling match. I've been keeping tabs on you since, boy. I heard you are a great shot and cool as a cucumber. That's what I need. I want you to join me here. There is a bunch of us up to no good."

He left out a big belly laugh.

"Its all hush hush, you know, boy, but I want you in. We are creating a different kind of war here. The fucking British don't know what's going on. We have infiltrated their intelligence network. You know the bastards that design this whole fucking mess. I'll tell you boy. We will take them out one by one. These are big league fuckers, boy. I want you to be part of it and get them back for your Da. Are you in?"

Mattie felt a surge of excitement. "Yes sir."

Collins then rang a bell on his desk and in came a smartly dressed man with sharp features and intelligent eyes.

"This is Paddy Daly, Mattie. I want you to take this young Cork lad, Paddy, and show him the ropes, get him ready. Show him everything and include him in the squad. Is that OK?"

Daly nodded and Collins came and put his hand on Mattie.

"I'm proud of you, boy. I know you won't let your Da or Cork down."

With that, the audience was over. Mattie left the room with Paddy Daly and began an unrecognisable life, a netherworld of sorts but it was one that was to fit him like a glove. It was a moment in time, sealing his future and it seemed to him also sealing the destiny for which he had always longed

The Drowning of Innocence

Cork City

17th July 1920

There was no doubt in Lt. Colonel Gerald Brice Ferguson Smyth's mind that these people were deluded and the sooner they were brought under control the better. He was a man who had seen the world and understood his place in it. It was clear to him, very clear, that the Catholic population of his country, the country he loved, needed to be saved from themselves. He could see the dangers of the papist foot soldiers spreading their ignorance and guilt, spoiling the country. He also knew, as only a man of his breeding and intelligence could know, what a privilege it was for his beloved Ireland to be part of this great British Empire.

He was outraged when he thought of these troublemakers, Sinn Feiners, spreading disorder throughout Munster and particularly Cork, bringing the county to economic ruin. He did not fight in the Great War and sustain being wounded five times for this. These people needed to be stopped at all costs. He owed it to himself and the many, many gallant Irishmen who had fought by his side at the Somme and Ypres to defeat them by any means necessary and he had no doubt that sharp lessons would have their effect.

He was happy he had government approval for his strategy although he understood that with the American elections coming up this could not be made public. He was aggrieved though. Firstly he had been shocked that his own force, the RIC, the command of which he had recently assumed, had rebelled against him when he had issued his "shoot on sight" policy. He had made that speech to reassure his force that in going about their work, they would not face repercussions, to give them confidence that they were on the side of right, of law and order. 'Shoot on sight', if only they had known what he really thought about these Fenian curs; How shooting was too good for them, how he would have liked to maim them, torture and then execute them and all those stupid gombeens who were harbouring them.

But it had all backfired on him. Some men had mutinied and resigned there and then. Afterwards he had been hauled over to London and given a bit of a ticking off. He had resented that but was now back and ready to rid the province of these scum.

He admitted quietly to himself that he didn't like this kind of a 'war', where the enemy was nowhere to be seen and yet were all around him. He thought of these scumbags as lily-livered cowards, gangsters, reprobates, degenerates, barbaric. What he would do if he could get hold of Collins……….., this fantasy occupied his mind for a few minutes and became a focus for all the rage he had felt at returning home victorious after a bloody war to find this mess.

There were compensations of course. And here he was enjoying one of them as he sat on the comfortable arm chair in the smoking room of the club, at the end of another week, the only way really to honour a Saturday night. Among friends and colleagues who honoured him, who recognised all he had given for the security of Empire. With them he was able to relax. With a glass of Bushmills in his one good hand, he had eased himself into the evening, had forgotten his 'dressing down' and was reminiscing about the 'good old days'.

It was his time off. Here, he was at home. His adjutant had prepared his cigar and he had dismissed him for the evening. He had watched him carefully and always loved this moment of anticipation, the ritual, the adjutant creating the ample, smooth opening without damaging the slender, delicate structure of the cigar, exposing a surface of cleanly cut filler leaves. He then carefully lit the cigar himself, taking his time, allowing the flame of the lighter to hover near the tip which he revolved continually in his good hand. It always reminded Smyth of the joy he used to get in toasting marshmallows as a young child on expeditions, camping trips with his father in the hills above Murree, delicately allowing the flame to toast the sweet flesh of the marrow, not getting too close for fear of charring. It was the same with his cigar, allowing the glow to slowly appear and then fan it gently giving up a reassuringly cool smoke, a grown up version of his childhood treat.

When the cigar was fully lit, he took a deep draw on it and melted back into the seat of the finely carved and beautifully upholstered leather chair. Here he was in the Cork county club, a long line of experience of such privilege in his life stretching back to his early childhood in India. There may be a growing madness outside these walls but inside, here in the club, all was as it should be.

The Empire he had given himself to, the glorious rule that he had witnessed bringing efficiency to the savage and over-populated subcontinent of India, that had also triumphed on Flanders fields, was and would remain inviolate. It gave him almost a sense of immortality, this rich heritage of which he was a part, this triumphant incarnation that had bequeathed so much to the world, its law, its sense of decorum, its technology, rail system, shipping - even afternoon tea!! He smiled inwardly amused at the juxtaposition of thought. The longevity and supremacy of Empire was his only way of explaining how he had survived being injured five times and had come back to tell the tale in clubs such as this, which were everywhere in the four corners of the world,

                    The Drowning of Innocence

providing deserved rest, relaxation and privilege for those who worked tirelessly for Pax Britannica.

He loved the smoking rooms in the various clubs of which he was a member; the delightfully carved wood panels on their walls, the beautifully shaped cornices, the chandeliers, the drapes on the stately windows, the finely upholstered leather furniture and regal standard lamps but above all the company of men, exclusively, and of military men, to be trusted, even loved.

He had looked out of the window earlier in the evening over the River Lee flowing just underneath and had to concede, as an Ulsterman, that this city was beautiful, its many hills rising from the centre, the river itself parting and creating an island of beautiful streets, as it meandered through and out to the estuary and harbour beyond.

He also reminisced about the good times in Cork before this madness had taken shape; How this city had been an imperial splendour, a welcome home and indeed playground for British royalty, a city which had always celebrated with gusto the reign of Empire and the trappings and festivals that accompanied such obeisance. He would, by God, return this city to such a point again. He thought of the magnificent harbour at Queenstown, sadly the last port of call for that great ship the Titanic, and his thoughts wandered to the river Lee estuary. He reminded himself that he must take time to explore it with his camera to see if he could get any of his pictures published again. He could see already that it was a haven for many unusual birds.

Suddenly the door of the room burst open and four men charged in, revolvers in their hands. Time seemed to be suspended as they moved to the corner of the room where Smyth was seated, drawing on his cigar. The others in the room were shocked into paralysis, unable to take in what was happening, almost imagining themselves in a film, a deep sense of unreality inhabiting the space, incapacitating their minds, freezing their reactions, rendering them immobile, fixed to the spot. Inspector Craig, sitting next to Smyth, was left with the indelible impression of one of the men, a young whippersnapper, swaggering in wearing his suit in a dapper manner, his floppy cap perched on his head in a jaunty cavalier fashion, for all the world like a cheap Hollywood gangster, a curl on his lip betraying a sneer and a deep, deep obfuscating hatred in his eyes, venomous as a snake.

It was that guttersnipe, he recalled later, who emptied the revolver into his commander. They heard the man say something but in their confusion and the thickness of the Cork accent, could not recall it accurately afterwards. They did not know whether it was in English or that guttural language, like a throat infection, they call Gaelic. The whole incident lasted about one minute, but in its wake, the men were gone, disappeared as if they had de-materialised and Lt. Colonel Gerald Brice Ferguson Smyth lay dead, slumped half out of his chair, his good hand reaching for his gun, two bullet holes to his head had made his face unrecognisable with blood, gristle, shards of bone and brain splattered everywhere, incongruously reducing the immaculately decorated walls to those of a slaughterhouse.

An inner sanctum had been exposed, blown open, and the men left behind in the room, although they had seen horror and trauma before, were left trembling and in shock at what they had witnessed and left in no doubt that to control the carnage that was being visited upon them now, had become well nigh impossible. Within minutes however, the paralysis lifted and was replaced by a paroxysm, an all consuming rage, a fury, a fierce indignation. Their commander was dead and by God, by God, they would get back at the fuckers for this.

The gloves were off. No quarter had been proffered and from now on, by God, no quarter would be given. "Fuck the Hague Convention!!!" It had no place here in this God-forsaken country. They rumbled and roared and teared around like mad bulls seeking something which would replace the powerlessness, the rage, the incredulity at what had occurred. In the months to come they would find many such targets.

                      The Drowning of Innocence

Mattie was deliriously happy after he had been summoned by Collins for the second time.

"I've got the very job for you, boy," Collins had said, "We have been tracking the bastard who ordered the 'shoot on sight' policy and he is back from London. A gobshite called Smyth. He's back in Cork this Saturday from our information. I want you in on this boy. You deserve it. We're going to take him out. Don't let me down, OK."

Mattie floated out of the room. He felt honoured to be chosen for such a mission. It was his opportunity to get the man who was behind the shooting of Da.

On the train to Cork, he had plenty of time to think, to reflect. As he gazed out the window at the tranquil countryside drifting by, he felt a change come over him.

"This cannot be about just revenge," he realised, "Its something more. Deeper. Stronger."

There was a momentum, he realised, a sense born from the last month he had spent in Dublin that this was the moment for Ireland to break free from British rule. He thought about his Da. Although he loved his Da deeply and missed him greatly, he reflected that his father's life had been lived under the shadow of this rule, a second class citizen in his own land. He was of a new generation that had come to question that. Because of the relationships forged with his peers, he had a new hope, a strong conviction.

He thought deeply about his time in the Irish college, where they had absorbed the passionate idealism of the 1916 revolutionaries. Patrick Pearse, his hero, that romantic visionary, captured his imagination. Now he saw him, in his mind's eye, this frail schoolmaster, standing on the steps of General Post Office in the centre of Dublin, just four years before, preposterously reading out his proclamation. Such audacity. To stand in front of the British Empire, that 'foreign people' and as a simple poet and soldier, declare that their rule was over and Ireland was from that moment independent and free. What courage.

Mattie, as others in the college, had committed the proclamation to memory as a foundation stone of their new belief. Sitting on the train to Cork, on his first mission from the Irish government, he called it to mind and recited those words in his head, almost like a prayer:

"We declare the right of the people of Ireland to the ownership of Ireland, and to the unfettered control of Irish destinies, to be sovereign and indefeasible. The long usurpation of that right by a foreign people and government has not extinguished the right, nor can it ever be extinguished except by the destruction of the Irish people. In every generation the Irish people have asserted their right to national freedom and sovereignty; six times during the past three hundred years they have asserted it in arms. Standing on that fundamental right and again asserting it in arms in the face of the world, we hereby proclaim the Irish Republic as a Sovereign Independent State. And we pledge our lives and the lives of our comrades-in-arms to the cause of its freedom, of its welfare, and of its exaltation among the nations."

The words had a powerful effect on him. He knew what was being asked of him, now. Like those who had gone before him, he would dedicate his life to this cause, to Irish freedom and sovereignty. He instinctively knew that the road ahead for him might not be understood by others in time. He was not stupid. He also realised, as his conviction was established, that Collins was right. The only way to challenge the might of Empire was to sow seeds of terror and mayhem. Any other way was to surrender to an unequal fight and predictable defeat.

Tom Hales and Florrie O'Donoghue recognised this conviction in his young face when they greeted him at Cork station and gave him his briefing. "It seems Collins was impressed by you, Mattie. But this is a big one. Get it right. We're depending on you."

He was part of a group of seven Volunteers from the 1st Cork Brigade and they all seemed like good, determined lads. Mattie however assumed control. He could see that the short amount of time he had spent with Collin's men had given him an aura, a sense of authority, calmness and presence. He welcomed this within himself as the most natural of manifestations. After his tryst with destiny on the train, he was confident that no feelings or sentiments would get in his way, that there was a steeliness about him which captured the attention of the others and gave them confidence in his actions. He even imagined himself possessing the calm bravura of Owen Conway, the hero from his favourite film 'Regeneration', suave, good-looking but someone to be held with respect, even fear. He self-consciously walked with a strut, the cocky air of someone who was now claiming his rightful place in the hierarchy of things.

The operation was planned to a T. Smyth was staying and spending the evening at the Cork and County Club. With great difficulty, the intelligence group had infiltrated its staff and recruited a waiter. Collins would be proud of them. The party arrived outside the club at ten o'clock, a warm, balmy July

     The Drowning of Innocence

evening. The sun had just set and there was a bright pink glow on the skyline over the whole city. It seemed to be as a portent, a sign, a harbinger shouting loud and clear to all who wanted to hear "Now we are taking our land back. This is how we are going to do it. Not by your rules, you fuckers, oh no. By your rules in the past we have always lost. This time we create mayhem, as Collins had said with a belly laugh 'up to no good'. The tables are turned. This time and more times in the future, you won't see us coming and a lot of you won't see us going either having been despatched to the only place you deserve to be."

Mattie, as he expected, experienced a deep sense of calm, a meticulously prepared anticipation yet it was curiously matched with a quiet exhilaration. This was his moment. The doorman would be distracted by a Cumann na Mbán girl, a pretty, sexy young thing, whose appearance had also thrilled him. He had enjoyed looking at her on the way there in the Model T, her shapely body, the way her legs crossed over and declared her ankles and the promises made by that simple act. He had caught her with a grin and a wink and was not disappointed by her response. Maybe he would catch up with her later. He would rise to the task of making her wet, indeed as meticulously, as carefully, as fully present as he was now to what faced him. He thought how he would move his hand under her skirt and sneak two fingers past her silk drawers to her hole. Then he would gently, imperceptibly, sensitively glide the two fingers over the open wet lips, feeling her clitoris with every contour and ridge of his fingertip, gently, gently massaging to reduce her to a paroxysm of desire. The two were intertwined weren't they? Making love to a beautiful woman and killing a British Army fucker. He couldn't tell at this moment which one he enjoyed most.

The seven of them entered the club quickly, found the waiter, who directed them to the smoking room where Smyth was seated. They walked up the stairs, Mattie noticing that the stair rod had come adrift on two of the steps, making the carpet loose. "I'll watch that on the way down," he thought, exulting in his command of the situation. He reached for his beloved Smith & Wesson and cradled it lovingly in his hand, sure that it was reliable and prepared. Four of them remained outside and guarded the door of the smoking lounge, the two others burst into the room alongside Mattie.

This was his moment. Mattie found that as he entered this ancient room, an ethereally calm frame of mind overtook him. He approached Smyth quickly and confidently. He took in the detail in everything, almost microscopically, noticing the frayed edges on the drapes, a slight cobweb on one of the standard lamps, the men seated in the room rooted to their chairs, one of them had a small stain of gravy grease, presumably from dinner, just above the knee of his tweed trousers - a curious dirty brown inappropriately mixed with the green and blue fleck of the fabric. He took great delight in the horror and fear which clouded their faces, the evident paralysis, "who's in charge now, boyos" a phrase repeated and repeated inside his head like a mantra, delightfully enshrining his consciousness.

Never feeling more alive and possessing this power, this immense power of life and death, he approached Smyth, who was staring up at him, surprised but still seeming to possess in his very stature his sense of entitlement, an arrogant bearing in his mien which was a deliberate affront, a challenge to a duel.

Mattie quietly intoned, "You issued orders to shoot on sight, you fucking langer, well now you're in my sight, this is for my Da."

He pulled the trigger continuously and proficiently emptied the chamber into Smyth, two to his head, two to his heart and he didn't care where the rest went, so full was he with this sublime sense of exaltation.

He put his gun away, turned the collar of his shirt up, grinned at his audience and strode with a deliberately cocky gait, alongside the others, out the door and onto the broad landing.

On hitting the street the men bolted up Grand Parade and separated, melting into the gathering gloom. Mattie on the other hand, nonchalantly, went in search of the Cumann na Mbán girl. With instinct on his side, he spied her at the entrance to the English Market. He quickly made up the ground and grabbed her. At first she was startled but on recognising him, melted into his embrace.

She had been a hit alright, she giggled, with the doorman and he had asked to meet her later when he got off duty, something that would now never happen for the stupid fellow.

"Siobhán's my name," she said as the two of them found a room together in Lancaster Lodge and hungrily, voraciously so, after the tension and electricity of the evening, threw themselves at one another in the privacy of the room, surrendering totally to their need to expurgate and celebrate life after death. When he entered her, when he was enveloped by her warm, wet, lubricious cunt, they both let out a yelp of delight, sensing a liberation, a breaking of the shackles, an overturning of an old order and the uncovering of a new. Mattie

The Drowning of Innocence

had never felt like this, this mixture of exhilaration and desire, it felt as if the act of sexual congress was designed for this moment, for the two of them and it was well into the small hours of the morning before both of them felt satiated and, still holding one another fiercely, fell into a deep, restful, dreamless sleep.

Cork,

1st November 1920

For Eileen the day had been an ordeal, rekindling the meaninglessness of loss, the chasm of emptiness that refused to be accommodated, regurgitating the vacuum of her Da's absence. "I have to go" had been the insistent refrain in her head carrying her through the pain and devastation. She would stand silently, with dignity, at the side of the road, lending her frame to the thousands of others as they lined the streets of the city with unbearable intensity finally laying to rest their Lord Mayor Terence MacSwiney; Fittingly so, on the eve of All Saints. Without Micheál at her side it would not have been possible to endure it.

Stories had reverberated through the crowd of their Lord Mayor's courage and determination, taking on the might of Empire, challenging the authority of British rule. Over the past two and a half months, his principled hunger strike in a Brixton prison cell had drawn the attention of the world and had become a lightening rod, a touchstone of resistance; His words from the dock at his court martial defiant, proud, determined. It had been the topic of conversation throughout the city.

"The British Crown has no jurisdiction in Ireland. The Dáil declared Ireland a Republic two years ago and my arrest, trial and incarceration has therefore no validity."

Those words had become a rallying cry, transforming the inchoate rage of ordinary people into a vivid synopsis of the audacious illogicality of foreign rule and jurisdiction.

The city had been transfixed with his struggle. Day after day headlines filled newspapers and circulated the globe. The story of an articulate, constitutionally elected Irishman, on hunger strike, starving to death, evoked a resonance with the million others who had perished in the Great Famine of 1846. The British administration, Lloyd George, Churchill, Shortt were powerless against such vulnerability. Stone by stone, the edifice of their authority in Ireland was being dismantled. For seventy four days, the world was gripped by the drama, Terence McSwiney questioning his incarceration, taken from his fireside, separated from his two year old daughter and prepared to surrender his life for the dream and vision of a Republic. In the end, as he prophesied, he had come home in a coffin and Eileen knew she must be present at the side of the road, joining the hundred thousand others to mourn his

     The Drowning of Innocence

passing and to continue his defiance at the illegitimacy of this foreign rule.

Now, imbued by the memory of the previous day and all its symbolic gravitas, she was on board the ferry from Passage to Queenstown with Micheál and Brother Paul. They had missed Paul's company as he had been away in London at McSwiney's side and they had agreed to leave the city behind to spend a day together. Seeing Paul's face and bearing, Eileen recognised the chaos of loss, its bewildering, incoherent void. He was struggling to do ordinary things.

Paul had loved Terry deeply and now his friend was gone. It was not a surprise to her when on the deck of the ferry, and their eyes met that Paul broke. Her instinct was to hold him as he let himself go, wordlessly cradling this big man in her arms. They embodied an incongruous image, a burly Franciscan in his shabby habit and cincture cradled by this beautiful young woman as they sat, side by side, on a wooden bench of the rickety old ferry traversing the bay of Cork on this cold November morn.

Paul did not care. Her softness, the intimacy of her touch, filled him in a way he had never experienced and acted to expiate all of his sorrow, a cleansing, a catharsis.

Micheál gazed at them both. There and then, he was struck by the commanding beauty of Eileen. His Eileen. It took his breath away; this elegant, serene, gorgeous presence and he wondered how it could be possible, in all the world, that they were together; that they were in love. His heart brimmed over with a delicious joy and gratitude. When he looked at Brother Paul however, at this forlorn figure, his eyes brimmed with tears, and he was forced, once again, to watch someone close to him encounter the eviscerating nature of loss.

Paul let the images that had haunted him rise and be quenched by the redeeming tenderness of his companions. The moments where his blood had risen; The intransigence of the British; The assault of the Black and Tans as they commandeered Terry's coffin from the Holyhead train and diverted it from the ship bound for Dublin and a State Funeral to slip into Ireland through Cork harbour; The rage he had felt as they leered back at him from the deck of the vessel as it left Holyhead harbour, irreverently lounging on Terry's coffin, it wrapped in hessian, smoking their cigarettes, provocatively gesticulating their 'triumph'. All these thoughts and images left him in Eileen's embrace, freeing his spirit and leaving him purged, exhausted but renewed.

The ferry pulled into Queenstown. On arrival at the dock, they all felt lighter somehow, as they came ashore and gazed at the beautiful town spread before them, rows of houses rising steeply up the hill from the promenade and the Holy Ground to the east, Saint Colman's cathedral dwarfing the vista, its roof with the line of lace-iron fretwork and tall steeple blending and stippling a painting in charcoal against the slate blue sky.

Later, seated in the tea room of the Queens hotel, with the fresh smell of scones and tea brewing, the elaborate cake display, the soft lighting from the chandeliers and the calm, hospitable efficiency of the staff, their spirits were lifted and they began once again to sink into the familiarity of one another's presence, diminishing the painful months of their separation.

Eileen and Micheál began, visibly, to relax and even seemed to breathe easier in this good man's company, his humour restored and his gentle eyes twinkling again. They began to feel safe, rooted somehow in a deeper, more immanent reality than the one that had overtaken them since Da's murder and Mattie's strange disappearance.

The tea arrived in a delightful Staffordshire pot, a double rose motif emblazoning the side, the elegant handle and spout trimmed in gold leaf. Eileen poured for them and they tucked into fresh scones, hot to touch, the butter and jam melting as they savoured the taste, consigning their shared ordeal of the previous day to memory.

Micheál was again overcome by her loveliness, the soft, subtle, silkily-smooth light picking out her delicate features, the warmth of her smile, the vibrant animation in her emerald green eyes, catching the light, catching the mood of her soul, bringing the wild Atlantic from the bay beyond into this cosy yet splendorous room. He adored her.

Paul broke the silence and spoke first. "What's been happening for you." He asked, looking consciously at Eileen. "How have you been managing? How is your Ma? Is she bearing up?"

"Oh in the beginning she was very bad. She hardly ate. She had never been without Da and now she was lost. It was hard to look at but we could do nothing. The family rallied around and she went back to her people's place, Grandma and Grandpa Bride in Nad. She is better there away from our house and memories."

"They own the shop in Nad, don't they. I can't think of a better place for

                    The Drowning of Innocence

her. Sure the people would look out for her up there. They are good people."

"Its Mattie that troubles us," said Micheál, "he's a changed person since his Da was killed. We haven't seen him for weeks. He's with Collins now in Dublin, but he's become very hard. Unrecognisable really. We are at a loss what to do, how to reach him."

Paul looked at both of them, taking in the deep concern so evident in their eyes, Eileen looking so forlorn. This hardness they described in Mattie he had seen time and time again over the years, a change that had come over so many bright, young men.

It reminded him of the steely-eyed men he had been alongside in France in '14 and '15, the way so many had lost touch with their deeper, more true selves in the foul, rat-infested trenches. The horror of this new and deviant actuality forcing them, each and all, to create an alternative personality, a new and different way of looking at the terrible beast that had morphed in front of them. He remembered thinking at that time "what young men before, in all the history of creation, had killed twenty or more other men and had witnessed the slaughter of hundreds almost before they had reached manhood, their innocence drowned in the sea of blood, guts, mud and poison gas that was their daily sojourn?"

And now it had come to Ireland, to Cork, to Mattie, changing everything utterly.

After a long, long pause, time suspended by this epochal contemplation, Paul sighed and said,

"There's very little to be done. War sweeps many away with it. You can only pray for him. Some don't know how to withstand the hatred and bitterness that comes when violence arrives. It robs us of our true selves. Others, I'm sad to say, begin to enjoy it, the strange elixir of excitement and power that overtakes them when they hold a gun in their hands. I don't know about Mattie but I do know that the men Collins has gathered around him are ruthless, determined, fixed on doing anything that the Big Fellow asks. We can only wait and see. Mattie is a good lad."

"I do understand how he must feel, though" said Micheál, "The 'Tans' were merciless towards Con. That was hard to take. And you yourself have seen how ruthless the British were with Alderman McSwiney. If we want our freedom, a new Ireland free from their tyranny, we have to fight for it. They're not going to give up their power easily."

"That's all very well, Micheál, but I am concerned how much we will lose as a people along the way. The vision you have, that simple desire for Ireland to be free, self governing, a caring compassionate country including all its people from all walks of life is not something that others will necessarily share. Times are telling. Its too often the case that the idealists, the romantics like yourself are eclipsed, indeed obliterated by others, who have less scruples. When the gun comes in, everything changes. It brutalises those who use it, permanently. The gun becomes the feature of their lives and they can't leave it behind afterwards. Then, there are others, scheming, waiting for their chance, queuing up to exploit the chaos that arrives. Those people will use the times we are in for their own ends. So Micheál, all I can say is please be careful nurturing your dreams. They may become a nightmare."

These simple phrases, words that came from Paul found a way into the deepest recesses of Micheál and Eileen's souls. Long afterwards, hours, days, months and years after they left the tea rooms of the Queen's hotel, refreshed by one another's companionship, these words would come back to both of them independently, prophetically encapsulating all that had yet to transpire, to take shape, as they walked the stately promenade of Queenstown harbour to find the ferry back to the city. Each in turn would find it to be an unassailable truth. The dream they still held at that moment, that instant, as they gazed out at the vast cove of the bay and the mysterious Atlantic beyond, this dream for Ireland, its vibrant self, a new and equal place in which to live together and raise their children, a place redolent with the rich heritage of their celtic forebears would in time be eclipsed by a mad scrambling for power in the vacuum that only a crumbling hierarchy leaves in its wake; the unscrupulous, unseemly machinations and posturing of gunmen, politicians and princes of the Roman church would sadly fulfil kind, wise, Paul's oracle and turn this, their cherished dream, into a frightening incubus.

     The Drowning of Innocence

Dublin

Sunday, 21st November 1920

"What is that fucking gurgling noise?" It was Charlie Dalton. "Blood gurgling, gurgling, oh shit, up from his throat. Fuck, can't someone stop it. I can't settle. I want to run. I just want to run." He wouldn't shut up. On and on he went and it was driving Mattie wild. They were in Phil Shanahan's, a safe dosshouse in 'Monto', a place they often hid after an operation. A place to wind down, drink, have fun with the girls and celebrate a job well done in a gaudy room, three sofas, a piano, uileann pipes, fiddle and the all important bar in the corner. Dalton was spoiling it. The others trying to reassure him with a naive observation "it's just a dripping tap." It didn't seem to help. He kept at it. As far as Mattie was concerned he had lost it. That was surprising as Dalton was one of them, a young fella, although just seventeen, nevertheless, you would expect this morning's operation to be just grist to the mill to him.

Mattie was also fed up with the others who had joined the squad this morning, useless fuckers from the Dublin brigade, making up the numbers. Afterwards they never stopped whining "this is not what I signed up for" and "it's just not right". Fuck them, all of them and their scruples. All very well for them to have a conscience, but work had to be done. Didn't the Boss himself make it very clear to everybody at the briefing yesterday. Mattie had listened to him carefully then, as they sat around the table at the O'Toole's club and could repeat every word and phrase.

"Listen men" he had announced, commanding their attention, standing proud, supreme, in front of them all. Mattie was struck with awe and pride as he regarded the measure of the man, his leader. The clear intellect, homely Cork accent, vibrant words, a charisma that exuded confidence in what he was doing. He looked magnificent. "D'y'know, I'd follow that man to hell" Mattie thought to himself.

"Listen up hard. The fucking British have upped the ante. They have brought in a bunch of experienced spies to work with the G-men. Fuckers who have cut their teeth during the war. These are serious people, undesirable bastards, who will make life miserable for ordinary, decent citizens here. The atrocities these fuckers have committed in the past is proof of that, let me tell you. Torture is their second name. So no qualms boys. They are dangerous reptiles and the very air will be sweeter in Dublin without them. We will take them out, one by one, tomorrow morning. These fuckers have left no calling card in the past, so we will pay them back in their own coin. I want you to hold your heads up high. Tomorrow is a great day for Ireland as we get rid of them and knock the British off their throne. As I have told you before, we are not playing by their rules. That leads nowhere. Our job is to create mayhem. Do you hear me, mayhem." Collins paused, visibly animated by the importance of what he was saying, conviction underlying his every word.

"OK, so here's the plan. It's not possible to do this job on our own. It's too big. So we have drafted in Volunteers from the Dublin Brigade to join us. They will help you out, drive you around, stand guard. We will meet with them later. But most of the killing will be down to you. I know you won't let me down."

When Collins spoke to the forty or so Volunteers, at night-time in Painters Hall, he was vehement.

"It is vital for the success of our fight that these spies are removed. No country has ever had any hesitation about shooting enemy spies in war time. So I want you to listen to me carefully. If any of you have any moral scruples about going on this mission, I am giving you a chance now to withdraw. No one will think any the worse of you. I want every man of you to be satisfied in your conscience that you can properly take part and do your bit to bring freedom to Ireland."

When he thought about it now, it was not only Dalton's wailing that was irritating Mattie. He had the Volunteers' voices going round in his head also, on and on about "how wrong it was to shoot men in their pyjamas". They didn't even know how to shoot. Useless. Useless. Useless fuckers, they were. And what's more of the thirty five G-men on the list to be executed, they had only got seventeen. Mattie had no time for this. He was a perfectionist and took pride in his work. And this was just not good enough.

It was all so different at eight thirty that morning as he strolled along Warrington Place, along the banks of the Grand Canal. How he loved Dublin and how it embraced him with a cloak of anonymity which was thrilling. Here he could find a new identity. He had no past, he didn't even think of a future, he just had the now, the glorious, vibrant now. He was full of the vigour of youth, loved the feel of energy rising inside him like sap, conscious he radiated animal magnetism, suffused with charm.

He had chosen his sharpest suit to wear, with its thin black and grey stripe and narrow double breast, a crisp white shirt and paisley cream and navy tie, topped with a light grey trilby, cocked as ever in a cavalier fashion, the look

    The Drowning of Innocence

completed by a dark gabardine overcoat, unbuttoned. Didn't Collins say he
should look smart, always, so as to blend in, avoid suspicion? He thought he
looked every inch a gangster, not the 'Oirish Mick' the British were looking for.
He often laughed that the 'Big Fella' himself cycled around the city, looking
like a solicitor, the most wanted man in Ireland, under their very noses. Here
in Dublin, Mattie could even be 'Owen Conway', for indeed the girls had seen
enough of the 'flicks' to recognise that in him.

As often the case with Mattie, he burst softly into song to keep himself
company, his soft and sweet voice and musical ear beautifully interpreting that
old melody,

"This morning early I walked on
While my darling was in a dream
The last sweet days of summer bloomed
And dressed the trees in green
Then soaring high in the gleaming sky
From far across the bay
Came a fearsome roar from a distant shore
At the dawning of the day."

He loved strolling this neighbourhood of the city, with its imperious
Georgian houses, exuding class. He studied the fanlights as he passed by, their
designs of sunbursts and petals, individually crafted, the sumptuous railings of
wrought iron decorating each house. The craftsmanship in each exquisite. The
lines of the buildings, as they dominated the facade, magisterial. He promised
himself that this would be where he would live in the new Ireland. The
thought delighted him as he continued to sing to himself,

"Then I called my men to follow me
Knowing well that the view was dim
Though tired and worn, how they fought all morn'
As time was closing in
And my heart was sad though sore with pride
For brave lads all were they
As the angels fly, how they climbed so high
On the dawning of the day"

At that hour of a Sunday morning, there were only "early birds" about,
maids and servants, dashing for nine o'clock mass. He nodded to those who
passed by, paying particular attention to the pretty ones, making sure they got
the full weight of his smile. When in couples or in threes, the girls giggled

sweetly as they passed, some of them flushed with excitement. He knew he had that effect on them. Oh what a time to be alive, he thought. So many rich pickings, he thought as he sang as if to them all,

"Forgive me love, I'm going now
So very far away
When darkness falls, only think me near
And do not be afraid
And please don't grieve when I am gone
Abide in what remains
'til the shadows end and we meet again
On the dawning of the day."

As he was singing softly, two young girls passed him. Their mood seem to pick up as they gazed on this smart young man, gaily singing as he walked, the very picture of innocence. Mattie laughed inwardly at the thought of his Smith and Wesson, carefully hidden in the holster underneath his jacket and coat.

The canal shone brightly, the trees lining the banks, majestic, the last of their leaves dancing, fluttering their amber and russet shapes in the light breeze; the early morning lateral sun, behind him as he walked, casting his long shadow on the pavement ahead. The air was redolent with smells from the gasometer tanks at Ringsend and surprisingly, the salty smell of the bay all the way from Sandymount. Mixed with the chimney smoke of early morning fires from the stately Georgian houses on his side of the canal, it evoked hidden, indescribable feelings in him. He thought it strange that such an acrid smell could be so dear to him, but there was no mistaking it was. It somehow rooted him to his new life, fixing him in Dublin and away, very far away from his past, from Cork and all that his county represented.

He rounded Herbert Place and turned into Lower Baggot Street. Up ahead he saw the others arrive in a model T Ford. They parked on the corner of James Street alongside the Mercy Convent. Mattie had always made a point of arriving at a rendezvous, separately, on his own. He wanted only to look out for himself, and he didn't trust the vagaries of driving with others. Although he knew the address of his victim, he only kept that and the person's name in his memory while the mission was underway. Afterwards, the details disappeared from his recollection. He treasured his anonymity and strove to keep it that way. He also did not like to expose himself to the nervousness and tension of the others in the party. It was enough to endure their frailty during the operation itself. He composed himself and strode over to meet them.

   The Drowning of Innocence

Madeleine Newberry was content. She was a woman of simple tastes and in her early forties, possessed a quiet confidence that she was loved by her family and admired by her friends. She did not make excessive demands on life, was demure in her appearance and possessed a reserve that befitted her station in life as wife to William, a senior serving officer in the British Army.

Dublin had been good to her and as a couple, they had put behind them the difficult years when he had to take work where he could find it. She remembered the years exiled in Canada as being particularly hard. She was a 'home bird' really and always liked to be in easy striking distance of their families in Devon. Somehow their current position in this stately city was perfect. She so enjoyed its ambience, loved walking through Stephen's Green, stopping at the grandstand where the music was often of a particularly high standard, then taking in the shops in Grafton Street, Switzers and Brown Thomas being her favourites. Her afternoons were often spent with friends for High Tea at the Shelbourne Hotel, where she kept up with all the gossip.

She enjoyed the simplicity and splendour of their rooms here in Baggot Street. There was no doubt in her mind that Georgian architecture was not only aesthetically pleasing but also functional. She had spent a lot of time and effort in decorating their homes over the years and felt a thrill of pride in her success in that. The compact space in their lodgings here afforded a challenge that she had, with ingenuity, overcome. On this Sunday morning, the fire was blazing in the hearth and she was looking forward to the day ahead.

She had come to love her lazy Sunday mornings with her husband. It had become their tradition to have breakfast in their pyjamas, a 'full Irish', with tea and soda bread from Findlaters and bacon and eggs cooked just the way they liked it. It was the highlight of the week.

William was not a very communicative man. She had always known that but he was a good man, worked hard and took care of her and their now grown-up daughter, who worked in London. In the last few years since they had arrived in Ireland, he had withdrawn further into himself. He never talked about his work now and she had guessed that he was involved in very secret but important affairs.

Ireland had changed over the last year and its beauty was being undermined by a gang of seemingly dedicated criminals who were trying to wreak havoc. She didn't understand what they were up to and wondered why anyone would want to continue with upheaval after all the years of suffering during that terrible war. Most of the trouble was in Cork and thankfully

Dublin was calm and peaceful.

This morning, William had seemed particularly tired. She had just received their breakfasts on trays and set about waking him. Five months pregnant, she felt ready to eat. Indeed she had felt recently she was eating for two. They needed an hour to get ready for morning service at St Stephens, "The Pepper Canister" church as it was affectionately called. Fortunately that was just a short walk away.

Suddenly she heard a commotion on the stairs outside their rooms. She was surprised and taken aback by this. It was usually such a quiet and orderly house. She heard a loud knock on the door and fatefully moved to open it. As she did so, she was overwhelmed by three men who burst into the room changing her life forever, dismantling, over the next fifteen minutes, her carefully assembled security, the settled nature of her existence, her quiet and peaceful contentment, her grasp of what was normal, casting her into a world of trauma, darkness and despair.

The Drowning of Innocence

Mattie greeted the others as they stepped out of the car and although some of them were much older than he was, self-assuredly, assumed control. He knew their names from the night before. They moved towards number 92, casually in twos, Mattie having already given instruction to the five of them; the three who would guard the entrance and the two who would accompany him into the house. At nine o'clock, on schedule and as planned to coincide with other climactic incursions spread throughout the city, they knocked loudly on the front door.

It was opened quickly by the housekeeper, an older grey-haired woman in her fifties. On seeing the six men, she screamed in horror and turned to run back into the hallway. Alert and as quick as a flash, Mattie sprang and grabbed her and with his hand over her mouth, quietly but with authority said, "This will go very much easier for you, dear lady, if you cooperate and be a good, decent woman. Tell us, which room belongs to Captain Newberry?"

The woman was trembling like a leaf but managed to splutter out that it was rooms on the first floor. Mattie looked at the others, O'Keefe and Dolan. They were ashen-faced and shaking. "I'll not get much help there" he thought, "but let's see." He gesticulated to them to follow him up the stairs. At the top of the first flight, the broad landing led to the door of the Newberry apartment.

Once again, Mattie politely rapped on the door. He heard quiet, ruffled movement inside and the door was opened tentatively by a timid looking woman in her forties. He saw the horror on her face as he sprang inside, dashing past her quickly and scanning the room. The door led straight into the bedroom, a wide and spacious chamber, with high ceilings, an impressive chandelier, open fireplace with a blazing fire. At one side he noticed a table freshly laid for breakfast, the rich smell of a fry-up dominating the air inside.

Captain Newberry was in bed, now bolt upright in his blue and cream striped pyjamas and at that very moment scrambling towards his bedside table. Mattie darted across the room and quickly opened and retrieved the revolver from the drawer, Newberry's 'insurance policy'. He ordered the man to get up.

The woman by this time had retreated in blind panic to the corner of the room beyond the breakfast table, close to the window.

"We have no money or anything here," he heard her wail, "We don't have any valuables, please leave us be, please, please."

Mattie grinned and continuing to look at Newberry exclaimed, "This is our valuable, a stóir, This man here is the jewel in our crown."

Newberry, at this point with his hands in the air, exclaimed, "What are you going to do with me?"

Mattie calmly spoke the words that reverberated through the room and their lives, all of them, including the Dublin Volunteers.

"By order of the Irish government, you are to be executed, before you cause any more damage."

He turned to the others and issued his command, "Now men, take aim and fire."

O'Keefe and Dolan raised their pistols, their hands, trembling, shaking, their bodies quivering, shuddering with the momentous nature of what had befallen them. Shots rang out and bullets flew everywhere, their aim askew. One hit Newberry in the arm. He ran towards the door to the back room of the apartment cutting a pathetic picture in his floppy pyjamas, the quintessential depiction of vulnerability.

"C'mon, for fuck sake, again," ordered Mattie watching with a curious, detached interest at the incapability of the Volunteers to take aim and hit the target from such close range. The men tried again, this time five bullets missing and one hitting Newberry in the leg. Screams of terror and panic emanated from his wife now huddled in a foetal position in the corner, for all the world, like a wounded, stricken animal.

Newberry was now in the other room and making his way towards the window overlooking the back garden. Mattie studied him for a moment, waited while he wrestled with the knobs of the sash seeking to release the frame and presumably jump out to what he hoped would be safety. When the window was open and Newberry was dragging himself out, in pain and awkwardness from his wounded arm and leg, Mattie took careful aim with his Smith and Wesson and executed him at that spot, leaving the body suspended over the ledge, blood pouring from his head and long frame, down the heavily patterned wallpaper, gushing like a geyser from his temple to the garden below.

"Much fucking use you are," he turned to O'Keefe and Dolan.

He walked over to the breakfast table and quickly made a rasher and egg butty from the spread. "Fuck, I didn't realise how hungry I am," he said,

          The Drowning of Innocence

munching eagerly on the bread, the melted butter dripping from the side of his mouth. When he was finished he exhorted the others, "C'mon, lets make ourselves scarce."

Without another word, they departed, leaving behind their victim, straddled on a windowsill, life ebbing from him, his wife traumatised, sobbing in the corner of the room and mumbling incoherently senseless words, over and over again. The trauma debilitating her, reducing her so that within a fortnight she had to endure the further loss of her unborn child.

This was a scene that was re-enacted contemporaneously that morning in various houses and hotels across Dublin; Seventeen men shot in their beds on orders of the Irish government, rocking the British Administration to its core. Acts of terror that sent shockwaves through the establishment and left British rule in Ireland hanging by a thread.

On reaching the street, all six sped towards the Ford. When they were safely away, travelling through Merrion Square and along Westland Row towards the quays, the other men turned on Mattie. "That was so fucking wrong. This is not what we signed up for. You don't just go around killing men in their pyjamas. And in front of their pregnant wives? For fuck sake. It's barbaric. How can we fight like this? You bring shame to our cause. You're nothing but a guttersnipe, a murderer" On and on they went, expelling their words in a fury and rage.

On the quays, Mattie had enough. "Let me out here, for fuck sake." When the car came to a halt, he got out quickly, and headed towards Mulligans in Poolbeg Street, sure and certain because of the docker's trade, that they would be open this Sunday morning and he would be able to relax in the snug with his well-deserved pint and whiskey chaser.

Phil Shanahan's Pub, Dublin

Late evening, Sunday, 21st November 1920

Dalton was still wailing, when Joe Dolan burst into the room, early in the evening, with sweat pouring down his face, animatedly shouting,

"They've hit back, the fuckers, like we thought."

Tom Keogh grabbed him and told him to sit down and calm down.

"Take it easy, Joe. Get your breath back."

"Fuck it, Tom. Breath back for fuck sake? I've just come from Croker, from the game. The 'Tans' came and opened up on the crowds. Brazenly. It was fucking madness. Never seen anything like it before in my life. A fucking huge scramble. People running everywhere. Running for their fucking lives. Fuck knows how many they killed."

"What? They just opened up on the crowd. No warning?" A chorus of voices greeted his words.

Keogh was again the more measured of those who were scrambling around Dolan, shocked by what they were hearing.

"Take it easy, Joe, Tell us slowly what happened. What you saw."

"Oh fuck. You have no idea." Joe stopped, took a deep breath and continued. " I suppose the crowd was tense before the game. You know, everyone was talking about this morning's shootings. The papers were full of it and people were sure there would be a reprisal. But when the game began they began to relax, just focussing on the teams. Fifteen minutes in, we heard rumblings of trucks on the bridge over the canal behind us. We heard some shots and I looked behind me to see a young lad fall from a tree and then immediately afterwards another young fella sitting on the wall behind take a bullet and drop from where he was sitting onto the road outside. All hell broke loose then, I tell you, people started stampeding towards the gates. There was a fierce crush. Some fell over and I could see them being trampled on. I saw people throw off their overcoats so they could run faster. Some ran onto the pitch. The 'Tans' just kept firing into Hill 60."

Mattie was listening to all of this and when he heard Dolan mention Hill 60, his mind raced to Claude and Charlie Hays, all those years ago in Gallipoli and

 The Drowning of Innocence

the price they paid. The irony that British Soldiers were firing into the mound which commemorated the battle for the Dardanelles was not lost on him.

Dolan continued

"I saw one of the Tipp players, what's his name, the corner back?"

"Hogan, Michael Hogan. Good lad."

"They shot him, out on the field. Can you fucking believe it? They shot one of the footballers. And the crowd, the fucking chaos. It was just a mad scramble to get away. Fuck knows how many they have murdered. We managed to squeeze our way out through the James Avenue gate in the initial stampede, before the British locked the gates to search everyone. After I had got out, soldiers surrounded that gate and let off a volley of shots. I looked back briefly and saw people turn in fear. The 'Tans' were shooting in the streets too and nowhere was safe. Most people were squashed into nearby houses. They were packed in there to overflowing, stifling. All of them full of people in a wild panic. I went to look for the lad who had fallen off the wall. I felt so helpless but this was something I could at least do. 'Willie Robinson', he said his name was and 'could I tell his Da he was hurt bad'. I managed to get him on an ambulance to Jervis Street and then made my way to the lad's house in Little Britain Street to tell his Da his son was in hospital. Then I came here."

"What's it like outside now?" Keogh was immediately on the alert, wary.

"You could cut the tension with a fucking knife. No-one is around now. The streets are deserted. Its like a fucking ghost town out there. The whole city is like a morgue."

Hearing all of this was too much for Mattie. He had enough for the day. He needed to get himself under control. His first instinct was to go out and take on the 'Tans', on his own, now, this evening. The pure fuckers. All this he was hearing. Every detail that was pouring out of Dolan reverberated in his head and brought Da to mind. Thoughts, images resounding in his head, his Da's face as he knelt over him on the Blackrock Road, that simple, kind, even beatific countenance, as he held him in his arms, the sobs shaking his own frame, the pain, the unbearable, stupid pain of loss and desolation. And the fucking 'Tans'? Off somewhere in their fucking barracks. Here it goes again. Resurrected by the same fucking 'Tans'. Listening, as he heard, without wanting to, Dolan's fearful telling of what happened just a mile down the road in Croke Park, at a football game, for God's sake, between Dublin and

Tipperary. He fumed inwardly, "It's a long, long way to Tipperary" for those people and their families now.

"Where will this all end," he cried out, involuntarily, startling them all. "When will we get these fuckers to stop?"

"Mattie, Mattie," Tom Keogh, now took hold of him. "Take it easy."

"Easy? Fucking easy. I want to go out and take the fuckers out now."

He stopped, recognised he was losing control and looked up at Keogh and the others and just waved his hand, dismissing his thoughts, recovering his equilibrium. He heard Tom Hales' voice in his head reminding him of the discipline needed. After a few minutes he was calm again.

"Sorry, lads. Fuck, I just needed to let it out. I'll be alright in a while. I just need to clear my head."

He got up, touched Keogh on the arm and said, "I'm going to the other room to be on my own. This fucking madness can get to you sometimes? Eh?"

Keogh smiled and said, "That's the spirit, Mattie. You did well today. You just need to relax."

He picked up the fiddle and went next door to the snug. The small room with its rich oak panelling closed in on him like a womb. He tuned the fiddle quietly. Then, softly, sweetly he played 'Caoineadh Eoghain Ruadh', a lament that had haunted and beguiled him since his childhood, dedicating it in his heart to those who had perished that day, their families, to Michael Hogan, the young footballer, the two young lads, who had just sneaked in to watch a football match but were now gone. And all the others, God bless them and their families. The piercing, plaintiff notes of the tune filled the snug and became a prayer, a remembrance, a dedication to those who had their lives abruptly taken from them, that they would not have died in vain. It had been a bloody, bloody day. One he thought he would never forget.

When he was finished, he wanted company. To recover, as a distraction. To eliminate the memory? He remembered a girl he had seen in the house before. She had besmitten him. A young woman from County Mayo, Gráinne, her name. He asked if she was around. Within minutes, she appeared in the room, her entrance like the breath of Spring, the very air changing, her simple beauty taking his breath away.

     The Drowning of Innocence

Gráinne stood before him, taking him in, this forlorn and lost figure in front of her. Her long hair a deep russet, auburn colour sweeping over her shoulders, her emerald green eyes beautiful beyond imagining, penetrating with a deep soulful, vulnerable simplicity.

Mattie was taken aback by her presence, saw in her the image and personification of all those girls he had known at the college, with their rustic charm and promise of a future. It was a moment of revelation for him. A scythe splitting him irrevocably from his past self, the young lad he was, carefree, easy, happy-go-lucky; now gone forever. The life he had now chosen, had dedicated himself to, issuing in a dramatic separation from the lad he was. He realised in that instant he could never be that man again. He was lost to himself. Cataclysmically, ruptured from his embryonic self.

The events of the day began to overtake him. He murmured to Gráinne that he was sorry. He realised he needed to be alone and gave her far too much money as compensation. He reassured her that she was beautiful and kind to come to him. Gráinne smiled a delicate compassionate smile, a deep look of concern in her eyes, thanked him and left.

Mattie just about held himself together as she walked out the door of the snug and when she was out of earshot, broke down, sobbing quietly for his loss of innocence, his Da, and the awful mounting deaths that were taking place and would continue to grow, in order to wrest the country he loved from the rule of its foreign invader.

After a time, he did not know how long, he gathered himself and knew he could not afford now or in the future such a capitulation, such an indulgence. He steadied himself, asked for a bottle of Jameson and set about drinking himself into a safe and secure oblivion.

West Cork

Sunday, 28th November 1920

It was a wet and dreary November night. A dark cloud, pregnant with rain, followed them through their forced march, a muscle-draining slog over the Shehy mountains, all thirty-six of them singing in unison to safeguard their timing and temperament.   The weather, turbulent and boisterous, the boreens unkempt and overgrown, drew them to the back of beyond. Hermits and wild men would be at home in the forsaken places they passed through; Recluses enduring the buffeting of the elements, stoically battling through life, their existence pared down to that of mere survival with the wild, untamed, tempestuous landscape providing the template for their search into the mystical and profound.

The wind-swept and deserted mountain road had a lonesome, ghostly quality about it, but there was safety in that. The wind itself stroked their faces like a clump of soft feathers, making them feel alive, exhilarated by their mission. Of all the places in the county, this was home, safe, off limits to invaders - The Gaeltacht. The 'Tans' and Auxiliary forces would not venture here, and certainly not at night. Even though the dismal weather seeped into their clothes, making them heavy and allowing the cold November air to pierce their insides, their spirits did not flag.

From time to time, they came across farmhouses and supped tea and ate soda bread in the yard, longingly gazing into the kitchen, the sparse interior brightened by the turf fire stoked in the hearth, its smoked sweetness beckoning them in to rest from their labours, beseeching them that comfort and cheer was their calling, not this fearful trek over the west Cork countryside in the dead of night. They were encouraged by the welcomes and the heartfelt blessings given on their departure; Some of the old women grasping their hands fervently and with a hopeful, compassionate, even prayerful look in their eyes saying:

"Go mbeire muid beo ar an am seo arís." (May you be alive and well at this time next year)

and

"Go n-eirí an t-ádh leat" (Good Luck).

In the darkness of the night the gorse bushes lit up their way, yellow stems, bedraggled now, fading from their splendour as the winter air pinched them,

The Drowning of Innocence

but picked out nonetheless by their lanterns. Just after two in the morning, as they came down from the Keimaneigh pass, and over the bridge at Drohidaspaunig, the moon burst through the clouds, three nights past full, it spread its light like butter, picking out the glorious features of the landscape. The waters of the Guagán Barra lake lapped the shoreline fiercely in the breeze.

In his weariness, Micheál took deep breaths and filled his lungs with the cold mountain air and marvelled once again at the deep, still, panoramic beauty of his native county. This is what drove him on. "Talamh agus Saoirse" "Land and Freedom". He could pick out places on the far shore of the lake where he and Eileen had courted during the summer of the previous year, their rich conversations, the deep thrill of falling in love, searching, exploring the landscape of each other's soul. His heart skipped a beat as he remembered her. For Eileen he would fulfil their dream, an Ireland of their own for themselves and their children. Free, second-class no longer, nor subservient to some foreign crown.

The old women in the farmhouses attesting that this was no idle fantasy, but something dreamed about for centuries, deeply embedded within the collective memory, that wounded memory, seared by Cromwell, famine and humiliation. His heart filled with a deep desire and he knew that, although he had butterflies in his stomach thinking about what faced him, he would be strong, buoyed by this deep conviction of a free nation within their grasp, a place for him and Eileen and their future together.

A month before he had been summoned by Florrie O'Donoghue.

"We are stepping up the campaign, Micheál," Florrie had said, "We realise that we are sitting targets for raids now and we can't let what happened to Tom be a pattern. We have to take control back. This fucker Percival knows too much about us so we have to get on the move."

The Cork brigade had been incensed by the treatment meted out to their commander, Tom Hales. He had been picked up by Major Percival's 'Essex Battalion Torture Squad' in July. Micheál had always liked Hales from the very first moment he had been sworn in by him into the Movement; A quiet, educated, studious man who developed and received, in equal measure, genuine affection among his men, devastating them when word got out about Hales' treatment from Percival's gang. Micheál could hardly take in the horror of it. He had been beaten, dragged along the road from the back of a lorry, his fingernails ripped out with pliers and his teeth extracted. It seemed that Percival had travelled to new levels of barbarism to wipe out resistance to

British Rule. If the bastard was hoping to send out a message, a deterrent, he was sadly mistaken. He had only served to strengthen resolve, to furnish conviction that Britain and its rule must this time be eliminated, banished from Ireland.

Florrie continued, "We have a new man working with us. Tom Barry is his name, a quare fellow indeed, a Kerryman. He comes from an RIC family and served in the British war but now he wants to get involved in the struggle. There's no doubt he is experienced and has great ideas, but not all of us trust him."

"Where is he based?"

"He's over Clonakilty way. The thing is he wants to form a column of full-timers who will be on the move all the time. He grandiosely calls it a 'Flying Column'. Anyway, he has asked the various brigades to pick men to join him and that's why I am talking to you. You know Micheál you are the best shot in the county, so you will be useful to him as a sniper. But more importantly we would also like you to keep an eye on this Barry fellow and give us reports. He has not earned his crust yet. Are you up for it?"

"Full time? You mean I have to give up work and go on the run?"

"Yes that's what it means. You won't see home or Cork for some time. Once you join the Flying Column you will become a marked man and will spend the rest of the war bunking down in safe houses."

Micheál paused to think for a moment. In a way none of this came as a surprise. He knew such a sacrifice was coming. The economic situation in the city was poor anyway and it had been a struggle to keep the kiln going. Eileen and he had talked. That had not been easy, they had come to rely so much on one another's company and support and to be parted like this would be hard for both of them. She would understand, though. The die had been cast. Freedom now or never.

Still Micheál knew that by accepting this commission he was putting himself in danger, he was putting their future together in obeisance. He thought of his brothers, of their eagerness to go to war, of those innocent days eight long years previously, before the full tumult of the thing had exploded in their midst. No naive search for adventure this time. Such a dalliance was wasteful and a distraction to the cause. He had learnt from Charlie and Claude, and was growing up fast.

     The Drowning of Innocence

Joan, of course, would not approve of this. She had lost too much and would be distraught to see her little brother go to war.   She mustn't know. These thoughts roved about his mind, churning up his insides, but all along he knew he could not live with himself if he walked away from this summons. He never felt closer to his brothers or his Da. Deep inside, he was a 'Hays', determined people, to be relied upon, dutiful and committed. Of course none of his family would understand his devotion to the 'Fenian cause', but they would know he could not walk away from this challenge. If he was not ready now, he never would be. He looked up at Florrie, who was grinning back at him.

"You bastard, Florrie. You knew I wouldn't say no."

"Well there you go, Micheál, that's why they make me Director of Intelligence, because I know what everyone is thinking before they know it themselves."

They laughed deeply and Florrie threw his arms around the young man and gave him a comforting, reassuring hug.

"Off you go, Micheál, show those culchies in West Cork we are not soft here in the city. And strike a blow for Tom Hales and Freedom. Saol fada agus breac-shláinte chugat." (Long life and health go with you.)

"Agus tú féin, Florrie." (and you too).

Saying goodbye to Eileen had been very difficult.   He forced himself to drink in the moment they were together. Deeply, deeply present to her so that he could carry that immanence with him to the wild country of West Cork.

"Micheál, a Stóir, don't worry. I will be fine. I have so much work to do for my finals next year. You just concentrate on what you have to do and be careful."

He had spent the month since under Tom Barry's command, being trained in warfare in the hills beyond Dunmanway. He was shocked when he first met the man, Barry's youthful twenty two years defying his authority, experience, knowledge and wit. Indeed if it were not for Barry's confidence and self-assurance, Micheál would have found him slightly comical, his Kerry accent delivered in clipped enunciation. But he also saw ruthlessness, someone who would take no prisoners, demanding the utmost commitment. On one occasion as they listened to his briefing on strategy, Barry was vehement in tone and intention,

"This war has changed completely. What happened to Tom Hales means the gloves are off. We will meet them with their own weapons. They have gone down into the mire to destroy us and our nation, and we will go down after them. Mark my words. I tell you now, I have no respect for these feckers."

Micheál felt a chill run down his spine as he listened to Barry and was wary, remembering Florrie's words of caution. He would be vigilant.

From his early days in the Movement, Micheál had been entrusted with a Short Magazine Lee Enfield rifle, a precious commodity among the Volunteers. He had embraced this weapon, been at one with it, feeling each part of the machinery with the delicate tips of his fingers. He knew from the intimacy of guiding and bringing life and shape to amorphous clay on the potters wheel, how to bring the best out of the materials given to him. With the Lee Enfield his prowess was quickly established.

Although ammunition was scarce, Barry wanted to assess his expertise. In training, in the hills, they set a target. Micheál loaded and cocked his rifle, put it to his shoulder, took aim, and with his being equally as transfixed as in shaping a pot, with calm, steady, efficient hands, fired. Remarkably to the utter astonishment of those around, he never missed. They found it difficult to comprehend how this elegant gun could be so deadly in his hands. Barry was suitably gratified. He was ready for action.

Now on this Sunday morning they were on their first mission. After the march through the night, they arrived at their destination, just after dawn, a damp mist rising from the bracken and hedgerows, creating a dank atmosphere. Kilmichael. Cill Mhíchil. Micheál ruefully thought about the name and hoped it was not an omen. When they reached the spot, a bend in the road Barry ordered them to stand easy as he spoke,

"Men, this is the ambush site. Take a good look at it."

He gestured with his hand pointing at the surrounding landscape. There was precious little shelter here, the ground was level and sparse, just the occasional crag of rock behind which they could take cover and mount an attack on the road.

"The lack of cover is deliberate. The British won't be expecting an ambush here, so surprise will be on our side. These Auxiliaries are experienced soldiers, battle-hardened so you will have to be ruthless. You can see there is

The Drowning of Innocence

no hope of retreat or escape from here, so kill or be killed. We can't take prisoners. What are we going to do with them, anyway? Where can we hold them? How are we going to force-march them alongside us? And if we let the feckers go, I promise you they will come back for us, one by one, and then we will face the same treatment that was given to Tom Hales."

Micheál looked at the other men and saw the occasional flicker and tremor as Barry's words took effect. Barry's demeanour was commanding, even intimidating. He was leaving his men no option. This would be a battle to the death. Micheál could feel the tension mounting as Barry continued,

"You have been hand-picked. You are the cream of Cork's brigades and I know you will do your job. We have it within our hands to deliver a devastating blow to the British. Show them we mean business."

The gloomy day became more gloomy as Barry had spoken. Micheál felt that something momentous was taking shape, that he was part of an action that would change the struggle for better or worse. Everything building up to this moment. Not just the years since '16 when those romantic idealists, led by Pearse, had stood on the steps outside the GPO and proclaimed the Irish Republic, but everything, The O'Neills and O'Donnells, The United Irishmen, Wolfe Tone, Éire Óg, the men '98, all that troubled history, all leading up to this day. They were being asked to pick up the mantle and carry it forward, a bloody quest for freedom and glory.

"Listen," Barry continued, "for the last two months since they arrived in Macroom the 'Auxies' have been throwing their weight around, terrorising people, beating ordinary citizens up, running amok. They regularly take trips in their Crossley's around here, taking potshots at people working in the fields. They are arrogant bastards, imperious feckers. They're looking for a bloody nose, to be taken down a peg or two. And we're the ones to give it them. They always take this route back after their 'sport'. So I want you to bed yourself in, make yourself as comfortable as you can, as it will be a long day."

Barry then proceeded to split them into sections carefully planning the logistics of the ambush, two sections covering the bend where the vanguard of the Auxiliary patrol would be stopped, one covering the rest of the patrol. A remaining section would act as cover and back up if the patrol was larger than anticipated. Two men were despatched to warn locals to avoid the road when travelling to and from Sunday mass. When he was finished he strode over to Micheál.

"Hays," he said, "I want you to take that high point up there commanding the road."

He pointed to a rocky crag that had a view over a good portion of the bend.

"When the 'Auxies' come, I will step out onto the road to stop them."

At that moment, Barry opened his great coat to reveal his British Army tunic inside.

"This will confuse them. When I gesture to them to stop, I will blow my whistle. I want you to open fire and kill the driver and those in the cab. I'm relying on you."

Micheál saluted and made his way up to the craggy rock. When he reached the vantage point, he lay down and got his bearings. From here his view of the road was clear. The boggy marshlands beyond painted a deserted and desolate vista. The mist was hanging over the landscape like a veil with just enough vision to pick out what he wanted but sufficient also to provide cover and camouflage. He applauded Barry's genius. He could see that this would be the last place the British would expect an ambush.

He was perturbed however. 'What ifs' circulating unhelpfully in his head. What did Florrie mean when he said few trusted Barry? Is this a set-up? Is Barry going to deliver them all to the enemy when he calls for their convoy to stop?

He was in for a long wait. These thoughts and others circulated round and round in his head as the day dragged on. Lying on the cold, wet ground became unbearable at times, the seeping wetness seemed to be everywhere, the permeating drizzle penetrating to his very bones, as he looked at the road and grizzled bog beyond. He had the company of a wren, its cheerful chirping defying its diminutive body throughout the day as it foraged about in the undergrowth oblivious to Micheál's presence. At times he found the little fellow captivating, charming, taking him out of himself and away from the intensity of what he was about to face. At other times, he concentrated, checking his sight picture on various objects all along the road, building his confidence that when the time came, he would not be found wanting.

At four in the afternoon, as dusk was beginning to settle on that sombre day, and after he had long given up hope of any action, he heard a rumble of vehicles in the distance. A low groan, getting louder, its ominous tone as a prelude, the opening symphony to a fierce, dark melodrama. Tension gripped

The Drowning of Innocence

his stomach. Adrenaline coursed through his veins far worse than anything he had experienced before any hurling game. He felt nauseous with it. He looked down from his vantage point and saw Barry rise from his place in the command centre, a rocky outcrop beside a boreen leading off the road. He observed the confident stride as Barry headed out onto the road having shed his great coat. He looked resplendent in his British Army uniform, standing there imperiously, as the first Crossley rounded the corner. 'This is it,' thought Micheál, 'this is where it is all resolved.'

Barry raised his right hand with authority, gesturing that the convoy stop.

'Now what,' thought Micheál, 'Is this the moment we are all sold out, down the river, like a bunch of eejits?'

The leading tender began to slow down and as it did so, Barry did two things. He reached into his pocket for a grenade and at the same time blew hard on his whistle. Micheál, his rifle already cocked, with almost consummate ease, took aim, fired and the driver slumped onto the wheel. Without waiting, Micheál drew back the bolt, releasing the cartridge, pushed it forward and with calm detachment aimed and killed one of the soldiers on the back of the tender. Barry's grenade exploded in front of the vehicle and out of control, it slumped to a halt into a small bank at the side of the road, its wheels sinking into the bog, and lurching violently to one side. The occupants on the back of the tender were thrown off balance and exposed and within minutes all were dead. Micheál's concentration had been fully taken up by the task in hand. "Kill or be killed" Barry had declared and he had reloaded and fired round after round during the three minutes of the assault. He hit every target but could not be sure if he had been the only one as Volunteers below and closer had also discharged their weapons, surging out on the road and onto the vehicle. Gunshots obliterated the calm normality of the landscape sending a paroxysm of movement through the wildlife. Lapwings, Curlews, Plovers took to the sky in terror, Hares shot from their forms and bolted across the bog, zigzagging as they raced away in a blind panic.

When it was over, Micheál turned his attention to the other attack. He could hear the fierce exchange of fire around the bend and out of sight. He made his way carefully until he could see the vehicle and 'Auxies' crouching behind it and under the ditch beside the road. As he was approaching, he thought he saw two of the British throw their rifles away. He couldn't be sure. Then everything became a blur. He saw two volunteers stand up to rush down onto the road, but immediately shots rang out and he could see their bodies twist at a queer angle and fall to the ground. Before he could reach the site, all hell had broken loose. The Volunteers had overwhelmed the 'Auxies' and he could see them shooting, almost indiscriminately, time and time again, reloading and firing, reloading. After five minutes, when there was no movement from the surrounds of the 'Auxie's' tender, the Volunteers moved forward with greater confidence, still shooting and bayoneting the corpses lying on the ground.

By the time Micheál reached the second tender, it all was over. Many of his comrades looked grey-faced, traumatised. Some had been overcome and were vomiting at the side of the road, retching and puking into the boggy ground. Chaos and disorder reigned. A nervy, incoherent, unsafe bedlam decimated their focus and actions. In the midst of it all, Barry strode in and commanded, demanded their attention. Many of the men were lost to themselves and with a great effort of will, Barry dragged them back from the abyss and got them into a kind of formation. He then issued instructions,

"Gather the dead and lay them on the side of the road with their identification tags clearly visible," He ordered one large group.

Then he ordered others to put their dead, O'Sullivan, McCarthy and the injured Volunteer, Deasy on stretchers stressing that speed was needed to move out and away as quickly as possible. Micheál with three others were ordered to torch the vehicles.

Barry's force of will brought order to their panic and disarray and the operation was completed efficiently. Plumes of smoke rose into the darkening sky, wet with rain. It was a bleak, dismal sight. Micheál grudgingly admired Barry and acknowledged to himself that there was no replacing experience in combat. Fighting back tears, he thought of Charlie and Claude and understood their holocaust of learning as the same as Barry's. "Is this what it turns you into," he thought, dejectedly.

They got away from the site quickly, almost involuntarily, leaving behind seventeen dead men at the side of the road, each one of the Volunteers overwhelmed by the memory of what had taken place, pleading that time be reversed but knowing, nevertheless, that it would stubbornly not be overturned.

Sadly for each of them it would remain fixed, stood still, paused, segued into an overdrive of remembrance. That hour between four and five in the afternoon, on the deserted road near Dromleigh, in West Cork, on a bleak Sunday in November in the year nineteen twenty would remain in their consciousness for the rest of their lives. Something to remain hidden, a

                         The Drowning of Innocence

shameful taboo, not talked about, kept to themselves like a perverted oath of allegiance.

They traversed over the hills out of sight from man and beast, first reaching Shanacashel where they handed over the bodies of McCarthy and O'Sullivan with the hope that a priest could be found to administer Extreme Unction. They gave Deasy to a farmer to be taken to hospital if that could be possible that night. Then they moved on quickly, wordlessly through Coolnagow, Balteenbrack and crossed the dangerous Manch Bridge in the dead of night.

Micheál's mind was in a turmoil as he marched, question after question, assailing his brain. What had caused this unleashing of fury, of mayhem? Was it Barry's exhortation to leave no-one alive, to take no prisoners? Was it a kind of primeval fear he instilled in them all that if recognised, a Volunteer would be hunted down, captured, tortured and killed like others in the past? Was it the recollection of torture of their comrades? The murders in Croke Park? Was it some visceral hatred of the British that had accumulated genetically through centuries as time after time, their people had endured humiliation and cruelty? He did not know. Some of Volunteers were murmuring about a false surrender and that was why O'Sullivan was struck, standing up from his position, believing it was all over, killed as he moved to accept the British capitulation.

But as Micheál looked at his group of comrades, he could see that they had been changed by the experience. He saw a degenerating atrophy appear in their manner as the full extent of the horror of what had happened unleashed itself on them. Ordinary men, farmers, tradesmen, they had become for thirty minutes in their lives perpetrators of this onslaught, this carnage, this slaughter and it was to be something that would haunt each one for the rest of their days. At that moment Micheál desperately needed Eileen and felt bereft, keenly longing for her touch.

On the other side of the Bandon river, they found a safe house and rested fitfully for the night, their consciousness dominated by terrible nightmares. The last thing they felt then was that they were heroes, saviours of their country, to be remembered fondly, to have songs composed of their exploits and sung in pubs late in the evening. That to them was unthinkable. On that long night, as they sought sleep and unconsciousness, all their energy and will power fiercely expended in forgetting not remembering; In elimination not preservation; In grasping for anything that would take them away from what took place that day at Kilmichael; Take them to years later, the day buried in understandable silence, glad then the war was over and the places it had taken them, consigned to oblivion.

That, for them was the epitaph of their day.

The Drowning of Innocence

9, Careys Lane,
Cork   *13th December, 1920*

Micheál,

Where are you? I am worried sick. I went over to Eileen and she told me you were called away and that it's best I don't know where you are in case the authorities come for you. She said if I wrote then she would try and get the letter to you. I am scared for you and don't like this one bit.

Oh Micheál, we have had a terrible time of it. Awful. You will have heard they burnt the city to the ground on Saturday night. On a rampage they were, Tans and Auxiliaries. It was so, so frightening. Patrick Street is no more, all the shops are in ruins, it's unrecognisable. We were lucky in a way that the direction of the wind took the flames away from Careys Lane, otherwise we would have lost our home also.

It all started at nine in the evening when we heard loud explosions and gunfire, so close it felt it was outside the door and so different to what we have heard before. Within minutes, Claude had lost his reason. It looked to Seán and me as if he thought he was back on the Front Line. I have never seen a look of such terror in anyone. He was like a frightened animal, rampaging around the house. Then all of a sudden, he darted for the front door. Seán tried to stop him but it was impossible. He burst out the door and onto the street, screaming and yelling like a man possessed. We could do nothing but follow him as he headed up the Lane and onto Patrick Street.

On Patrick Street, he seemed to shudder and collapse. All around us buildings were on fire, the flames shooting up into the sky, bombs exploding and shots being fired in the air. Detachments of Tans and Auxies were running amok, most of them were 'worse for the wear' with drink and very, very dangerous. They were in a mixture of clothing but you could tell straight away who they were, Glengarry caps and English accents, striding down the centre of the street. We didn't know what to do, as Claude continued ranting and raving towards the elements, like a lunatic, drawing attention to us. We couldn't quieten him. He had become feral.

Seán and I were in shock as we tried to contain him and at the same time take in what was happening to our city as the flames engulfed Grants, Cash's, the Arcade, all those lovely landmarks disappearing in front of us. We were scared it would get to the English Market and destroy that too. We saw soldiers looting in Mangan's jewellers, large suitcases in their hands, they were a frightening sight.

We could hardly breathe from the terror, the smoke and the fumes, as black palls of it descended from the sky. The blaze was totally out of control and we feared for our lives, but there was nothing we could do. We couldn't abandon Claude, not then. He was uncontrollable, fierce, strong but so forlorn, weeping and crying at the flames.

We saw the fire brigade arrive and thought there was hope, there would be some respite, but they immediately came under fire from the soldiers who cut their hoses when they were hooked up to the hydrants. It seemed they were hell bent on destruction. We saw one fireman going up Grant's fire escape with a hose trained on the building. Next minute a Gordon Highlander came out of Market Lane, very drunk and fired twice at him. The Highlander discharged the rest of his revolver, luckily missing him. The language he used was obscene, terrible. The soldiers were all filled with so much anger, rancour and hatred, staggering about, laden with cases full of finery, coats, hats and other things they had looted. They were sacking the city.

Claude was in an agony of confusion. I'm sure he didn't know where he was. Was he in Cork, Ypres, or Krithia? He had truly lost his mind.

Auxies stopped a tram near us and ordered the people inside to disembark and lined them up against a wall. Our luck ran out as they grabbed us as well. They set fire to the tram. I was frightened out of my wits. They had absolutely no respect and were out of control, striking Seán on the head with their rifle and sending him flying onto the street. They pushed me over and I fell badly on my knee. But all I could think of was Claude. I was worried that he was so out of control, they would kill him as it seemed very little provocation would push them over the edge. As he was screaming, they belted him with a rifle butt and when he fell they kicked him repeatedly and roared at him to repeat "God save the king". They also demanded he say (Oh Gosh) "Fuck the Pope." Do they hate Catholics so much? It was terrifying and we were helpless. The anguish in Claude's face was truly heartbreaking.

Fortunately for us, two O'Gorman brothers, Danny and John, who had been travelling on the tram, had the sense to grab hold of Claude and lift him up. They pleaded with the Auxies that he was suffering from delusions and had served in France. I don't know how they managed it, maybe it was that the Auxies got bored or wanted to get on with their looting, but somehow they let us go.

Danny and John took us up to their place in Blarney Street. It was so tough leaving Patrick Street behind, not knowing if by morning our house would be gone. But we were glad of it, to get away from the mayhem.

As we walked up the hill, and looked back over the city, it resembled a scene from Dante's 'Inferno' with flames boiling up in a foment. When we reached number 55, Danny and John's home, we heard a deafening explosion and looked back to see the City Hall and Carnegie Library engulfed in flames. We couldn't understand it. How could this happen? The wind was in the opposite direction and so the flames could not cross that distance of the river. We knew then that they had also set fire to those beautiful buildings and we didn't know what they would stop at and whether by morning Carey's Lane would also be gone.

    The Drowning of Innocence

But at the same time it was good to be safe, away from it all. Danny and John were great with Claude and he began to settle down with a cup of tea and a Paddy. But it is a big setback to him. I thought he was settling into a routine and slowly picking up his life again, but I fear this night has put him right back to square one. I am so sad for him. He is such a different person from the young man, our dear brother, we knew all those years ago. We love him so much. He reminds me so much of Charlie that it breaks my heart to see him this way.

It was only when we relaxed in the O'Gorman's that Seán thought of the shop in Maylor Street. He had been so busy thinking of Claude. John O'Gorman and he went back down the hill to check on it. I suppose he had to do it for his peace of mind but I was terrified all the time they were gone.

They came back an hour later looking white, like they had seen a ghost. They had come across this tall man in King Street who was wandering around like a maniac, shooting at firemen, shooting indiscriminately. They overheard him say in a cold, menacing voice, "My brother got killed in an ambush and I am here to get my revenge." We guessed he was talking about Kilmichael. They managed to stay hidden from him and ducked down Harley Street out of his way. It was about five in the morning when they got to Maylor Street and fortunately everything there was under control. I was so glad to see them back with us.

The O'Gorman's were lovely, so hospitable. They walked back with us to Carey's Lane on Sunday afternoon, after dinner. Walking through Patrick Street was sobering and deflating. Our city is gone, wiped out in a night. There is this congealed filth everywhere on the streets from the water and soot, buildings have collapsed and our beloved skyline is no more. It is heartbreaking.

But we are safe. We are back home. Claude is recovering and the doctor has been to see him. We are alive. Thank God for that. It's as much as we could have hoped for in the middle of all that turmoil. But I will only fully rest if I know you are safe. Please, please let me know. I am worried sick. Please, please write and let me know you are alright.

Love, Your sister Joan.

Riverview

Blackrock Road   13th December 1920

Micheál a stóir,

I miss you my darling as I pass on this letter from Joan. I hope you can keep your spirit up, take courage and be safe. I know things are very tough. Remember we talked about this together. We knew it would not be easy. We knew that the British would not give up without a fight. But we don't want to live in an Ireland ruled by a foreign power where our children will be always be second class.

So I am alongside you, my darling, in what you have to do. God keep you safe and bring this bitter thing to an end soon.

Joan is distraught, bless her. She has not the same understanding of what this is all about. I see it in others too. A weariness. Many of the neighbours are longing for it to end. There are no jobs. There is no money. Thousands have lost work because of the devastating effect of the burning of the city and people are going through desperate times. Bless them.

You remember the Delaney brothers from the summer school. At the same time they were sacking the city, a bunch of 'Tans' burst into their farmhouse on Dublin Hill. The two lads were asleep in their beds when they were shot. I went to their funerals and one of the sisters told me it was horrible. She had to sit by her brother as his life ebbed away from him, holding a crucifix to his lips and praying for his soul. Oh Micheál, when will this end? I am so glad you are on the run. Its not safe anymore to be in your own home. There is something about Cork people when they are roused though. They are determined. I believe everyone wants this to continue to the end whatever that is.

I can only hope that the British see sense soon and give up. Although I doubt that very much. So I must urge you to stay strong. Feel my touch alongside you. You are the light of my life. I love you so much,

A stóir, Your Eileen XXX

                    The Drowning of Innocence

Truce

"I will arise and go now, and go to Innisfree,
And a small cabin build there, of clay and wattles made;
Nine bean rows will I have there, a hive for the honey bee,
And live alone in the bee-loud glade.
And I shall have some peace there, for peace comes
dropping slow,
Dropping from the veils of the morning to where the
cricket sings;
There midnight's all a glimmer, and noon a purple glow,
And evening full of the linnet's wings.
I will arise and go now, for always night and day
I hear lake water lapping with low sounds by the shore;
While I stand on the roadway, or on the pavements gray,
I hear it in the deep heart's core."

"The Lake Isle of Innisfree"

W.B. YEATS

"The SF [Sinn Fein] cause and organisation is breaking up …there is no need of hurry in a settlement. We can in due course and in our own fair terms settle this Irish Question for good"
Hamar Greenwood, The Chief Secretary for Ireland

"There are of course one or two wild people about who still hold the absurd idea that if you go on killing long enough, peace will ensue. I do not believe it for one moment but I do believe that the more people are killed the more difficult a final solution becomes"
Commander in Chief, in Ireland, Neville Macready

"I call on all Irishmen to pause, to stretch out the hand of forbearance and conciliation, to forgive and to forget, and to join in making for the land they love a new era of peace, contentment, and good will."
King George V

"To say that we were jubilant would be untrue. It was more bewilderment. Through the years of struggle, the hangings and executions and sufferings had generated in us something unchristian. Our lust to kill had not been satisfied."
Volunteer, County Monaghan

University College, Cork

Monday, 11th July 1921

Eileen was nervous as she boarded the train at Blackrock on her way into the city. She had chosen to wear her light blue chemise dress with its delicately designed lace collar and her white pumps. The previous day she had her hair cut into a fashionable bob and she was hoping the look of her would provide the confidence she needed as she faced the ordeal of her finals. She had fitted a cloth portfolio around the frame of her finished piece, to help with its ferrying to college. "If I am not ready now I never will be," she thought to herself as she had closed the front door of Riverview. It was the day her Da had longed for, but would not see. She owed it to him to be at her best.

She had prepared long and hard for this day, had dreamt many times of being in front of her examiners with her work displayed before them, vulnerable in all its simplicity. Would it capture enough of what was inside her? Express, to their critical, even censorious eyes, the vision she had set herself to portray?

The months without Micheál had been long and hard, fretful about his whereabouts and safety, missing his comforting presence, his reassuring voice, his encouragement. His absence like a dull ache to be endured. Things had gone from bad to worse in the country. The very air had become bitter and the city and county had sunk into a morass, a labyrinth of killings, murders, reprisals, burnt-out houses, terror, viciousness, hatred, enmity, hostility and fiercely held antagonism. Killings and reprisals doubled by the week as 1920 ground on into 1921. It was as if the people were continuously holding its breath, awaiting the next atrocity; ordinary people going about their daily lives under a cloud.

Eileen looked at this very real contagion, and guided by the memory of her dear Da, sought a different view. She wanted to excavate the beauty of her county and its people, capturing their aboriginal spirit in her creations, in her art. Obligated, in the middle of all this turmoil, to forge a pastiche of the land which distilled all its wild beauty, the deep dignity of its people in their daily quest for life, their acquiescence to the unknown and the mysterious; uncovering their identity and soul; simple ordinary unsophisticated folk, women and men, making their peace with life.

During the winter months she had lived in Sherkin island. Sherkin. Replete

The Drowning of Innocence

with memory. How she loved that island, her own 'Little Isle of Innisfree'. The family had spent many happy holidays there in her childhood in Mrs Roche's house. Everything about the place had enraptured her from the very first encounter. Vivid recollections of stepping into John Willie's boat as they sailed from the harbour at Baltimore, excitedly looking forward to the days ahead. The rich green expanse of water washing away, cleansing them as they headed to that magical place, landing, disembarking in gleeful anticipation, past the ruins of the Franciscan Friary and up the hill, the overgrown boreens winding their way to the Atlantic side, in and out of fissures of land and water, mystical in its intrinsic beauty, capturing the soul of the land and its island people, the very air teeming with the sweet aroma of summer.

Long days in the sun on Silver Strand or Noreen's bay; Searching the rock pools, bracing the cold waves rushing in from the ocean beyond. Mass on Sunday in the little chapel, a chance to meet with new found friends and reflect on the glories of weeks past and adventures planned.

Her Ma had been alive then, alive and captivated by the place. She remembered days with her, stalking otters in Horseshoe Bay, following their spraints, rewarded by glimpses of their proud heads above the deep green water, fishing; Picking wildflowers for the table; Scanning the rock pools for gems. Mattie and Da joining others in fierce games of hurling on the smooth strand. In the evening, as Mattie and she were tucked into bed with a glass of milk and a marietta biscuit, counting the indents on its circumference to prolong the pleasure, her Ma and Da would trek across the island to John Willie's for 'ceól agus craic'.

Sherkin was the place to guide her reflection. At the beginning she felt daunted. How could she give expression to the thing that was resonating inside her. To bring forth its beauty. She trawled the island, seeking inspiration, gathering quintessential materials; Driftwood, shells at the Atlantic shore; Roots, berries, bark; Turf from bogs carried with such dignity to light and warm winter fires; Arran weaves that spoke a family's name; Perfection in lace filigree; Discarded fired fragments from the potter's kiln; Stones from rock pools and creeks to mirror her precious find, sandstone, lime, chalk; Thatch golden from the sun; Wild grasses dried in the wind. She spent hours in Mrs Roche's, grinding, dissolving and extracting the pigments, firing them in clay kiln that Micheál had shown her how to construct, melding the raw materials of the countryside to form a subtle yet untamed image, a prospect, textured and worn, which characterised the deep soul of her people and depicted their celebration of blessing and life.

She surrendered herself to the process, all the time open to where it would lead her, curious, energised, inquisitive. There were moments along the way which authenticated her voyage of discovery. Enamoured, touched deeply by Native American rock art, it's pared-down simplicity pointing to mystery, a treasure of a life lived in community and solidarity, in union with the immanent cosmos. The Conquistadors, seeking gold and fortune of a temporal nature, had missed and obliterated the real wealth of heritage and understanding inherent within the vision and lifestyle of the many tribes they had overrun. Instead they brutally and in ignorance slaughtered people in their thousands and consigned to oblivion the wisdom of centuries.

Eileen wanted to mine, explore, reveal and exhibit the quiet self-esteem of her people, their deep connection with the earth, wild and glorious, the land perched as it was on the edge of the Atlantic, the last outcrop of Europe, somehow carrying in its essence the mystery of the eternal in the now.

After the winter of exploration and composition, today was the day when all her efforts, her reflections, her work would be placed in the open. Her notebooks, scrapbooks replete with her commentary, understanding and vision: The finished work, a framed image, textured, layer on layer, to be seen, touched, felt, seeking to celebrate identity and origin. Her heart beat faster with the thought of it, the uncovering of her soul.

When she alighted from the tram on the Western Road, she saw a group of her friends gathered at the quadrangle of the college. There was something strange about their gait. Were they as nervous as she was? And yet, their expressions didn't seem to exhibit a strain. Instead, even from this distance, their faces were wreathed in smiles, arms clasped around one another in some sort of communal embrace of exhilaration. On catching sight of Eileen, struggling as she was with her portfolio and satchel, walking towards them, they turned and rushed over to her, screaming, screeching with joy,

"ITS OVER, EILEEN, ITS OVER!!!!!!"

The jubilation in their faces astonishing to Eileen, a transformation she had not seen before, an iridescent eruption of exaltation.

One of her friends, Úna, grabbed her and spun her around,

"The British, they've called for a truce. Its over. We've won."

Eileen could hardly take it in. Is it true? The conflict gone? The news cast her into a tumult of emotions. Relief, oh blessed relief. She would have

                         The Drowning of Innocence

Micheál back. But pain and sadness. Her Da not there, gone and missed now, keenly so, taken by the turmoil that had won this day. She fell to her knees and sobbed. Úna was taken aback for a moment and did not know what to do. In the midst of her own unconfined joy, she was brought back to earth, with a crash, remembering the cost of this day. She was suddenly transported, as others were throughout the country that day, into a conflicted state, thoughts colliding violently, in a clash of syllogisms, differing ergo's falling, tumbling from scrambled minds and hearts.

"Isn't it great. The day has finally arrived. Its here!!!!"

"Why did it not happen earlier?"

"We can begin to dream again! Life can start now!"

"Why did we lose so many? Oh if he was only here!"

"We can be at peace in a new Ireland!"

"Why so much hatred? How can we escape that?"

"We can build our own nation, our own, free identity!"

"Why did we have to suffer the destruction of our city?"

There were no answers. The pain of sorrow and loss was inextricably and inherently bound up in the ontology of this new day, this new dawn, this new frontier. Eileen was comforted by her friends as they gathered her to her feet and held her. Tears of inconceivable elation and bliss were mixed with profound sorrow and anguish as she allowed the news to sink in, to become absorbed into her very being.

The exams were cancelled as was everything else. The whole city seemed to expel its breath and spontaneously, here and there, at street corners, crossroads, pubs and shops, people burst into song and dance. Neighbours, friends, comrades who had travelled together in the terror and wrath that had engulfed them, now embraced and reached out to one another with a different consciousness, glad to be alive and present to one another, knowing with certainty and conviction that, as they come through this, they could, together, endure anything that the future threw at them.

As ordinary men and women greeted the rapture of that glorious day, the 11th July 1921, no-one knew or could have guessed that within a year, just a short twelve months from their celebration, from this ecstasy, all would be plunged into a conniption of hatred, an outpouring of fratricide, a division of bitterness that would wound immeasurably and hopelessly all their desires and dreams and leave each one, in their own individual torment, paralysed, trapped by memories of what could have been and should never have happened.

The Drowning of Innocence

Loss

"All day long, in unrest, to and fro, do I move.
The very soul within my breast is wasted for you, love
The heart in my bosom faints to think of you, my Queen,
My life of life, my saint of saints,
My Dark Rosaleen, My own Rosaleen
To hear your sweet and sad complaints, My life, my love, my saint of
saints,
My Dark Rosaleen!

Woe and pain, pain and woe are my lot, night and noon,
To see your bright face clouded so like to the mournful moon.
But yet will I rear your throne again in golden sheen;
Tis you shall reign, shall reign alone,
My Dark Rosaleen My own Rosaleen
'Tis you shall have the golden throne, 'Tis you shall reign, and reign
alone,
My Dark Rosaleen

I could scale the blue air, I could plough the high hills,
Oh, I could kneel all night in prayer to heal your many ills!
And one beamy smile from you would float like light between
My toils and me, my own, my true,
My Dark Rosaleen, My fond Rosaleen
Would give me life and soul anew,
My Dark Rosaleen"
From 'Dark Rosaleen - James Clarence Mangan

We had fed the heart on fantasies,
The heart's grown brutal from the fare,
More substance in our enmities
Than in our love; O honey-bees,
Come build in the empty house of the stare.
From 'The Stare's Nest by My Window'

W.B. YEATS

"Our only fear was that there would be no more loyalist homes to destroy."
Tom Barry

"To allow them to come unconditionally (viz. to the Treaty negotiations) - would be to admit that the British Empire is an open question ... I propose a direct question to them – 'If you wish to come to a conference on the basis of the integrity of the Empire, come, if not, not'
Winston Churchill

"A Commission consisting of three persons, one to be appointed by the Government of the Irish Free State, one to be appointed by the Government of Northern Ireland, and one who shall be Chairman to be appointed by the British Government shall determine in accordance with the wishes of the inhabitants, so far as may be compatible with economic and geographic conditions the boundaries between Northern Ireland and the rest of Ireland, and for the purposes of the Government of Ireland Act, 1920, and of this instrument, the boundary of Northern Ireland shall be such as may be determined by such Commission."
Article XII of Treaty

"Think what have I got for Ireland ... Something which she has wanted these past 700 years, will anyone be satisfied with this bargain, will anyone? I tell you this, early this morning I have signed my death warrant"
Michael Collins

"Now, with regard to the oath, I say to anyone – go truthfully and take this oath, take it. If they take it under duress there may be some excuse for them, but let them remember that nobody here took their Republican oath under duress. They took it knowing that it might mean death; and they took it meaning that. And when they took that oath to the Irish Republic they meant, I hope, every honest man and every woman – I know the women – they took it meaning to keep it to death."
Constance Markievicz, January 3, 1922

"War by the Irish on the Irish is the kind of development which I observe with great pleasure."
"There is no danger that the Boundary Commission would make drastic alterations in the boundary."
Lord Birkenhead

"If the Treaty were accepted, [by the electorate] the fight for freedom would still go on, and the Irish people, instead of fighting foreign soldiers, will have to fight the Irish soldiers of an Irish government set up by Irishmen..........would have to wade through the blood of the soldiers of the Irish Government, and perhaps through that of some members of the Irish Government to get their freedom."
Eamon DeValera

General Registry Office, Roscommon, Ireland

July 2011

Alannah was relieved that Mr. O'Rourke was a kindly man. Peering over his half-rimmed glasses, the lines in his face etched more from mirth than censorious frowning, his grey, almost silver hair personifying his dignity, he was, finally for Alannah, an embodiment of reassurance and compassion.

To get this far had been a struggle of phone calls, emails and blind alleys. Alannah had often wondered how people could spend their lives toiling in administration, in a tight bureaucracy, surrounded by rules, paper, walls and circumscription. This was not a judgement on their choice of life, but more a sense of awe that they had the capacity to surrender to their defined place in the scheme of things. Mr. O'Rourke was different, unusual. He did not seem formed by his role, was able to touch the edge of things, the margin and open up the bewildering world of paper and records, and make it accessible to those who found their way to his desk.

"So what is it you want to find out then, Alannah?"

"I have hit a brick wall, Mr. O'Rourke. I have been searching for my mother's birth records and they don't marry with what I know to be true. She learnt she was adopted when she was a young teenager. When she was told, she never pursued any questions then or after. I guess it was the time that was in it. Let sleeping dogs lie and all that. The records however name her adoptive parents as her birth father and mother. Surely, this can't be true. There is no record of her birth parents. Its confusing, frustrating and distressing."

"I'm sorry Alannah. All too common I'm afraid, several hundred birth records in fact. All falsified. But let's make a start. When and where was she born?"

"From what I know so far it was Waterford in February 1923."

He drew up the record on the screen of his computer.

"Oh bless her, right in the heart of the Civil War. Well, you've come to the right place but I'm not sure I will be of much help. There have been many sad stories passing through my desk over the years. People searching for their family origins. There was a lot of illegal adopting done and it was often hidden through registering the adoptive parents as the birth parents."

"Oh dear, that seems so heartless."

"Well, Alannah, different times really. Its hard for us to pass judgement.
Definitely there was a great deal of nefarious goings-on, but not always."

"What do you think happened?" Alannah looked quizzically and
beseechingly at this kind man in front of her. Mr. O'Rourke melted and was
taken aback by the exquisite beauty of those deep, blue eyes. "Bless her," he
thought, "I will do as much as I can to help her along."

"There are as many stories as there are people, my dear. Some
heartbreaking. I try myself not to establish too much of a pattern. I think it
somehow does more justice to the individual lives of each child to give him or
her a unique place in our history rather than to reduce the records to 'patterns'.
Your mother, Rose, was born during a time of terrible animosity and confusion.
Your adoptive grandparents are Church of Ireland people, right? and they
must have gone through a terrible time. There were killings in Bandon at the
time and then a lot of country houses owned by the Protestant Ascendancy
were burnt to the ground. Who knows what could have happened? There
were so many dark secrets hidden from that period. I think people were afraid
to talk afterwards lest a word out of place would resurrect the awfulness of
what they had gone through."

"So there are no clues in the documents?"

"None at all I'm afraid that would help. The records were filled in as if
everything was above board. The only thing I can say is that the nursing home
where Rose was born is linked with the Franciscan Friary in the town. They
may have some knowledge of events leading up to it. It's all I can do to help
you. As far as everything else is concerned, the records are a cul-de-sac to you.
You will have to be imaginative if you want to find out what happened. But
don't give up. People have long memories and although not many talked
about the Civil War, you will be surprised what turns up if you dig around.
Sorry I can't be of more help to you. I have found though that if you suspend
judgement, the story opens up by itself. I know the newspapers have been full
of the shame of it all over the recent years. For myself, I don't see that does
much good. All this 'holier than thou' revisionism. Alannah, my dear, we have
to go with an open heart and if you do that, you will find your answers."

Alannah was touched by his kindness and stood to say goodbye. She was
surprised and nourished by his words of encouragement - 'to continue on';
'never know what might turn up'; 'Go with an open heart.' It was, she realised,

                    The Drowning of Innocence

what she needed to hear.

Three days later, a letter came in the post from her cousin, Nicholas, in England. She hadn't heard from him in years and so already the letter was something that had her trembling with anticipation. He had been going through his mother's papers, he wrote, and had come across a letter from Alannah's Grandmother, Elizabeth to his Grandmother, Maud sent way back in 1923. He was aware of the sensitivity of the discovery and did not want to intrude on family matters. He had deliberated long and hard before sending it but in the end thought it best to go ahead as Alannah would have a chance to judge for herself. He hoped she didn't mind and that he had done the right thing. With trembling hands, Alannah opened the envelope and drew out the letter, the colours faded but the cream paper and sepia ink resonated and reverberated in her very being. The handwriting on the envelope that of her Granny Elizabeth, familiar yet stronger and more fair than she remembered. She unfolded the letter and with a beating heart read,

Waterford *January 4th 1923*

My dear Maud,

I hope this letter finds you well. Charles and I are both in good spirits and have the most exciting of news. We are going to have a baby. There I've said it. I know you will be overjoyed for us as you, above all people, have watched our struggle with this for years. Maud, nothing has changed of course but the wonderful news is that we are going to adopt. It's all very hush-hush, so not a word to anyone.

We don't know the mother and have to be very strict in not asking questions. All we know is that she, bless her, is convinced it is for the best. I have to say I struggle sometimes with what she has to do, give her baby away. But you know, I can't think like that. I have to think of the child and I know, am convinced, that with Charles and I, the baby will not want for anything.

The birth is some time in February, so we are on tenterhooks, fiercely praying that all will be well. Our contact, is a lovely man, a Franciscan Friar. Brother Paul is his name. I can tell by the way he has approached us and how he talks that he deeply loves the girl and is very committed to her. That gives me some comfort in the early hours as I lie awake, worrying about her. I know from the time I have spent with him, that the mother finds herself in an impossible situation and so am reassured that this is for the best.

So there you are Maud. I want to ask you to help me with this whole thing. Charles and I have gone away to the countryside near Waterford so that we can keep up the whole facade. You are the only one who knows, dear Sister and I know you will be thrilled for us.

Alannah read and re-read the letter. It was a moment of revelation, a cornerstone on which to build her future. For years she had wrestled with Ma's simple words that she had been adopted and didn't know her origins. In the last while she had doubted herself, wondering if she was pursuing a fantasy. But here in front of her now was the evidence, the first piece, confirming the rightness of her search.

The letter had transported her in time, visibly, into the lives of two important people in her life. Her Granny Elizabeth. Here she saw her softness mixed with trepidation and unrestrained excitement. A mixture of feelings. And then her own unknown grandmother. She reflected again on the pain, the mystery surrounding her giving her baby away. She wondered what had taken place to make this a reality for her and how she had managed after.

She read and re-read the letter fraught with the emotions of the time. But there was a lead in the letter. It confirmed the link made by Mr. O'Rourke that the Franciscan Friary may have some clues. For the first time in months she allowed herself to think that maybe, just maybe, she might be able to find an answer to her quest.

She placed the letter carefully among her documents in her bedside cabinet. As she opened the drawer, she picked out the postcard from the Ha'penny market. She now had a plan. She was going to Cork next week. She would visit the address in Cork city to see what it may open up for her about this extraordinary postcard. On her return, she would talk to the Franciscans in Waterford. Two quests to occupy her. She would be busy, she thought.

Nad, County Cork

St Stephen's Day, 26th December, 1921.

The sky was an icy blue and the lateral sun framed the vibrant crowd lining the road between Kanturk and Nad, etching their outline against the luminous green backgrounds of the hedgerows and copses, as they passed through, avidly cheering their champions on. The county road bowling championship was underway and this ten mile stretch of road was chosen for the event.

Eileen, Micheál and Mattie had travelled to Nad for Christmas and were among friends and family in the spreadeagled crowd. Everyone had looked forward to the day, the first championship for years; Its recent suppression leaving a foment of bottled energy now exhilaratingly released.

The whole village had been woken early that morning by 'The Wren Boys'. Young lads and lassies, dressed up in straw hats, an assortment of clothes, faces decorated with burnt cork, toured from house to house, demanding treats. The quiet peace of the morning disturbed by the cacophonous rending of the ancient song,

> *The wren, the wren, the king of all birds,*
> *St Stephen's day got caught in the furze,*
> *Up with the kettle and down with the pan,*
> *Give us a penny to bury the wren."*

All of the children steeped in the stories surrounding their self-made pageant. How the wren got its crown on the day of the great competition in the animal kingdom; The title of king being allotted to the bird that could fly the highest. The wren, light, imperceptible, hitching a ride on the Eagle's back and as its carrier reached its pinnacle, the little rascal took off from its vantage point and soared to claim the prize. And how in the first century, Stephen, the first Christian martyr, fleeing from Roman centurions was betrayed by the wild chattering and wilful flight of the bird as he lay hidden in a copse. It mattered little. What thrilled that morning was the treats doled out from house to house as they circled the village, sweets, a penny here and there and Christmas cake. Eileen had found the occasion charming and delightful, a tradition living here in the countryside but dying out in the city.

Now they were on the road, waiting for the contest of the day to begin. The two finalists took their turns to wind up their run and hurl the iron ball fiercely and with accuracy through the crowd-lined road, skipping on the hard ground, clipping corners, desperately seeking the advantage of yards on one another. Groans of despair and mad whoops of joy accompanied each shot taken, money changing hands as believers staked their claim on their individual champion, the cold air being held at bay by the many hip flasks of poitín, generously handed around.

Sauntering on the road, neighbours greeting one another, Mattie and Micheál passed through quiet murmurs of adulation, the stories told of their involvement in the struggle "doing their bit" travelling before them. Micheál was not comfortable with this. He hated the swagger he had seen in colleagues, fellow revolutionaries since the Truce. But he shook it off, his arm around Eileen, for reassurance and comfort. Mattie, a few strides behind, courted the attention. The men siding up to him seeking snippets to embellish stories of 'The Big Fella', ferreting a way into the reflected glory of their man. The girls, shyly from a distance, but not unnoticed by Mattie, giggling softly to one another as they stole a glance at him.

"OK, Micheál, I bet the first round on Séamus' next shot. Are you a coward or what? You Cork city fella's afraid of taking a beating from us culshies."

Mattie had thrown his arm around Micheál's shoulder and gave him a playful dig in the stomach.

"If you want to throw your money away, Mattie a chara, then there's no sounder man than myself to pick it up."

Eileen found the playacting between the two of them affecting and laughed heartily.

The Corkman's next shot hit a stone in the middle of the road and was diverted into the ditch. Mattie jumped on Micheál with whoops of victory.

"You lucky bastard."

"Sure there's no luck to that at all, boy. That's the superior skill honed in the countryside through hard work."

Laughter overtook the group as Micheál grinned gamely.

The final part of the championship was thrilling. The two players tied on number of shots over the course, everything dependent on the length of their last throw, the tension palpable. The Cork city man's shot had gone a full hundred yards beyond the finishing line. It was all down to the local man from

     The Drowning of Innocence

Banteer, Séamus. His road-shower taking a line near the edge of the road to gain maximum advantage in the length of shot. Séamus wound up his run, skipping in the air as he hurled the bowl under arm. It flew from his hand and scooted along the road, passing the finish line with speed, accurately traversing the line mapped out by the road-shower. Hearts in mouths, local people held their breath as the bowl flew along the road. As it came to the bend it traversed and skirted the fringe and just as it looked like it would overtake the Corkman's shot, the ball hit the root of a Hawthorn bush that had encroached on the road, stopping the ball in its tracks and sending it spinning into the undergrowth on the other side of the road, no more than five yards short of the Corkman's final shot, to the crushing disappointment of the majority of the crowd gathered from local areas in anticipation of victory.

Supporters gathered around the Corkman and raised him aloft. The locals from Banteer, Kanturk and Nad graciously conceded defeat and clapped the Corkman's triumph. The score was over. Micheál, Eileen and Mattie with others of the family retired to the Nad pub. The light was going out of the day, the sun sinking in the west had barely registered any warmth all day and now as night was closing in, everyone dreamed of the fire.

Inside, the main room in the pub was warm, simple and inviting, the turf fire blazing in the hearth, crudely-made oak tables and chairs, and behind the long, sturdy counter, Paddy Bride, the owner presiding. Behind one section of the counter, taps of porter, and framed on the wall, whiskeys of various kind, Paddy, Jameson, Tullamore Dew and the new local favourite pot-still whiskey, Redbreast. The shelves in the grocery section lined with an assortment of tins and packages, Barry's Tea, Campbell's soup, Jars of Irel Coffee, Bovril, Fry's Cocoa, Fray Bentos Corned Beef, Mi-Wadi orange squash, Sunlight Soap; Tins of Woodbine, Navy Cut, Sweet Afton and Golden Flake tobacco decorating the shelves in a motley of colours and shapes. The wall over the fireplace enshrined with a framed icon of 'Our Lady of Perpetual Succour', a picture of Pope Pius X with his handsome face, a poignant handbill advertising passage on 'The Titanic' for six pounds and ten shillings. The victorious Cork all Ireland hurling champions of two years earlier had pride of place though, the famous 'blood and bandages' team togged out for the first time in the red and white, colours overpainted on the photo.

The crowd settled into the evening. Despite the celebration and things seemingly back to normal with the rightful restoration of the bowling championship back among the people, the day was overshadowed by events that had taken place in London, just three weeks previously. Arthur Griffiths and Michael Collins, along with others, had signed a treaty with the British Government which incorporated an oath of allegiance to the British Crown and fractured the island into north and south. The news had acted as a sharp cleaver to the soul of the nation, splitting families and former comrades in two, erupting into a fissure of volcanic proportions.

So seismic was the news that people dared not talk about it. Up and down the land, its promulgation had created rows and arguments that had already left deep wounds. Many felt deeply betrayed, mostly by 'one of their own' Michael Collins; His apologists left stuttering for words in their attempts to proffer justifications. An uneasy 'quiet' accompanied family gatherings and this St Stephens Day was no exception.

The men had ensconced themselves in the bar, circled around the blazing fire, fortified by stout and whiskey; The women had retired into the safety of the kitchen, busily preparing stew for all.

Mattie was pounced on. "Tell us about the Big Fella," The chorus loud and clear. Mattie took a long sip from the creamy pint in front of him and in full flow now, delighting in his notoriety, spoke about the immensity of the man, his grasp of everything, his indefatigable energy, his bright humour. He was energised, beside himself, on 'the pig's back' when abruptly interrupted by Micheál.

"I can't be listening to this, Mattie. Please not now. Not on this day."

"What's the matter with you, boy. Didn't the Big Fella beat the British at their own game," came the chorus of dissenting voices from the gathered group.

"And then he makes a right hames of it when it really mattered," said an unrestrained and unrepentant Micheál.

"And what the fuck does that mean?" said Mattie.

"He failed along with Griffiths to stand his ground for the integrity of the island and sold our soul for a mess of pottage."

"Get your facts right, Micheál. You're just reacting. He has been promised by Churchill that there will a boundary commission to examine the position of the six counties in the north. It's there in the treaty. Churchill told him that within months, they will be able to demonstrate the unviability of the six-county state. Craig will be left with Belfast on its own and that won't stand up.

          The Drowning of Innocence

Then we will have our unity."

"For fuck sake, Mattie. Churchill!!! He believed Churchill? Everything we know about the man says he is a duplicitous bastard. His father was prepared for civil war to be alongside and support the Unionists. In the Treaty document, the Boundary Commission is vague, leaving plenty of room for the British to wriggle out of it. They haven't stood up to Craig or Carson before and they won't now. Its a shibboleth, concocted by Lloyd George and Churchill and will come to nothing. Collins gave into them too easily. He was out of his depth."

"So why didn't your DeValera go instead then. That fucker knew that he couldn't get any better than Griffiths or Collins so he did his usual cowardly thing."

"He's not my DeValera. But one thing is sure, he knew the snakes he was dealing with. That's why he told the delegation not to agree to anything but to report back to the Dáil in Dublin with what was on the table. Dev knew that there would be underhand dealings."

"They didn't have that option. They were given a few hours to decide or else the British would return to war."

"C'mon Mattie, do you honestly think that Lloyd George would have been able to carry out that threat. He would have had to go against world opinion to return to conflict because of breakdown of the talks. He tricked Collins, pure and simple and your 'Big Fella' fell for it. And what's more to make us give an oath of allegiance to the King of England. What the fuck was he thinking of?"

"Mick says the fucking oath is not important. We will get rid of it in time. The Treaty gives us time to build our own nation."

"Are you kidding me? The Oath means that for the first time in seven hundred years we voluntarily agree to be ruled by Britain. If the Oath wasn't important, then why is it so important to the fucking British? Or the fucking Orangemen in the north? You and I Mattie, we signed an Oath of Allegiance to the Dáil, to the Irish people. A solemn Oath. We can't take that back and give it to some foreign ruler. An Oath is who we are. For fuck sake, Mattie, 'Mick says this', 'Mick says that'. Listen to yourself. Can't you think for yourself for a change instead of bowing to that domineering fucker."

Micheál had strayed over the line. There was a sharp intake of breath from those gripped by the tension of the argument. Maura Bride, seeing what was happening rushed for Eileen in the kitchen. Eileen emerged to see the situation beyond her control. She knew that when Micheál reached this stage in passionate argument, to try and stop him would only succeed in egging him on. She touched him gently on the shoulder, but Micheál was now gone from her, squirmed away into the confrontation. The crowd in one voice had risen to challenge Micheál. He had dared to call their hero 'a domineering fucker'. The hate and vitriol in their faces was terrifying.

Mattie retorted

"How can you describe him like that? How can you think of the man who single-handedly took on the British establishment and brought them to their knees, how can you use bad language to describe him?"

"You have been too long in Dublin, Mattie. The war was not won there, like you've been led to believe. It was won here and not by one man, not by Michael Collins. You are too much under his sway. You can't think clearly."

"How dare you say that!"

"Oh c'mon Mattie. You know there's always a price to be paid for greatness and its rarely paid by the so called 'Great' themselves."

"What are you implying?"

"Mattie, I am not implying anything. I'm simply saying to you and to all Collin's men, the Squad, as you like to call yourselves, think for yourselves for a change. Collins is not a saint, or someone who is owed unquestioning allegiance. Can't you see that he is a man who had no compunction in sending out young fellas barely old enough to know their own mind to murder in cold blood, there's the cost, to do his dirty work, while he sat behind a desk plotting."

This was too much for Mattie. This, not only an affront to his beloved leader, but a damning question raised against those he had fought alongside. With consummate rage, he flew across the table at Micheál, bottles and glasses flying everywhere, porter gushing up and drenching those standing by, he grabbed Micheál by the throat and wrestled him to the ground. Eileen looked on in sheer bewilderment that things had come to this, this explosion of rage, this eruption of unprecedented violence between two lifelong friends, soul brothers and it terrified her very being. Bystanders wrestled to pull Mattie off Micheál. Paddy Bride, rounding the bar, stood above both of them.

    The Drowning of Innocence

"Out," he screamed at Micheál. "Get out of my bar and don't come back until you can keep your tongue in check."

Micheál rose gingerly from the floor, touched Eileen gently on the arm and whispered "I'm OK" as he moved to get his coat and hat and stride out of the door of the pub into the cold night air.

An uneasy calm descended on the men in the room. One piped up by saying he always had his doubts about that fella, him being a Protestant and all and how in heaven's name could he call himself a true Irishman. This and Micheál's expulsion from her family's pub, gripped Eileen deep inside with nausea, horror and fear.

"How dare you," she exclaimed fiercely, "That man that you have asked to leave our home has Ireland deep in his soul, in his very being. You ought to be ashamed of yourselves. I will not have another word spoken by any of you against him."

And with that she turned and moved quickly to the door of the kitchen, to the safety of her family's quarters, desperately holding onto the tears that fought to stream down her face, her heart aching and beating fast, a pain in her chest that almost brought her to her knees and a deep cloud of despair and hurt encircling her mind and soul.

The cold air jolted Micheál back to reality. He strode fiercely out of the village taking the old boreen heading up to the top of the Boggeragh mountains. To be away was all he could think of. An all consuming sense of loneliness and desolation engulfed him. The night was dark, bitter and clear. The starry sky and constellations seemed to emphasise his sense of aloneness, gazing as he did out into space.

As he walked his thoughts came rushing at him with stampeding pace. "Why was it always like this," he thought. From his earliest memories, Micheál had found himself alone at the dinner table, holding onto his opinions and rationalism, as he faced his father and brothers' ridicule and disagreement. He had always thought that people disagreed with him because they did not understand what he was saying. "It must be so," he had thought over and over again, so sure was he of the conclusions he had arrived at. And so he had always vehemently pursued his line of argument, full of passion and conviction, little realising that others understood very well what he was saying, and had rejected it, and interpreting his manner, his passion, his invective as aggressive and hostile. He had never meant it to be so.

It was no different now. As he walked away from the village, from Eileen's family, he regretted his outbursts, not for their inaccuracy, for he fully believed the things he had said, but for their unnecessary airing, causing a rift, pushing people to take sides, alienating them and making himself a pariah. He felt he had done irreparable damage, first to his friendship with Mattie. That now, surely had been reduced to irredeemable tatters. And to the esteem with which he had been held by Eileen's family in Nad. They would not forget this outburst, of this he was sure. He had remembered their suspicion of him when he was first introduced, at Con Barry's funeral. Then they were taken aback that he didn't receive communion and understood that he was not of their faith and culture. The hard work, sensitivity he had displayed towards them in the intervening period, undone by the outburst in the pub, an incident now irreversibly etched in their consciousness.

As he reached the brow of the mountain and the land and universe lay before him, the sky sparkling with diamonds of stars, patterns etched in the cosmos, a barn owl hovered miraculously just above his head, almost oblivious to his presence. There was a stillness and quiet in its very being. The pure whiteness of its wings, as silent as falling snow. Its heart-shaped and still face encompassing him. It was as if the arc of its wings were seeking to gather him up and comfort him in his desolation, like the Holy Ghost himself, had come to minister to him and remind him of the eternal. To deliver balm to his soul and

     The Drowning of Innocence

hope to his heart.

He sank down on a rock and sobbed uncontrollably for the state of affairs he was in and the terrible pall of division that had encroached on the land, his nation, his people.

It was quite some time before energy returned to him and he was able to get up and make strides back to the village and Eileen. He could not, indeed the country could not, afford self indulgence now. It was a time to reach out if possible and bridge the divide visited upon them by this so-called Treaty.

Guagán Barra

3rd May, 1922

The gentle spring air enveloped both of them as they made their way along the boreen by the lakeside to their secret spot. The day itself enchanting; The sweet yet frenetic mating calls of small birds flitting in trees as they passed, the chirruping thrush, the sing-song of the blackbird, the staccato thrill of the wren, the glorious celebration of the skylark dominating the skyline, its shape framed by azure blue; The myriads of dandelion seeds wafting in the sunlight casting a myopic haze on the horizon; The Spring fragrance from the hedgerows; The gentle warmth of the Sun on their faces.

Part of the pathway took them through a shimmering carpet of bluebells, their honeyed sweetness, drifting in rivers and lakes of blue and violet, flickering ephemerally in the dappled sunlight. Three days after Lá Béaltaine, it seemed as if the hawthorn bushes themselves were contriving to enshroud Eileen, captured as they were by her beauty; A fertile queen in their midst.

A day it was from heaven. A day of promise. A day replete with intrinsic immanence to capture the heart and soul.

Yet within it all, Micheál's mood was incongruous, contrary, deflating. Cast deep in sombre thoughts, he was poor company; Trapped by disappointments he could barely articulate.

"Tell me what's up with you," Eileen reached out to him as they arrived at the mossy bank under their pine tree.

"I don't know how to say it. I'm in so much despair with what's happening. I can hardly begin to speak. How has it all come to this?"

"I think you just have to try and spit it out, Micheál. That's the only way."

She heard him give a deep sigh as they lay down side by side.

"I find myself questioning it all, that's just it. Everything. What was it all about? All that fighting and suffering? It seems to me we have woken up a beast in the middle of us and I can't make sense of any of it."

"Just let it out, Micheál. It will do you good."

"Well for a start, what is Rory O'Connor and his gang doing invading the Four Courts? And all those other shenanigans down in Limerick? I just feel

 The Drowning of Innocence

like we are turning on one another."

"Oh, Micheál, you seem to be right. I'm sad to say there was always a danger of that, wasn't there? D'you remember Brother Paul's words? When the gun comes in, things begin to fall apart. Some people just don't want to leave it go."

"Y'know, in the end, I've even begun to question the Rising. Was it the origin of all this? The very thing I thought was sacred now turned profane?"

"What do you mean?"

"Just that they, Pearse, Connolly and the others, were all convinced that they knew what was best for Ireland. No questions asked. But now we have every Tom, Dick and Séamus also thinking he knows what's best for the country too. And I include the 'Long Fella' and 'Big Fella' in that. I am very scared and worried about what's to come. I'm afraid we will turn, viciously, on one another. I can see signs already. I don't like what I see in my own comrades. Most here want to remain neutral but I can still see things turning for the worst. I have dreadful premonitions and it breaks my heart."

Lying on the ground together, gazing at the Spring foliage, the Sun creating dancing dappledness on their frames, she was moved by his vulnerability, his pain, recognising his fears for the future; Desiring him now as never before, wanting to comfort him in his isolation and despair.

She reached for his hand and with a boldness that shook him to his very being, guided it under her dress and undergarments to the moist lips of her quim. It caught his breath and enraptured by the sheer intimacy of it all, he turned with great urgency to be on top of her, kissing her with tenderness, while frenetically trying to move himself inside her, to that place he had fantasised about so many times. Waves of pleasure soared in his imagination, concentrating on the tip of him as he sought to enter her. She reached her hand between them and grasped his penis gently, moving herself towards him. It was too much; The willingness evident in her delicate, encircled hand, the touch, the moist and encompassing lips of her quim was too, too much. Maddeningly, before he could realise what he had dreamed of, before he could penetrate, he came, uncontrollably, in waves, pleasure seeping out of him, he trying to arrest its onset so ardently that he failed to surrender to the inexplicable joy of it all. In the end, he capitulated and sunk his head into her shoulders in embarrassment, helplessness and acute frustration.

"It's OK," She whispered in his ear. "We can try again in a little while."

They lay together. He, overcome with love, gratitude and peace; Filled with the wonder of her and the recognition that once again, she had taken the lead in understanding who they were together and who they had become; His mind, imagination, memory and now body gilded with hers. She confident now in their shared love and open to him like never before.

After a short while, he could feel desire rise in him again and he reached for her, this time gently, with a mixture of tenderness and awe. He moved himself inside her with delicate sensitivity, all of his being focussed on the sensation of their union, he inside her, moving slowly, exquisitely overcome with a pleasure that enthralled and intoxicated him. She felt him enter her, blissfully; Felt his movements and surrendered to them, coaxing him, comforting him, drawing him out of himself, happy to give herself to him now, especially now. The moss beneath her, soft and bruised, released into the moment a delicate aroma of new life; In the branches above and in the woods around them, other creatures mirrored their search for a mate and copulation. She anticipated and felt the moment of his climax and was overcome, shocked, surprised by it, her body taking over, leaving her behind, turning renegade as she reached up to him, grasping him, moving towards him to take him completely into herself until eventually in a paroxysm of uncontrollable delight and joy, her body writhed and shook with pleasure. His hands grasped her buttocks, desired since she came into his life again as a woman, and held her to himself as he came fully, exponentially, deep, deep inside her. One with her very soul, spirit and delightful flesh.

Afterwards she lay in his arms, both of them overcome with a rich contentment; In tune with their surroundings; The Spring day that was in it; Baptising their own special, secret rendezvous; A moment and its consequence that would stay with them forever.

Later in the afternoon, they made their way back to the city. It was the one and only time they would lie together. They did not know it then but they were soon to be separated. Abruptly, a few weeks later, Micheál summoned for duty by Tom Hales. The road to the fulfilment of his dreadful premonitions already beginning.

Within two short months of their love-making, a divisive general election had taken place setting pro and anti-treaty parties into further acrimonious conflict; Sir Henry Wilson was assassinated outside his London home for his part in the orchestration of sectarian, anti-Catholic violence and murders in the

The Drowning of Innocence

northeast; Common knowledge his execution ordered by Collins.

In ultimate, grim irony, Churchill demanded the Four Courts cleared. Collins, with British guns, opened fire and oversaw its destruction and the Civil War with all its savage, violent, caustic, bitterness had begun.

Within another month, Mattie and Collins lay dead, and he, Micheál, in desperation, a fugitive, on board a liner bound for America, abandoning Eileen to her fate.

A Field in Killumney, West Cork

22nd August, 1922

Major General Emmet Dalton looked to the skies in despair and mad rage as the rain poured down from the heavens onto the sodden, boggy ground beneath his feet. "This fucking, miserable Cork rain, piercing everything, sending me over the fucking edge." Overwhelmed by images of himself as Blake's 'Nebuchadnezzar', he was hanging from a cliff of lunacy.

"If I don't get a fucking grip, I'll be discovered stark naked, eating grass and railing at the elements like a latter day King Lear."

He had descended into Hades. The Rolls Royce, in which they had been traversing this boggy field, was now stuck definitively, decisively in quagmire; Its engine drenched, without a spark of life.

They were forced to take their beloved Commander in Chief, Michael Collins, out of the back seat where he had lain lifeless, his head cradled in Dalton's lap, as they had tried to make their way back to the city. Now, the men, his men, struggled and stumbled, slipped and slid, clambered and crawled over the grassy, muddy field; Their leader held aloft, undignified, the back of his head no more, as from a gaping hole oozed blood, shards of bone and brain.

They had entered a nightmare and at every twist and turn, the descent had become more pronounced and irrevocable. Twenty minutes before, they had been racing back to the city along the rough ground of the thoroughfare heading for Killumney, on the back roads to Ballincollig and the outskirts of Cork. Haring down their chosen route, following its features in the weak and almost ineffectual headlamps, they had come across a man furiously gesticulating them to stop, stood as he was in the middle of the road.

For a moment they had thought of ignoring him and driving straight at him, so great was the anger and dismay that had consumed them from the ambush two hours earlier which had left their 'Captain', 'The Big Fella', 'The Laughing Boy' dead.

But they had stopped and discovered the stranger had waved them down to prevent them driving precipitously over a bridge that no longer existed, blown up two weeks previously by 'Irregulars', those fucking, destructive, irresponsible, anti-treatyites; Arrested and saved from plummeting thirty feet to their deaths, adding a final devilish epitaph to this terrible, calamitous, catastrophic day; Now forced to take the man's advice and drive over fucking, boggy fields to find an alternative road to the city.

It had all been so different that morning, as they had left the Imperial Hotel in the city, at the crack of dawn. Collins in buoyant mood, looking forward to travelling through his beloved home county, a king in waiting, eager to encourage his troops and walk among his people. Dalton had been vehemently against the trip.

"Its too early, Sir. Its far too dangerous to travel yet. The 'Irregulars' are everywhere."

"Not at all, Emmet. You worry too much. Sure aren't I among my own people. I'm safe as houses here, boy."

"Forgive me, sir. But I don't think you appreciate the irony of that statement. There are no 'houses' safe in West Cork. Haven't been for years."

He remembered it now. "Fuck." The 'Laughing Boy' had just laughed it off.

"Yerra, boy, they'll never shoot me in my own county."

Full up as he was with his own mythology; Feeling, as he did, that the force of his personality, the love that existed between him and his people, even between him and former comrades now railed against him; This would triumph and bring the terrible acrimony of this bestial Civil War to an end. The man himself convinced that after the capture of Cork, it would all be over in weeks and then we could build together again.

Bitterly now, Dalton reflected on how they had got it so wrong, so horribly wrong. 'The Big Fella' brought down by the same hubris that had felled Nebuchadnezzar and King Lear.

"Had it happened? Is there any chance I might wake up and discover that this is not real? That it is just a visitation, a frightful incubus that inhabits the dark hours of a fitful night? That I will wake up soon?"

Dalton felt trapped, starved of oxygen, the centripetal force of this nightmare pinning him, keeping him fixed in the unfolding, degenerating horror. Struggling with all his might to escape it, to surface again to a different order of things.

He tried, desolately, dispiritedly, to imagine himself again, full of courage, insight and determination, on board the Arvonia, as it sailed into Cork harbour, no more than a fortnight earlier, to take that city and crush the anti-treatyites, the fucking Irregulars, once and for all.

"Surely I will wake up now. Wake up to the real present. Back to he night moving to dawn on 8th August. Be transported away from this diabolical visitation and be taken back to reality, to the optimism, the determination, the confidence I felt that morning, as we sailed into the wild wonderful expanse of that glorious harbour and set in place the final act, the crushing of opposition to the Treaty once and for all."

"Wake up," he wailed, "Wake up, for fuck sake. Let this all be a dream."

                                   The Drowning of Innocence

Cork Harbour and Passage West

Early Morning, 8th August, 1922

Mattie was summoned by Dalton to the deck of the 'Arvonia' as it rounded Roches Point; The lighthouse beckoning the ship into the wide expanse of Cork harbour; The moon full in the night sky cast an ethereal light over the wide expanse of the bay. It moved Mattie unexpectedly. He was coming home. To Cork. He had forgotten how beautiful the horseshoe-shaped harbour was as it opened its welcoming bosom to a returning son of the city. The countryside around so familiar to him, he was taken aback by the memories and emotions evoked by this vista.

He had grown enormously during the year. As part of Collin's squad, he had been given a prime appointment in the new National Army formed by the Provisional Government. His boss now everyone's boss and that had made him swell with pride.

Mattie had no use for the complicated, esoteric discussions that had taken place around the Treaty. His boss had signed it and that was enough for him. Now a Captain himself, one of the youngest, he had been singled out for special training in the use of the Thompson machine gun, a powerful weapon and one he carried with a swagger and which, he was confident, would bring the anti-Treaty rebellion into line. He looked resplendent in his uniform and wore it with distinction. Dalton, he had got to know through his brother and it was with a certain familiarity that he approached him on the deck, not forgetting to proffer the accustomed salute.

"We've heard from a British patrol vessel that the Irregulars have blocked the channel leading up to the city from the harbour, so we have to revise our plans, Barry. We can't think of landing at Ford's now. I've asked you here for advice. You're a local man, so I wonder what your view would be of the alternatives."

"What are your options, Sir?"

"Well, Queenstown would be one, but we think it may be heavily defended."

"I think you're right there Sir. The other thing is that getting off the island to get to the city may be difficult. We would come to a bottleneck at Belvelly bridge. That bridge is the only crossing onto the mainland, Sir."

"Have you any ideas, Barry?"

"Passage West, Sir. That's where my Da worked for years. I know it like the back of my hand. I think that would be the best place to land. It's a small dock but it can handle this."

"And the roads into the city from there?"

"I think they're manageable, Sir. We can cut up through Rochestown and Douglas. Our main problem, I think, will be the Landings. We don't know how well Passage is defended."

For all his eagerness to be getting on with it, Mattie could not help reflect on the stories he had heard from Micheál of his brothers' fate at Gallipoli. He knew that what they were undertaking, landing from sea into hostile territory, was dangerous and possibly foolish. He had a strong sense of foreboding.

"Thanks, Barry. Well done. That's what we were thinking too. The men will be kept below deck until the last minute. We want to make it look like an innocent landing. After we get ashore, I'll want you to command the lead group opening out the route into the City. Are you up for that?"

"Yes, sir. Very much so. Sure I know the road inside out. I've ridden it on my bike since my childhood."

"Good man so, Barry. We're relying on you."

With that, they saluted and Mattie turned and went downstairs to ready his Company, flushed with the news that he was to be the liberator of his native city.

The next few hours were critical. But they were not without tension. The Pilot, who had boarded, refusing to navigate the waters around the dock.

"It's too risky. Its probably mined and I have my responsibilities," He screamed at Dalton.

But Dalton now had his gander up and pulling out his revolver, pointed it at the man.

Reluctantly and with trepidation, the Pilot guided the vessel to the dockside, tying up without incident, finding the Irregular guards asleep. The cranes at the dockyard were insufficient to land the armoured vehicles. Within a few hours however, the full tide raised the ship to dock level and the vehicles

    The Drowning of Innocence

were driven off.

Landing had a peculiar effect on Mattie. Here he was at the place his Da had graced for years. He remembered days when he was a small boy and Da had carried him on his shoulders through the machinery; The big loud Saw Mill. It made him pensive, thoughtful. He had tried to block Da out of his mind. He really couldn't get on with his life if he kept remembering him. But this moment was different. Too intense, evocative, memories cascading through him like a vibrant waterfall.

At dawn, he was given his instructions and was glad to leave. He formed the men into combat lines and chose the lower road along the river front. In that way his right flank was protected by the river and he could concentrate on what was on his left as they moved carefully forward.

As the sun rose, he was overwhelmed by a deluge of conflicting emotions as they marched along by the river. The unique smell of the tide mixed with foliage of the elm trees brought back to him memories of his childhood and Micheál. He thought of the last time they had seen one another, the disagreement that had ended with him throwing himself at Micheál, across the table in the Nad bar. He laughed inwardly at it, thinking about Micheál's intensity, typically wrapped up in the conflict that had absorbed the whole country.

"I'm sure when we meet again we will be able to square it all over a couple of pints," He thought, "Sure, we'll have Eileen to help us both forget it. After we take the city and he realises the game is up, we can start again."

For now he must concentrate. He had men to lead. He barked instructions to them, expecting and getting immediate compliance, a leader who took his place right at the front, where the greatest danger lay. Demonstrating unequivocally to them that he was alongside them and with his innate courage and self confident swagger, impart a strong sense of invincibility in their ranks. They moved on towards the city, expecting little resistance.

Capuchin Monastery, Rochestown, Cork.

Midday, 8th August, 1922

Micheál's troop had been rushed back to Cork from Kilmallock on the Cork-Limerick border when news of the landings were heard. He had passed a hectic and exhausting journey by train through the night, with little sleep. The weeks he had been away had been frustrating. Full of mock battles, he had no enthusiasm for fighting his fellow countrymen. He had witnessed men on both sides discharge their weapons indiscriminately, wasting ammunition, filling the air with the resounding crack of gunfire, but all to no avail. Opposing forces had swapped positions like a game of musical chairs. The whole experience approaching high comedy if it were not for the bitterness that was growing between former comrades.

He was exhausted by it all. The separation from Eileen he had felt keenly. He kept himself sane with a private reflection of the day they spent together at Guagán, playing over in his mind the passionate intimacy they had shared. Communication between them, however, had been impossible and he had no word from her for more than six weeks. In his mind, he could not wait to see her and had imaginative, elaborate plans of taking her again to Guagán, falling on his knees and asking for her hand.

Back in Cork and met by Tom Hales, he had no time to see her, responding in shock to the news that the 'Staters' had landed at Passage and were making their way towards the city.

"I need you out there quickly, Micheál. Find a spot to snipe and hold them up."

He had taken his bike to the Capuchin Monastery at Rochestown, a familiar place. Somewhere he had played when younger. The view from the tower covered the road from Passage. He banked on the fact that the 'Staters' would come up that way.

Now in position, he carefully adjusted his visual axis and waited. It was getting toward midday and the air was clear. From where he lay, his rifle loaded, he had a perfect sightline.

Then he saw them, moving forward with a swagger that shocked him, about fifty of them, in their now familiar 'Stater' uniform. He was jolted by the wave of emotion that overtook him then.

  The Drowning of Innocence

"Who the fuck do they think they are? Fucking Dublin Jackeens waltzing in to take over my city. Fuck them."

In his rage, he knew this was to be no mock battle. Proud as he was of the resistance put up by his Cork comrades during the war with the British, he was not about to roll over for some fucking Jackeens who had a different view of how things should be. "How dare they? How fucking dare they?" He fulminated. Although he agreed with most of his comrades that this war against one another was futile and wasteful, these fuckers striding up a Cork road to take his city was just too much provocation. Now he was engaged. Now he would stand his ground.

He prepared carefully, drew back the bolt and cocked his rifle. In his sight line he could see their leader striding ahead, carrying a Thompson machine gun. He had been instructed earlier to concentrate on those bastards.

"There are not that many who know how to use them, Micheál," Tom Hales had informed him, "But they are very dangerous. They can do a lot of damage. If you can get a bead on anyone carrying one, you will save a lot of lives."

Now with experience, he breathed calmly, pressed on the trigger and felt the explosion of the gun. He saw the fellow fall and others around him run to his aid. As they grappled with him, his cap fell off and Micheál could see with unfolding horror and increasing certainty that it was Mattie. Mattie, his childhood friend, known to him as he knew himself.

"How did I not recognised you before, mo chara? What devilish trick did my eyes play on me?" He wailed and slumped in his position, nausea overpowering him and leaving him wasted. "Mattie, oh Mattie, what are you doing here?"

From his vantage point, he watched those around Mattie with increasing dread, recognising from their frantic expressions that the man they were seeking to help had already passed beyond their aid, and had slipped from them into the next world.

He did not know how long he lay there on top of the tower, hidden from view. But later in the afternoon, he moved from his position, recklessly, carelessly, his life now as good as over, found his bike where he had left it hidden in bushes and cycled mechanically, like an automaton, away from the scene, away from the city, away from everything that had been familiar, constant, reassuring, certain, and into the dark, dark darkness of his thoughts and life; Into the anonymity of the verdant countryside.

Riverview, Blackrock, Cork.

Early Morning, 10th August, 1922

By this stage, it had become monotonous for Eileen, humdrum, tedious. For weeks, endless bouts of sickness passing through her, waves of nausea, a dull thud in her stomach; Continuously feeling like she was on board a ship, tossed to and fro, her stomach always teetering out of control; The paradox of life seemingly seeping out of her as new life was being conceived within her very being.

She had woken up to it again, foregoing food, the very thought of it exacerbated her symptoms. Thrilled with the thought of her baby growing inside her, she had no capacity to enjoy it. In the kitchen, surrounded by her familiar things, she cradled a cup of tea in her palms, seeking comfort.

A loud knock on the door shook her from her absence and she moved cautiously towards it. "So early," she thought, "What in heaven's name could this be?" She had been aware of shots in the distance the previous two days and rumours accelerating into fact, that the Free State troops, the provisional Government army, had taken the city. She had no appetite for any of this. This a world that she was now steadfastly seeking to blot out, eliminate.

Opening the door, she was greeted by a smart, good-looking but sombre figure, an officer of that army. By instinct her shield was up. She had spent the last few weeks protecting her unborn child from the madness that had overtaken the country, retiring into herself, nurturing this vulnerable person within. She would not let down her guard now, whatever the provocation.

"Good morning, Ma'am. I am very sorry to disturb you but I have been instructed to tell you that your brother, Matthew, was shot and killed as we took the city. He died a very brave man."

Maybe the unbelievability of what was being said and the sheer stupidity of the way it was phrased preserved her. She stared back at him in incomprehension, exhibiting no feeling, no reaction. The soldier was taken aback.

"Ma'am, I have been sent to inform you that his body will be taken back to Dublin by ship overnight. Along with the others, there's planned to be a state funeral in the capital. We can make arrangements for you to travel with him."

Eileen's will kicked in, strong and fierce. These unfathomable and gauche words would not penetrate, would not breach the place she had retired to with her unborn. With no expression, just a simple nod, she closed the door and left him blank and uncomprehending on the other side, unsure if he had fulfilled the awkward commission he had been given.

The day that followed was full of upheaval. Scores of friends and relatives arriving at Riverview. All trying to root, establish and place what had occurred, oblivious to her need for retreat. She found no comfort there. She walked in their midst as a ghost, unengaged, removed. Tiny snippets of bitter conversations reached her ears as unwilling guests; Vitriolic words spoken against Micheál, whispers, furtive utterances. "The fucker." "I never trusted him." "Fucking prod." "Rue the day Mattie took up with him." "How can you do that to a childhood friend?"

In the afternoon, she took herself off into town to Carey's Lane. Along the Quays and Patrick's Street, she tried to keep aloof, oblivious of the turmoil in the city; Crowds cheering as the "Staters" swaggered about imperiously.

Joan opened the door and wordlessly from deep inside herself saw her distress and greeted her, reached for her and gathered her in. Almost instinctively seeing the forlorn girl of Crosshaven all those years ago, now tossed violently by waves of life. They didn't say much together. It was not needed, just enough that Eileen found temporary refuge, a sense of belonging and intimacy that reached back to less turbulent times.

It was early evening when she made her way back to Riverview, having received no further knowledge of Micheál's whereabouts. But these things seemed to fade from her. The temporary sanctuary of Careys Lane had established her resolve. She would take herself and her unannounced child, her secret, away from it all. The rest could wait, Mattie, Micheál, Ma, all of it, put on hold. For now, her unborn child was everything and for her, (she somehow knew she had conceived a daughter), she would avoid trauma, heartbreak, pain and seek a place of peace, order, security, shelter, sanctuary and refuge.

There was still a crowd at Riverview. She was told that Ma had been informed and was being looked after in Nad. There was some relief in that. Steadfastly, she made her way through them all and took to her room. There, undisturbed, she packed. She passed a fitful night's sleep after the house became quiet and the last ones had left. Then early in the morning, she left silently and made her way to the railway station and caught the Baltimore train, changing at Skibereen. Unaccustomed to taking flight from life's

    The Drowning of Innocence

vicissitudes, she knew this time it was her only option. She would be safe,
undiscoverable in Mrs. Roches house on Sherkin. Wrapped up by the
simplicity of the island; The Atlantic and Roaring Water Bay providing a
bulwark against the nightmare that had arrived elsewhere. The boat from the
harbour at Baltimore their 'Ark'. The wild and soft boreens, the small wooden
gate, the welcoming turf fire, simple food, quiet, peace. These would be her
gift to her child. On that tranquil island, surrounded by the wild Atlantic, she
would nurture, nourish, commune with, cherish and protect her child as she
grew within her. This would be their time together. Intimate, profound,
transcendent.

Cork City.

August, 2011

It was a glorious summer's day and Alannah was back in Cork. There was something about the city which made her feel like she was coming home. The river dividing in the middle with its juxtaposition of confusing bridges and the hills surrounding the centre offering a kind of amphitheatre and context to the vibrant, raggedy-edged enthusiasm of its natives.

These days, however, the city had suffered. The world's economic downturn and crisis affecting the whole country had hit it hard. But it had also remained assured, ebullient even, self-confident in a way that should not surprise. Cork had always had its cornerboys willing to despatch their wit and performance to all-comers. It was alive with commentary and self-deprecation. Alannah adored that about it.

She was on a mission of course which enabled her to cover the ground of the city with purpose. Her postcard carefully packaged in her bag, she was on a quest to find out more about the occupants of 9, Carey's Lane, way back in the mist of time. She wandered down Patrick's Street with its wide palatial bearing, Roches Stores standing commandingly above it all. She passed busy shoppers, absorbed in their obsession.

She was not prepared for Carey's Lane when she turned into it. Her research and scanning of old photos in a library in Waterford had unearthed its history as an old quarter, largely populated by refugees from persecution in France in the 17th century. Huguenots, who had fled the reign of Louis XIV and found a safe haven in Cork. Carey's Lane had been their oasis, their port after a storm. But as she turned into the small lane off the main street, she was struck by the bohemian nature of its current incarnation, cafe society at its finest. Its elegant boutiques and restaurants spilling out onto the narrow street. Alannah was overwhelmed. This bore no relation to what she had pictured in her mind and rapidly her sense that she might discover some answers to her questions evaporated. She needed to sit down and take stock of this, to absorb it all. A cup of tea would bring back some sense of equilibrium, so she headed straight to Fellini's tea room, a place she had heard about.

Ensconced in this elegant space, she ordered a cup of Barry's tea and some soda bread. It was a moment to breathe in. To think. Who was this Micheál character who had inspired such devotion in the post card? He had, presumably, lived on this very street. She tried to capture his spirit among the

     The Drowning of Innocence

other ghosts in this hallowed place, the street's existence and origin as a place of refuge surely housed a multitude. She already felt at home, though, as if she had walked into her own past, bizarre and all as that seemed.

An older man walked in, holding himself tall and straight, a smart Fedora hat on his head, and dressed in an old fashioned manner as if dolled up for Sunday mass. He held 'The Examiner' in his hand and sought in vain for a place to sit and read up on the news. Catching his eye, she gestured to him that he could take the seat opposite her.

"Sure, that's very kind of you, girl," he pronounced in his mellifluous Cork accent. "You're sure you don't mind?"

She smiled at him and nodded. He took his seat and made to read his paper.

"No. I won't do that. I would be chastised by the Missus if she caught me. 'Rude', she would say, 'have you no manners?'"

"You'd better not then or you'll get a hiding when you get home."

"Sadly she's gone now. A few years ago. The flea in the ear will happen a bit later, when I get to heaven or wherever else I might be going. She's there alright but I might only see her as I pass down to the other place. Finbarr's my name by the way."

"Lovely to meet you, Finbarr. I'm Alannah."

"And what brings you into Fellini's, Alannah? I haven't seen you here before."

"Oh gosh that's a story, Finbarr."

She proceeded to tell him of her quest to find the enigmatic person to whom the postcard was addressed, handing it to him to view.

"Well that's amazing, indeed. As you can see there are not many people living in the Lane now. But I do know someone who might be able to help you. Breda Russell. She has made it her business to know everybody over the years. She's quite frail now I would say. I haven't seen her for a couple years. She must be in her mid nineties. I'd say, if she doesn't know who the Hays family are, you might as well give up. She lives up in Sunday's Well. Sure we can hop on a bus after we're finished and head off up to give her a call. She'll be delighted to help you, girl."

Alannah immediately became excited. How sweet of him to offer to help her. Full of excited chatter, they finished their mid morning snack together and left just after Midday.

They found their way up to Buxton Hill in Sunday's Well. Alannah marvelled at the view, the river Lee meandering below them as it wound its way into the city, and the city itself, in all its glorious splendour, spread in all directions. They opened the gate of the Russell household, an impressive house, whose gardens sloped below the gable.

Finbarr knocked on the front door. After a few moments, it was opened by a woman in her late fifties.

"Oh God preserve us from all harm, but look who's here, Ma." She let out a whoop and roar of laughter as Finbarr gave her a hug.

"Bless you, Niamh," Finbarr exclaimed, "Is the mischief herself about? I have a visitor for her. This is Alannah."

"Well, you're very welcome Alannah. Come in, come in."

They went into the living room with its wide bay windows framing the city below. A lightly-built, frail-looking but alert older woman was sitting on a chair, beaming at them as they walked through the door, visibly excited by their presence.

"This is Cork royalty, or as near as be dammed you'll get to it, Alannah. Say hello to Breda Russell."

Alannah grasped Breda's hand gently and took in the laughter and perspicaciousness in her eyes.

"Suigh síos agus lig do scíth, mo chroí. (Sit down and relax, love)" Breda gestured to the armchair opposite her.

After the small talk was over, Finbarr explained the quest to her as Niamh went to make tea. Alannah showed Breda the post card. A tiny necklace of tears appeared on her face. "Gosh that's so lovely. It just takes me back. 1949! That's another time altogether. Sure wasn't I falling in love myself at the same time.

"We wanted to know if you knew anything about this fellow. Do you know the Hays in Carey's Lane?"

    The Drowning of Innocence

"Well Carey's Lane. The Huguenot quarter. Let me think now. I don't know a Micheál. But there was another Hays fellow there I remember, lived with his sister way back. Sad fellow. I think he hit the bottle too much. You'd often see him walking around the town. A lost soul he was. What was his name, now. Unusual name for a Cork man, I remember. But of course it would be. I think the family were Protestant. That's it. Claude. His sister I seem to remember better. Joan her name was. She was very devoted to him. I think he fought in the Great War. She married one of the Kelleher's. You remember them Finbarr? They used to own a shop on Maylor street. Seán the owner. Sound man he was."

"Indeed I do. Gosh that takes me back. I can remember going in there in the forties. Lovely old shop. Full of sweets. Great for a young lad, like. They had all the fancy stuff. And one of those cable cash carrier systems. I used to watch it in fascination and awe as it sped up and down from the accountant's room upstairs. Not there anymore. All gone now thanks to that dreadful Roches Stores extension out the back. Some great old buildings lost to that."

Alannah was transfixed by these recollections. How sweet that in just a short time from meeting Finbarr she had the beginnings of a lead to find the elusive Micheál.

"Do you think they are still in business?"

"I wouldn't know that at all, I'm afraid," said Finbarr. "I think you'd have to check the golden pages."

"Do you mind?" said Alannah as she whipped her smart phone out of her pocket.

"What are you going to do?"

"I'll just look it up."

"There you go Finbarr. Sure they've left us all behind. They can buy and sell us now without leaving the house."

Finbarr and Breda laughed together as Alannah put in 'Kelleher's confectionery' into her search engine.

"Do you think this could be them?" She showed them the page that came up. 'Kelleher's fine chocolatier and dried fruits.'

"Gosh they've gone up in the world from boiled sweets, like, if it is them," said Finbarr.

The address showed the Clogheen trading estate, on the outskirts of the city.

"Do you think I should give them a call?"

"Sure what harm?" said Breda, encouraging her.

Alannah did not like the phone, but she had come so far and with the three of them in the room, looking inquisitively at her, already captured and enraptured by the adventure, she felt she had no choice. With trepidation, she entered the number laid out on the immaculate website she had brought up, rich with its delicate chocolate designs, tempting, beguiling.

The phone call was answered quickly by a young woman singing in a delicate Cork accent.

Alannah stumbled over her words.

"This is a strange phone call, I'm afraid. I am looking for a family who lived in Carey's Lane, donkeys years ago. Their name was Hays. I am told that one of the girls married a Kelleher who used to trade in Maylor Street. I'm calling on the off chance it might be you."

"Gosh," said the young woman on the other end. "That's my Great Granny you're talking about. Amazing. Yes, we're the same Kelleher's."

Alannah was taken aback. In such a short time, she had made so much progress. How thrilling. How exciting.

"Oh, I have a postcard that I picked up in a flea market. I think it was probably addressed to her brother. I promised myself I would try and get it back to the rightful owner. It was sent over sixty years ago."

"My goodness, that's great. Are you in Cork now?"

"Yes."

"Well what I suggest is I call my Granddad and see if we can fix up for you to meet him tomorrow morning. I think he would be the best to help you. Oh Seanair will be thrilled. He loved his Ma dearly. This will touch him."

"So the morning, then?"

"Yes. We have a small shop in the English Market. You can meet him

     The Drowning of Innocence

there."

"I'll pop by at about eleven. My name's Alannah, by the way."

"Look forward to it, Alannah. My name is Siobhán after my Great Granny."

Alannah closed the phone. Whoops of joy encircled the room. They had all been drawn into this excursion, this excavation of a love story.

"Of course, of course. Kelleher's in the English Market. The same people. How stupid of us."

Finbarr said he would join her in the morning.

"Are you sure?"

"Of course. The government pays me now to do nothing so I might as well be useful." He said with a wicked grin.

They spent the afternoon talking about the old days in the city. Alannah beguiled by tales which opened up its intimate community life. She could see it was more of a village than a metropolis.

Later in the day, she travelled back to the centre, to her hotel, said farewell to Finbarr and made arrangements to meet in the morning.

English Market, Cork.

August, 2011

It was the extraordinary blue eyes that struck Seanair Kelleher when he was introduced to Alannah in the small coffee shop next to their store in the English Market.

"Gosh you remind me so much of my Ma when she was young," he said as he shook her hands vigorously. An elegant man, still strong in stature, in his early eighties, he had startlingly blue eyes himself, unusual in Cork, and in Ireland.

"Ah go on, Seanair," said Siobhán, laughing heartily, standing by his side, "You're always seeing Great Grandma everywhere. You adored her so much"

They sat together and took one another in. Siobhán, his granddaughter, a sweet effervescent young woman, ordered coffee and selected an array of fine chocolates from the store.

Finbarr chipped in first, telling Seanair that he had often gone into the store in Maylor Street in his early teens. They sat reminiscing together about this for a while.

"It's my son Seán who changed the business. Very proud of him we are. He got the bug of making chocolates when he was in his early twenties. Took himself off to France to learn the trade from a chocolatier. He convinced me that it was the future. D'ya know, he spent a long time explaining to me that sweets were not good for people and he wanted to move into a more healthy line of business."

"I wish my waistline would tell me that chocolates are healthy," Alannah said. "I can't resist them."

The display of chocolates had arrived as if to emphasise the point.

"We make them all ourselves, right from roasting the cocoa beans to enrobing and decorating the final piece. It gives us an opportunity to establish our very own brand and signature. Each chocolate is decorated by hand. Great fun."

They all examined the chocolates displayed in front of them, exquisitely decorated with miniature fruits on each one.

     The Drowning of Innocence

"The moulds are handmade. You can see which fruit is in the chocolate. We get great enjoyment from it."

Alannah reached for an oblong chocolate with a fig delicately carved on the top. As she placed it in her mouth she was astonished by the delicate flavour of the fruit that permeated the perfectly blended chocolate centre.

"Wow," she exclaimed.

"We source the best dried fruits and add no sugar. We try and keep the taste natural, drawing out the bitterness of cocoa beans with the sweet natural sugars and flavours of the fruit. We have spent years perfecting it and continue to learn. Its a lovely way to spend your life," Siobhán laughed.

Alannah felt an embracing familiarity with them. An ease and friendliness that gave her reassurance in her quest, enhanced by the chocolate feast of flavours - almond, date, pear, pomegranate, apple. So many delights.

Suddenly, strangely, she felt nervous. She became aware that she was about to show this family something extremely intimate. She recalled the moment when she first read the words on the back of the postcard herself at the stall in the Ha'penny flea market. *'You are in my heart always. Not a day goes by, when I don't think of you. I love you, Eileen.'* What would these words open up for this family? Would they be aware of this Eileen? Is Micheál still alive? Are there ramifications to the two generations in front of her, a story hitherto untold, a secret? Alannah suddenly felt overwhelmed by the responsibility of it all. She reflected on her own situation and the words that her cousin Nicholas had written when he had sent her the letter from her Granny Elizabeth.

"Well, why did you want to see us. Alannah? I heard from Siobhán something about a postcard. Do you have it with you?"

The die was cast. Alannah knew she could not stall the revelation. She reached into her bag and drew out the postcard.

"I don't know if I'm doing the right thing here. I'm a bit nervous, you see. I found this postcard in a flea market in Dublin and it captivated me and intrigued me. I felt compelled to find the rightful owner and see if I could hand it over. In fact I made a stupid bet with the man who gave it to me. But now I am a little scared that the sentiments expressed are so intimate that maybe they should remain private."

"We're not afraid of a little intimacy in this family, Alannah. I'm sure it will do us no harm to see it."

Alannah opened the tissue paper which surrounded the much valued postcard and with reverence, handed it to Seanair and Siobhán, seated together. They held it for a long time, lovingly, sweetly, without a word. The image, the painting with its extraordinary vibrancy and colour moved them deeply.

"Very strange. I was born in Carey's Lane myself, but we moved when I was five. It's peculiar to see the address here on a post card. To a Hays. To dear Micheál. Ma would often talk about him. Her youngest brother. We never saw him, of course. He left Ireland long before I was born and never came back. All we have is a vase he made in his early years. Ma said he was a talented potter. Indeed this pot is unique, a beautiful glaze on it, deep greens and blues. It was Ma's pride and joy."

"When did he leave Ireland?"

"In 1922, I think. We don't know why he left. Ma or Da never said. Putting two and two together, we came to the conclusion that it was something to do with the Civil War. It was right smack in the middle of it. Just after Michael Collins was killed. All sorts of rumours. But it was never talked about. And I guess for good reason. Same as everyone else in this blessed country. Too painful. Too much terrible stuff happened at that time to dredge it up. What was it the Lord Mayor, Deirdre Clune said that time about the film 'The Wind that Shook the Barley'? Let me think. 'Oh God, do we need all this again, we've come so far, do we need it? We just should move on.' I think that summed up everyone's feelings about it all."

"That's why I'm so nervous about showing you the postcard. Opening things up that should be kept closed."

"Not at all, Alannah. This is different. We know very little about Micheál really and this will help us paint his picture. He's dead now. Died a few years ago. In the early nineties. Lived a good few years I think. In his mid nineties when he died. He married an American woman and lived all his life in New York, I think. Although a talented craftsman, I believe, he spent his life as a plumber. He has one son, Mikey. That's about all we know. But thanks for this. We can send it on to Mikey. We have occasional contact with him over the years."

"I'm not so sure about sending it now, Seanair," Siobhán interrupted. "I

The Drowning of Innocence

understand what Alannah is saying. This could be a time bomb disrupting his life. He may not thank us for it."

The weight of the story behind the postcard had grown. It was no longer just a charming love letter. Its impact and meaning on the lives of those who were descendants brought caution and hesitancy. Alannah felt bad about introducing this dilemma. An air of awkward embarrassment descended on the group.

Finbarr rescued the situation.

"I don't see how the unearthing of this card could have any bad effect. Sure, if you say the Micheál on the card left Ireland in 1922 and never came back, then he must have known Eileen before he left. That's what Eileen is saying isn't it. 'Not a day goes by.' Written in 1949. That's a helluva lot of days. My goodness, makes the hidden story even sweeter."

The logic of this took all of them aback.

"You're right indeed, Finbarr. Sound man you are. What an amazing thing. And I wonder what happened on Easter Monday, 1949 that prompted the card to be sent?"

"That's when we became the Republic of Ireland," said Finbarr, grinning wildly. "The plot thickens. Civil war, then finally a Republic. I can see now Alannah why you wanted to find out about the background. Sure maybe it's time for all of us to open the secrets of those years and let bygones be bygones."

The air cleared with this. It was if they had come together, to a fork in the road, deliberated and were, for a while, paralysed in indecision. Now they had found a solution together which enhanced the inherent beauty in the lyrical sentences on the postcard. They felt conjoined now in their quest, and part of a fellowship. Laughter and gaiety descended on the group as they swapped stories and personal history. Surprisingly, Alannah told them about her own, other quest to find her grandparents.

"Gosh, you're a brave, lovely woman, Alannah," Seanair said as he held her hand gently. "I wish you all the best in your search. I'll pray for you. We feel so fortunate as a family to have all our nearest and dearest around and close by. Except of course, Micheál's family. That's the missing piece for us. But of course we will try and make amends there and your postcard gives us the inspiration. We'll write to Mikey, bless him and send the postcard. We'll let you know what he says. But keep in touch anyway, my dear. We'd love to know the end of your own story."

They rose together and gave one another a hug goodbye. Alannah felt profoundly embraced, held, as Seanair wrapped his arms around her. The generous spirit of the man enveloped her and she was deeply moved. To tears.

"Forgive me. I don't know what's come over me. I guess it's also relief. Thank you so much for making me feel at home."

"Don't be a stranger, Alannah. Look us up the next time you're here. I'd love to spend more time with you."

Alannah almost skipped out of the English Market. The stalls rich in fragrance from the profusion of spices and abundance of flowers; Cheeses, vegetables, fresh meat and fish, all arrayed splendidly, carefully, captivated her. The vibrant crowd parting before her as she moved towards the street outside. She found it hard to believe that she had gained so much joy and exhilaration from pursuing such a simple quest. Her job was done. She had fulfilled her mission. She had passed the postcard back to the family of the addressee. A rich thrill of satisfaction embraced her. She hugged Finbarr goodbye as they left the market and she walked up Grand Parade.

   The Drowning of Innocence

Béal na Bláth, West Cork.

22nd August, 1922.

For two weeks, Micheál was in deep turmoil. When he hadn't returned from Rochestown, Tom Hales had sent out a search party for him. He was discovered, after two days, in a barn near Bandon, just before the fall of the town to Free State troops and was taken with others to safe houses near Béal na mBláth, the centre of Republican resistance.

He had been put up in a dorm in Long's Public House. There he wallowed in his misery, almost catatonic in inactivity. Hales had come to see him, to comfort him, talk to him. He had even sent someone, secretly, to Riverview, to discover how Eileen was. She had dominated Micheál's consciousness, full as he was in pain and despair at the consequences of his action on her life. He was divided hopelessly in himself. All his being wanted to be with her, to hold her, to comfort her, to fall at her knees and beg her forgiveness. But the other dominant and terrible aphorism that trapped him was the irredeemable harm he had caused her and their love. A nauseous fear overwhelmed him when he envisioned approaching her and seeing the imagined horror, hatred, bitterness which was, inevitably, the fearful consequence of his felling of her brother.

He could not articulate what he had done, not even to himself, so awful was the chimera and spectre that had invaded his life. The apprehension and premonitions that had dominated his consciousness for months had finally borne noxious fruit and he was in hell.

No word arrived of Eileen's welfare, just the awful truth that she had disappeared, vanished, dissolved, fading from his life as if it had all been one long, impossible dream. He was heartsick, barely ate and spent most of his days in self absorption.

This morning though, he had been awoken by a vigorous commotion. One of the lads was standing outside the pub, having a smoke in the clear morning air, when a Free State convoy came through. Lost and uncertain, they had sought directions. Nonchalantly, he had given it to them, taking a good look at the occupants of the three vehicles as they passed slowly by. When they had left, he ran up the stairs, screaming,

"Fuck me, you'd never guess who's just passed by. Fucking Collins himself."

The place became a hubbub of activity after that. About thirty volunteers gathered from the surrounding safe houses in the lounge bar of the pub. Deasy, the commander of the First Southern Division was emphatic that this was a brazen incursion from the chief architect of the Treaty and leader of the Free State government into the territory of its greatest, most ardent resistance. The provocation inherent in the act did not escape him.

"We must ambush them. There's only one way back to Cork and they'll come back this way. All the rest of the roads are impassable. This is our opportunity and we must take it."

Arguments raged on around Micheál. He could see that Tom Hales was quite emotional. As a life-long friend of Collins, the thought of mounting an ambush was abhorrent to Hales. Remarkably, Micheál himself was raised from his stupor by the heated discussion.

'Collins!!' His mind was sucked back to the Athletic Grounds, three years before, when he and Mattie had first been introduced to Collins. A grimace of disgust and pain enveloped his face as he thought of this memory, this incipient moment which had brought him to this point and his friend now gone. "Collins, here," he thought. "The brazen-faced nature of it."

For the first time in two weeks he felt alive, blood flowing back into his veins. He was alert, listening, the buried and inchoate rage and despair that had submerged his energy and life had found a focus. He listened carefully to the instructions. They were to commandeer a cart to block the road just up the way from the pub and mine a section where the attack would take place.

Micheál spent the day with Tom Hales scouting ambush points to cover the road's layout. There was an air of tension as they waited, uncertain as to when the convoy would return. It was late in the day and approaching dusk when they decided to abandon the task.

"They're not coming back today, now," Deasy explained. "It's more like they've gone on to Bantry. Wrap it up and we will get ready again tomorrow."

The engineers were despatched to disarm the mine and clear the obstruction from the road. Hales, visibly relieved, made his way down to the cart to supervise its removal and the dismantling of the mine. Micheál was left alone as he trudged back to Long's for the evening, to face the anguish of yet another night of agitation and restlessness.

He had reached the brow of the hill overlooking the pub when he heard gunfire from the ambush site, became aware of the motor engines of the

     The Drowning of Innocence

convoy and knew that it had returned. His heart was gripped with fear for Hales and the others left exposed as they dismantled the blockage on the road. It was late in the evening, almost dusk.

In great alarm he rushed back. He could hear the ominous sound of Vickers machine gun fire from the armoured car, as bullets strafed the fields, cutting into any undergrowth on both sides of the road, exposing previously safe ambush points.

He was heartily sick of it all, slumped to the ground and scanned the convoy. The occupants had disembarked and taken cover under the vehicles. Some were hidden by a bank at the side of the road. They returned fire sporadically. To Micheál it was a sham. Deasy came up behind him on the hill and urged him and others to fire their weapons and distract the column, draw their fire to his direction and away from the main ambush site. Deasy was worried about the men trapped on the boreen below.

Suddenly, a figure stood up from behind the bank positioned next to the Rolls Royce and began to run down the road towards them. Micheál was aghast at the foolhardiness of this move. "What's he thinking of?" he thought, "he's a sitting duck." Then, in amazement, he recognised the figure of Collins himself running towards him, with a bravado that was scarcely credible.

Micheál was taken aback. He trained his Enfield 303 on the figure, an easy mark. He could hit him fatally and effortlessly from his vantage point. Here, in front of him, in his sightline, was his nemesis, the person who had taken Mattie away, levered his friend, had turned the bitterness he had felt on his father's death into a powerful, coruscating weapon of destruction; The man who inspired hero-worship and unquestioning loyalty; The dividing point, the fissure who had brought the two childhood friends to the tragedy that now dominated his consciousness.

A furious rage rose up inside him. It was his moment. He could now blow away the memory of Mattie's death with this apocalyptic slaughter, consign to oblivion the moment when Collins had entered their lives. He took careful aim, pressed gently on the trigger and then, realised in an instant, that he could not do it, could not follow through and was paralysed into inaction. The very act of taking aim evoking in him deep resonances: Mortifyingly, the wretched moment when Mattie was slain, but then also echoes, reverberations of Kilmichael; The slaughter of bodies gruesomely inhabiting his consciousness.

He was sick to his core with it all; This pointless, futile violence. He was full of disgust, loathing and repugnance for what was taking shape before him, now. Another ridiculous chapter in an increasingly preposterous conflict. He was nauseated by the metamorphosis that had taken place in his own soul, propelling him towards hell on earth. As if to emphasise the moment of his conversion, the moment when he definitively decided that the whole charade was over, he moved the sightline of this rifle to a dry-stone wall to the left of the running figure on the road. He pulled the trigger with consummate rage and the violence of rejection, and with pernicious destructiveness, his rifle kicked back on his shoulder.

Immediately, and to his horror, he saw the running figure, Michael Collins, slump into a heap struck down in flight. Where had the shot come from? The confusion of gunfire lacing the valley made it impossible to judge. What was evident though was that Collins was slain and in serious trouble. He continued to stare at the prone figure stretched out on the road and could see a gaping wound at the back of his head, behind his right ear. He saw other "Staters" rush up the road, to the aid of their stricken leader. Around him, gunfire continued to rage from Micheál's comrades, encouraged as they were by the lull in return-fire from the Free State troops.

Cataclysmically for Micheál, this was it. He threw his rifle down in despair and knelt in the boggy ground, resting his hands joined in prayer on the rock in front of him and begged with all his heart to his God, the God of his beloved mother, to forgive him, to look down in mercy on him, on the man stricken below, on Mattie, Con, and all those whose lives had been cut short by this terrible visitation of bitterness, hatred, conflict and death. He prayed with all his might for Eileen, wherever she was, that the God who had inspired such grace and dignity, compassion and mercy in his dear mother's heart would visit his beloved in her misery and despair and give her strength to carry on, and comfort her in her deep sorrow. Tears streamed down his face as his grief broke, sobs wreaking through his body in uncontrollable anguish, the events below him like some Greek tragedy epitomising all his losses.

He was largely oblivious to the events railing around him, the continued gun fire, useless and intense. He hardly saw the armoured car being driven forward towards the prostrate figure, who was now being cradled by one of the 'Staters' as they tried to engulf his head in bandages. He didn't take in fully the back doors of the vehicle being flung open and Michael Collins being lifted on board.

The firing had by then abated, as if in recognition of the calamity that had fallen on the land and its people. He was still kneeling in his prostrate position

     The Drowning of Innocence

as the vehicles took off in formation, bashing the obstructing cart to one side as it made its way from the ambush site into the gathering gloom of that terrible, appalling night, a night when hope died and the country submerged into a slough of sour, virulent, acrimonious poison, from which it would not recover for generations.

Franciscan Friary, Cork City.

24th August, 1922.

Brother Paul looked aghast at Micheál. The young, bright, intelligent man he knew had evaporated, replaced by a troubled ghost looking twice his age. Crumpled inarticulately on the wooden chair in the small guest room of the Monastery, Paul was summoning all his experience and wisdom to reach him; To peer down into his desolate spirit and find a spark there that would stimulate some movement, some motivation.

The previous day, the aftershock of Collin's assassination had gripped the nation, triggering a tidal wave of anguish, grief and rage. Paul had been contacted by Tom Hales and had travelled alone to Béal na Bláth.

"He's gone from us, Paul," Hales has told him. "He's been distraught since the ambush. We can't get anything out of him. He just lies there. What's more, the word has got out that he it was who killed Collins. Goodness knows how that happened, because none of us here know for certain how the 'Big Fella' was shot, Lord have mercy on his soul. But the rumour is enough. There's plenty of fellows devoted to Collins who smell blood and want revenge. We can't protect him, even from our own. So I wonder can you take him and smuggle him out of the country? It's the only way to keep him safe."

Paul gazed long and hard at Hales and saw the compassion of the man. Somehow it exacerbated the madness and mayhem that had taken a grip on things.

After it was resolved, they moved fast and with Micheál dressed in Franciscan robes, he brought him under cover of darkness to the relative safety of the Friary.

"Micheál, I can't ask you to think about things now. That'll come later. I want you to be safe and you're not safe here or anywhere in Ireland for that matter. Nobody wants any more killing. I have to act for you. For Joan, for your family, for Eileen."

At the mention of her name, a strangulated cry emanated from Micheál, as of a stricken animal, a cóinín caught in a snare, desperately pulling away from the stake, the wire noose tightening fatally.

"We haven't been able to find her. She disappeared in the night two weeks ago and we haven't seen hide nor hair of her since. But she is a strong woman

     The Drowning of Innocence

and I am not worried for her. You must now be strong too."

There was no stirring in the man. The darkness into which he had been plunged seemed unremitting, all-encompassing. He didn't touch the food that was placed in front of him. He appeared inescapably lost.

On inspiration, Paul summoned Joan in secret. He knew that Collin's squad were probably staking out Carey's Lane already but he got word to her and late in the evening she arrived, surprisingly, with Claude in tow.

Joan's entreaties to her brother also seemed to fall on deaf ears.

"For me, Micheál, please. I can't lose another brother. Spare me, I don't think I can face another loss like Charlie."

To the wonder of all, Claude took control. He moved his chair close to the bed where Micheál lay forlorn, wrapped in a blanket of forgetfulness.

"Michael, brother, now is the time to be strong. To have courage. You will find it there in yourself. I know it. I am sure. Listen, when I lay on that beach in Gallipoli, with Charlie gone, I thought I could never again rise. I know where you are now. I've been there, sweet brother. I can only tell you that somehow and I don't know how, I got the strength. Mostly from the lads around me. I just had to put one foot in front of the other; Ma, even Charlie looking down on me. Let me lend you my strength now. You have to get out. We have a ticket for the Laconia, sailing from Queenstown on Sunday. We can get you there. Afterwards we will figure out what to do."

Miraculously, Micheál squeezed Claude's hand and raised himself to look at his brother, a deep sense of recognition passing between them. It was enough.

Three days later, Paul had moved him carefully through the city. Finally, there on the quay of Queenstown harbour, looking out at the wild Atlantic, Micheál opened up. There, almost on the very same spot they had stood waiting for the ferry the day after the McSwiney funeral, that prophetic day, he found strength to speak his last words on Irish soil.

"Look out for her, Paul. I love her more than life itself. But I know that we can never be together now. What has happened has opened up an unbridgeable gap. I cannot ask her to look at me again and see, in my eyes, her brother resting in the darkness inside. I love her too much for that. I know her, Paul. I know she will forgive me. I know she will not harbour any resentment and bitterness, but I can't ask her to take on an odyssey like that. It would cripple the very parts of her I admire and love so much. So I am asking you, my dear friend, to take my place and make sure she will be alright."

When Paul held him for the last time, it was all he could do to stand without crumpling into a dishevelled heap. In all his years of listening to and holding people in grief and disarray, he had never been reduced like this.

Micheál turned and, without looking back, walked up the gangplank to the deck of the ship, rupturing forever his dreams, his attachments, his sense of belonging. 'Talamh agus Saoirse' now behind him, a wasted, blasted delusion, a mockery, a chimera that had beguiled and unerringly led to disaster.

A few hours later, the Liner embarked, casting off the hawsers, dispatching him, adrift, into an uncertain and lonely future.

     The Drowning of Innocence

Sherkin Island, Baltimore, West Cork.

Autumn, Winter, 1922.

The island cradled Eileen when she arrived, exhausted and drained. Mrs Roche taking her in without questions or enquiry, as if it was the most natural thing in the world. She could see the distressed nature of the girl and knew that time here in her little cottage would help.

Eileen's days settled into a rhythm. That September, Sherkin shone in all its glory. The purple red fuchsia bushes, interspersed with delicate rabhán farraige, yellow agrimony, pink-red campion, cerise foxgloves, hedge bindweed, golden honeysuckle, heath spotted orchid, multi-coloured dog roses and flame-orange montbrecia all competing with one another for her attention. The sun appeared most days, peering behind billowing clouds, extending its warmth and light way beyond its usual and occasional summer foray. Somehow, knowing the land needed healing.

She spent her days in communion with her daughter, meandering through the places she loved. Noreen's Bay, Silver Strand, Cow Bay. She confided with this new life inside her, letting her daughter in on all the secrets she had herself discovered. The healing, shifting strand beneath her feet as the tide rolled in; Its grittiness sanding her skin to a rich smoothness. The game she always played with the surf, daring it to ensnare her with the occasional exploding wave travelling many feet beyond its previous mark, seeking to catch her out; Eileen herself with whoops of laughter skipping inland to avoid being soaked.

She clambered gingerly over rock pools, knowing her history and chuckling to herself at its remembrance; The pools themselves replete with barnacles, mussels, limpets and seaweed of all shapes and colours, the solitary fish caught out by a receding tide. She revelled in the wonder of it all.

Every day she braced herself and swam in the cold Atlantic, even into October, becoming colder and greater in challenge as the days grew shorter. It was like a cleansing and re-invigoration. She, swimming in the sea, her daughter mirroring her actions in her own amniotic fluid. They were together, as one.

On most days she walked the perimeter of Horseshoe Bay, following the trail of otters; watching them for hours as they fished. It was there she discovered the sound; The tumultuous noise the Atlantic made as it entered a deep cave under the rocks; The noise as of a benevolent cascade of armaments falling from the sky; Not frightening but uplifting in its power and vigour. It caught her out for a moment and she remembered Charlie and his last hours trapped in the hull of a ship off the coast of the Gallipoli peninsula, the fierce and inexplicable noise of exploding shells closing in on his world.

"Charlie," she whispered his name to her daughter and in a soft, gentle voice told her unborn child of the rescue of her young mother all those years ago, along the coast in Crosshaven. "Dear, dear Charlie." She remembered him and gave thanks for his short life, his boundless energy and vivaciousness, his athletic frame, warm spirit and generous heart.

On other days, when she felt stronger, she spoke the name of her love to their child. Holding back waves of emotion, she whispered silently his qualities, his courage and devotion, his deep sense of commitment to her and his people, his poetic soul, his brilliant hands that could turn their skill and adeptness to anything, great and small. His fondness, his adoration of her. She breathed his spirit into the depths of her where his daughter grew. She felt her kick with excitement in return.

In the sixth month of her pregnancy, in the middle of November, Mrs Roche came to her.

"I want to take you on a little trip, over to the mainland. It won't be far. We can have a day out. We can wrap up warm. We'll bring some soda-bread sandwiches and scones with us and a flask of tea."

Eileen loved the idea. They left after daybreak and John Willie took them by boat to Baltimore. There, Mrs Roche had a friend who loaned them a donkey and cart. The November air was crisp and bright as they made their way out by Ballylinch towards Barloge. Eileen shifted often in her seat to get comfortable but relished the salt air coming from the south and the Atlantic beyond, its vista framed by heather, gorse and low stone walls. When the cart sank into potholes they laughed, Eileen joking with Mrs Roche that her hostess wanted the child to come early.

When they reached the top of the hill they could see Loughine, spread below them in its emerald green glory, its deep waters fed and cleansed by the ocean. They made their way down to its shores by the Rapids. Mrs Roche built a small fire on the rocks with driftwood they collected. Then they rested, spread blankets and drank tea and ate their store.

Eileen became transfixed by the waters of the Rapids and fell into a deep

                         The Drowning of Innocence

silence. The torrent streaming over the rocks making its way to the Atlantic beyond looked unrelenting. Her thoughts were invaded then by the equally incessant and pitiless storm that had invaded their lives over the previous eight years. She had to remind herself that she was a young woman still, with her life ahead of her and yet it felt as if she had lived three lives already.

The storm of water began to quell and became serenely penetrable. Ever changing, it somehow also remained the same, constant and reassuring. Eileen lost track of time, lost to the world, gazing deeply into the stream and her soul at the same time. Anxieties rose within her, deep fear for her daughter's future, unwelcome as she would be, the child of her maligned father. A sickly turmoil took hold as she gazed on fearlessly at these thoughts and the cascade flowing below her.

Magically and without warning, the Rapids began to slow. The torrent evaporated and became a gentle stream until at last, it came to a quiet, peaceful standstill.

Then, out of nowhere, the hidden kelp, which had been swept to one side by the rushing torrent, rose above the still water, its stipes tall and erect, the fronds gently caressing the surface. It was as if time stood still and the earth held its breath, touched by the divine.

Eileen became enthralled, mesmerised. She was caressed deeply. At that moment, her anxieties melted, disappeared. She felt held and comforted. Filled with a great resolve she knew now what she had to do and that all would be well with her little girl.

Wondrously, as if it had all happened in her imagination, in some transcendent world, the waters started to flow again but this time in the opposite direction; The turning of the tide; Gathering speed, it captured the kelp in its vortex and swept it out of sight once more.

Eileen felt Mrs Roche's comforting arms around her. "I wanted you to see this, mo chroí. You see, things can change in an instant."

Eileen looked up at this kindly woman. "I don't know how to thank you. You took me in and didn't ask me any questions. You have taken care of me and put me back together. I am so much in your debt."

"Sure, not a bother. I love you like my own."

"Something happened just now and I have clarity for the first time in ages. I know what I have to do and I am OK."

Uncharacteristically, Mrs Roche reached across to her and gathered her in a warm, tender embrace. Eileen relaxed visibly, waves of serenity drenching her frame in a deep contentment. Later as the afternoon drew to a close, they packed the cart and made their way back to the pier at Baltimore and home to Sherkin, replete with the drama of the day.

Sherkin Island,
26th November 1922

Brother Paul,
Franciscan Friary,
Liberty Street
Cork

Private & Confidential

Dear Brother Paul,

I suppose this will come as a shock to you to see my handwriting on the envelope - such as it is. I hope you were not worried about me, but I suspect you know me well enough to gather I was all right. I needed to get away and the reason I will tell you later. I still don't want anyone to know where I am but you, of course, can let Ma know you have heard from me and that I am fine.

The thing is Paul, I am six months pregnant with Micheál's baby. This is the reason I had to disappear. To give my baby a safe place away from the madness that has consumed us. I am writing to you for help. I trust that you will be able to honour the difficult position I am in. I don't want Micheál to know. I think he has suffered enough in this and what he doesn't know will not harm him.

You see, Paul, I can't think of my daughter, Rosaleen, (I'm sure its a little girl), growing up with my family. I know them. I know they will not be able to forgive Micheál for Mattie's death, no matter how they try. And my dear girl will bear the brunt. There seems to be seeds of immense division, hatred and bitterness sown among us now that will take years to heal and I can't surrender my girl to that.

I came to a decision the other day. I'll tell you of the circumstances later but it was like a divine revelation. I knew for her own good I would have to give her away. No, I don't mean it like that. I mean that she will be a gift of life to a couple who desperately want a child and can't have one. So she will be chosen and loved.

That's where I need your help. Don't try and dissuade me, Paul. You know how hard enough it is for me to do this. But my life and wishes are not the most important things here. What is it you always say "Greater love hath no man than he lay down his life for a friend." Well, I'm doing it for dear Rosaleen and you know how strong I am when I make up my mind.

I am so much in your debt in this. I would like it best if you found a couple of the Protestant faith. I think that would honour Micheál and his family, particularly Joan, who has always been so kind to me. Not a Huguenot family of course as they are too small a community, hardly extending beyond Careys Lane. This will also take Rosaleen away from the horrors into which we have all been plunged. I trust you Paul with the most precious part of me. You are a good man and I know you will be able to find a way.

Love,

Eileen

Franciscan Friary,
Liberty Street,
Cork

1st December 1922

My dear Eileen,

My heart goes out to you as I hear your tale. I am so glad you are well and enjoying your child. I did not worry. You are a strong woman and I suspected there was good cause for your flight. Of course I will keep your news in confidence. I know you will have thought long and hard about your decision and I understand your reasons. God knows, things have got even worse and the Free State government have gone crazy with executions. Killing far more than ever were executed under the British. The residual effects of this are already seen as we turn on one another.

I spoke to your Ma and let her know you are alright. I don't think she can take much in, bless her. But she seemed OK.

Oh Eileen, to give your child up. How much that must cost you and part of me fears for you but I will of course honour your judgement.

I do have contacts. And I will sensitively enquire on your behalf. And I pray that God will be gracious to me in this quest. That I might find a couple who will cherish your and Micheál's child. Truly a special child indeed.

Give me time mo chroí. You have set me an onerous task but I will do my best to fulfil it as you desire.

For now all my love, Paul.

The Drowning of Innocence

Franciscan Friary,
Liberty Street,
Cork

20th December 1922

My dear Eileen,

Good news. I have found a couple. I have spent a good deal of time with them and as best I can see it, I believe they will be good parents for Rosaleen. They are in their late thirties and have tried for a child of their own for many years without success. I think this has caused them a great deal of pain and suffering but they remain strong together and very much devoted to one another.

They can hardly contain their emotions with the news, worried as they are that it may not come to pass. So I would like you to give it your prayerful consideration. As I have got to know them I see them as straightforward people, reasonably well off, but more importantly they show a kindness and hospitality that you would warm to. They are very concerned for you, which is something that touched me deeply. He is an engineer and she is a secretary in a school. They are Church of Ireland people but very down to earth, no airs and graces there.

Their home is comfortable and simple and they are devoted to the Arts, something I think which will matter to you.

As you have requested, I will not give you their details and I have only given them scant details of who you are. They wait with bated breath for your decision. For now all my love

Paul.

Sherkin Island,
Christmas Day 1922

Brother Paul,
Franciscan Friary,
Liberty Street
Cork

Private & Confidential

Dear Brother Paul,

Thank you, oh thank you for this wonderful news. I feel deep inside me that this is right. God knows, I need that as it's such a painful thing to do. I'm writing this on Christmas morn, my first and only Christmas with my daughter. Its such a lovely feeling and I am projecting grace towards all her many Christmas morns to come. So you can tell this family the good news.

I want to pass on two things to them, to accompany my daughter on her journey into the unknown future.

The first is her name - Rosaleen. I think of Da most days and what he passed on to me about Ireland and our people. His vision of a gentle, compassionate and including community fired his life and he handed it to me as a torch, fierce to hold, but one that has always shed light to my path. I see Rosaleen as that future, way beyond the acrimony that has recently consumed us. So she and others who follow her will embody the real Ireland and will, as so eloquently written by Mangan;

"......scale the blue air,

.........plough the high hills,

..................kneel all night in prayer,

(to) give (you) life and soul anew,"

Then there is the stone I found in Crosshaven all those years ago. Let it be a birthstone for her, carrying within its being all of what her name and heritage mean. Let it bring her joy and peace in the rough times ahead.

For now Brother Paul, thank you, happy Christmas and you have freedom to pass on the good news to these good folk,

Love,

Eileen

Franciscan Friary,
Lady Lane,
Waterford
28th January 1923

My dear Eileen,

As you can see, I have moved. I have found a new home for myself. I'm glad, in a way, as I found it difficult to balance the differences of position among my friends in Cork on the state of affairs, which continues to decline.

The good news is that I have found a lovely nursing home for you here near the Friary. They are happy to receive you for the birth of your baby and can be relied on to be discreet. So I plan to come and pick you up when you are ready and we can travel together. I can get hold of a car for that, so you will be safe from prying eyes.

I hope you continue to be well and I am really looking forward to seeing you. Then I will be able to be close by to you during your childbirth and alongside you as you say goodbye to Rosaleen.

I admire you so much, dear Eileen and you are constantly in my prayer and thoughts

Love

Paul

Iveragh Nursing Home, Ballyhack, Waterford.

16th February, 1923.

The thunderstorm rolled over the harbour in the middle of the night, great waves of it, shaking the room with its loud peals; The hail on the roof, a thunderous cracking of icicles; The heavy air all encompassing. Her room with its big bay windows affording her a dramatic and panoramic view of its pageant. It was another thing to distract Eileen. The searing pain of the contractions dominated her consciousness, her body betraying her and moving with a determination all of its own. Long and painful birth pains which well-nigh overcame her. In some ways she was glad of the pain, taking her away from her impending decision.

She had woken the day before when her waters broke, exhilarated and apprehensive and spent the day negotiating this new and surprising event. She fought with herself as she pined for Micheál's comforting presence and succour. It was not helpful to think of him now, so she just whispered his name and sent her love over the miles to him; He would remain oblivious of the phenomenal occurrence taking shape in this small nursing room; The birth of his daughter, his flesh and blood.

Brother Paul had arrived and spent time with her and now was anxiously pacing up and down the corridor outside, unused as he was, common to all men, of the private domain of childbirth. He was dreading what faced him, the support of this young woman as she enacted the most devastating decision of her young life.

Just before dawn the child arrived. As if in celebration, the storm eased and the sun found its way over the horizon alternatively scattering and lighting up the dense, billowing, powerfully shaped clouds with an orange red hue. The little girl was immaculate in every way and Eileen held her in her arms and moved her to her breast, in awe at her perfection, her exquisite shape, the beautiful and fully formed fingers and toes, with their delicate and unique print. Rosaleen looked up at her as she drew comfort and nourishment from her breast.

"So here you are," Eileen whispered to her, at that moment profoundly aware that she was not a surprise. Everything about this gorgeous baby she already knew. "Rosaleen," she whispered. "We have had such a lovely time together, but now I must let you go. You will be safe. You will be loved by me and your new parents all your life. I will never forget you." She carefully parcelled her stone, so that it would go with Rosaleen. "Its your identity. That you may always know who you are, where you've come from and that you are deeply cherished and loved."

Some time after the birth, Paul came in. Struggling to keep his emotions in check, he greeted the child lovingly and anointed her with oil, praying softly over her.

"May strong arms hold you
Caring hearts tend you
And may love await you at every step."

Too early, far too early for Eileen, the midwife arrived. "It's time," she said softly to Eileen.

Eileen gazed down at Rosaleen for the last time, drank her in, in all her beauty and wondrous vulnerability, and handed her over, watching the movement as the midwife made her way to the door.

When the door closed, she broke. A great upheaval of grief shook her very being. Violent sobs of anguish and desolation overwhelmed her. Paul moved towards her and held her in his arms, mirroring the moment when she had caught him on the deck of the ferry, the day after the McSwiney funeral. He silently hoped that she would experience the same exorcism by his touch, that she would find within herself the strength to carry on. With all his heart he tried to banish fear for her and her future as he commended her to his merciful and graceful God.

Brother Paul,   *19, St. Otteran Place,*

Franciscan Friary,   *Waterford*

Liberty Street,

Cork

New Years Day, 1926

Dear Brother Paul,

We are writing to let you know that our daughter Rose has become the joy of our lives. She is a beautiful child, now nearly three. It's a wonder to be part of her growth and development. Every day brings new things, new explorations, new words, smiles and bouts of mischief. We have been so rich and blessed.

I felt compelled to let you know this and will forever be grateful to you and Rose' mother for this gracious gift of life to us. She will not want for anything. We love her dearly.

Yours in gratitude,

Elizabeth & Trevor Morley.

     The Drowning of Innocence

Homecoming

" Come away, O human child,
To the waters and the wild,
With a faery, hand in hand,
For the world's more full of weeping than you can understand."
–William Butler Yeats, "The Stolen Child"

"Woman is by her nature fitted for home work and it is this which is best adapted to preserve her modesty and promote the good upbringing of children and the well being of the family"
Pope Leo XIII, Rerum Novarum (1891)

The State recognises the special position of the Holy Catholic Apostolic and Roman Church as the guardian of the Faith professed by the great majority of the citizens
Article 44.1.2 Irish Constitution 1937

In particular, the State recognises that by her life within the home, woman gives to the State a support without which the common good cannot be achieved.
Article 41.2 Irish Constitution 1937

"No change in the opinion of men, no new state of things, nor course of events can ever snatch woman, if she realises her mission, from that sphere which is natural to her – the family"
'Rights of Women', John Charles McQuaid ('JC')

"That Ireland which we dreamed of would be the home of a people who valued material wealth only as the basis of right living, of a people who were satisfied with frugal comfort, and devoted their leisure to the things of the spirit – a land whose countryside would be bright with cosy homesteads, whose fields and villages would be joyous with the sounds of industry, with the romping of sturdy children, the contests of athletic youths and the laughter of comely maidens, whose firesides would be forums for the wisdom of serene old age. It would, in a word, be the home of a people living the life that God desires that man should live."
Éamon DeValera St Patrick's Day 1943

"Later as the day cools and they have gone in, the cry of the corncrake will carry across those same fields and over the lake to the blue-hazed mountain, such a lonely evening sound to it, like the lonely evening sound of the mothers, saying it is not our fault that we weep so, it is nature's fault that makes us first full, then empty."
–Edna O'Brien, The Light of Evening

"Love … is like nature, but in reverse; first it fruits, then it flowers, then it seems to wither, then it goes deep, deep down into its burrow, where no one sees it, where it is lost from sight, and ultimately people die with that secret buried inside their souls."
–Edna O'Brien, Lantern Slides: Short Stories.

And for all this, nature is never spent; There lives the dearest freshness deep down things;

'Gods Grandeur' Gerald Manley Hopkins

To: Mr. Micheál Hays   *9, Carey's Lane,*

50, St Johns Place,   *Cork City*

Park Slope,

Brooklyn

New York

11th January 1932

My dear Micheál,

It seems it's always down to me to break sad news to you. I wish I could protect you, my dear brother for you have suffered so much.

Brother Paul died last week. His funeral was quite something, with thousands flocking to the church to say their goodbyes. I don't think I will ever forget it. I went there especially for you as I know you loved him dearly and he was the rock you could lean on during difficult times.

It seems like you were not alone. The Franciscan celebrating the funeral mass broke with convention and asked us to turn to our neighbour and tell one another what it was about this man that meant so much to each of us. Gosh it transformed the church for five minutes as the din of conversation and enthusiasm fairly lifted the roof. Very moving. Oh that we would all be remembered like that.

I saw Eileen there, bless her. She no longer lives in Cork. We didn't say much to one another. What could be said, really?

She seemed quite subdued, which was not surprising given the day that was in it. Nevertheless, we gave one another a big hug. She really is such a sweet girl.

I hope life continues to be good to you in the big city. You are lucky to have a job, I guess, as I hear many, many stories of those who have none. Life is tough. But you always knew that.

We are grand. Our baby grows day by day and is now two. He is into everything and reminds me so much of our dear brother Charlie. So I feel glad that we gave him his name.

                    The Drowning of Innocence

Seán is great and is very dedicated to the business. We feel very fortunate to be able to make ends meet.

Claude is Claude. He gets by from day to day. He works hard bless him. I think the activity keeps his mind occupied. He is very quiet though. We don't see much of him in the evenings. He is usually off to the High B for a pint and doesn't come back till closing time.

But I want you to know we are happy and there is no need to worry about us.

Again, I hope this letter finds you well.

With much love

Joan

Lismore, County Waterford

3rd April 1947

Méabh O'Connor stared at the walls of her bedroom in utter despair. The floral pattern screamed back at her; 'Conform, fit in, why do you always want to be different?' Walls were unfeeling. They were there to protect, isolate, give the illusion of comfort. She, on the other hand, didn't feel safe or comforted. There was no symmetry between what was going on inside her and what was expected of her. The suffocating aspirations of her parents, the inebriated preoccupations of her friends, boxed her into a territory and landscape for which she had no map or key. Here she was, twenty years of age, sitting in her bedroom, in this small town, at the end of herself.

"That Johnny Murphy is a nice lad. His father is the bank manager, you know, and he keeps calling. Wouldn't you think you could show a bit of interest Méabh or are you going to be single all your life?" Her friends had acclaimed the same Johnny as a 'fine thing' whatever that was when it was at home.

It had been years now that Méabh had felt this gnawing difference as a huge burden. She knew enough to understand the rules but felt in her heart that to surrender was to drown. She quietly cursed her teacher for occupying her head with nonsense. Miss Barry had filled her with hope when she had taught her the Leaving Cert Art course a couple of years back. How she had loved listening to her as she pulled a curtain back on the world. Walking into her class, like strolling in a meadow after a soft rain had fallen, so clear, so bright, so fresh was the touch on her imagination.

In those days, Méabh could ignore the clamour around her. Under Miss Barry's guidance and encouragement she had taken tentative steps. "Find yourself in what you express" was her teacher's mantra. "Excavate it. It's hidden there." And so during those precious years she had studied form and substance, being drawn inexorably to women artists and writers. "For too long Irish people and particularly us women, have had a proscribed, circumscribed, subservient identity forced on us," she would proclaim. "But there is a true, beating heart of integrity among us and in our shared history, if we only have the courage and perseverance to discover it." They had poured together enthusiastically over images of Norah McGuinness' paintings, relishing the delicate colours and shapes, the free-flowing imagination of the artist. Miss

The Drowning of Innocence

Barry had shown her evocative paintings of Irish life, 'Top of the Hill' and 'Going to Mass' catching her attention and she applauded Méabh's attempts to make sense of her own prism on the world.

Such fine words they were which had drenched her impressionable mind. The reality of the last two years, however, had trampled on them. The love she had cultivated for Art had been eclipsed by her mother's diktat of finding a job and she was now a fully trained comptometer operator in a local insurance company. She had forced the fingers of her hands which had loved the free flowing movement of holding a brush or shaping clay into the rigid, automatic manoeuvres required by the machine to multiply, divide, add and subtract big numbers.

Fitting into its regime, mirrored her own reshaping. The rules were clear, unequivocal and complicated. Subtracting numbers taxed her brain and withdrew energy from her spirit and soul. Adding numbers in order to subtract seemed such a paradox and yet every day spent in front of this metallic, brown machine stripped her soul, subtracted from it and added to it the weight of conformity, the body of fitting in. The grand totaler of this clanking calculator racking up how far she had travelled in such a short time from the vibrant optimism of her school years. The whole process had ground her down and left no room for the ideals imparted by Miss Barry. It had squeezed her into a queer shape.

Then there was all this nonsense of 'finding a fella.' She had looked in sheer astonishment at the transformation of her dear friends from engaging, energetic companions to giggling, frivolous hordes as they anticipated dances at the rugby club. Such occasions overwhelming her with tepid indifference.

"Méabh, can you not hear me? Are you deaf or what?" Her mother was standing at her bedroom door. "Where do you disappear to, for goodness sake? I need you to go down to McGrath's to order the meat for Easter."

Méabh dragged herself back to consciousness, tripped down the stairs, grabbed her coat, scarf, gloves and boots and walked out into that bitterly cold, winter's day. The air gripped her. The icy ground, treacherous from the continuous snowfall that had held the country to ransom for months made her journey along the streets of the town slow and tortuous. The early days of snowfall which had given an other-worldly, ephemeral quality to the outline of the town had long since disappeared. The pavements were transformed into icy, rock-shaped, slopes to be negotiated with care and precision. Her whole being was absorbed in this precarious activity when a voice called out to her, familiar and ringingly exciting,

"Well now, aren't you a sight for sore eyes."

There in front of her, in the main street, was Miss Barry herself.

"Oh, hello, Miss Barry."

"Era sure, none of that Miss Barry nonsense now, Méabh. Those days are gone for us. I'll be seriously upset if you don't call me Eileen."

Méabh felt her spirits inexorably lifting.

"Where are you off to?"

"I'm for McGrath's to order the meat for Sunday."

"Well can I suggest a grand detour then. I'd love to have a cupán té. I'm dying to find out what mischief you've been up to."

The look on Méabh's face made it clear that she was delighted to be rescued and they found their way together, arm in arm, to the tea rooms of the Lismore House Hotel.

As they walked into the tea rooms, the radiogram was playing Fred Astaire, the town's celebrity. Eileen caught Méabh by the waist and they both sashayed and waltzed their way to the table in tune with the sentiments and beat of 'They can't take that away from me' giggling provocatively, generating wide-eyed stares and some amused grins from those already seated.

"I haven't seen you in ages around the town. Have you moved?" Méabh asked as they sat down.

"No, not moved. I'm still in the cottage over the bridge, but I've a new job. I moved to Fermoy school last year and catch the train every day. But what about you, dear Méabh? I've often thought of you."

Tears began to well up in Méabh's eyes at this. She felt somehow as if the nightmare of the last two years had been interrupted and she was transported once again with a vision of optimism and hope, an incongruous sense that despite the boxed-in nature of her existence, here in front of her in beloved, sweet, gentle, Miss Barry, now to be called Eileen, was an acceptance, sensitivity, a welcoming of her whole, conflicted being that surely could be a passport to a life which she might endure, maybe even adore.

 The Drowning of Innocence

Eileen saw the tears and shadow pass over her dear young friend.

"Oh let's not talk about all that now. I have a better idea. Why can't we get away from the town tomorrow. I hate the enforced suffocating sombreness of Good Friday anyway. If you come to my place, I can make a picnic and we will walk along the Blackwater for the day. That will give us plenty of time to catch up away from prying eyes. For now, let's enjoy our tea."

The tea and hot scones arrived and they passed an hour together, parting with Good Friday fully planned. Méabh called at McGrath's to deliver the order and hardly noticed the journey home, revivified as she was by the encounter.

River Blackwater, Lismore

Good Friday, 4th April 1947

Somehow it was easier to talk as they walked side by side along the river. The steps they took, in synchronicity with their deepest heartbeats. Eileen put her arm through Méabh's as much for encouragement as warmth, the other arm looped around the picnic basket. The river flowed strongly beside them as the snow melted. They were alone with their reflections. The loamy soil pregnant with new life, the buds on branches forcing themselves to open against the intimidating cold. Spring finally emerging from the landscape as winter receded.

Eileen looked at Méabh and thought, as she often did, of her own child, just a few years Méabh's senior. While she had no way of providing comfort for her own in the storms and vicissitudes of life, she wanted with all her heart to give solace to this young woman who was clearly distressed. As they walked together arm in arm, Eileen thought of all the children born that morning and wished for them that they would be loved and would in turn give great joy to their mothers and fathers.

She listened intently as Méabh poured her heart out. The young woman was clearly adrift, without an anchor.

"When I saw you yesterday, Eileen," Méabh said tentatively, unaccustomed to the familiarity of calling her teacher by her first name, "It's as if the last two years hadn't happened and I was back dreaming again, full of hope for my future. But that's not what it's like every day. I'm usually under a terrible cloud. I can't seem to find my way out of it. And I have no confidence."

"What bothers you most?"

"Everything. I hate work even though I know I must go there. I feel like I am living a lie."

"Maybe you are."

Méabh was taken aback by the tender honesty of her companion.

"You know, one of the lovely things I remember about you was how fearless you were at expressing yourself in class. I loved watching you grapple with big ideas."

The Drowning of Innocence

"That's all gone now. I'm a continual stranger to myself these days. I don't know who I am anymore."

"Well, Méabh, we always have to work at who we are. We change and life, like art, throws up different challenges to overcome. I learnt that a long time ago from my Da."

"But everywhere I look, there seems no place for me."

"There's always a place for you. That's the first thing to get hold of. But it's rarely the one presented to you. Certainly not on a plate. Gosh, Méabh, if all I had was what was given to me by the Department of Education, my classroom would be the most stodgy place on earth."

"But you're different, Eileen. You're so confident."

Eileen laughed. "I feel the same way as you do Méabh. I have to fight my corner as well. All the time. And it mostly seems like a losing battle. When I was your age, I had so much faith, dreams for the future of our country and our place as women in it. But its been carefully stripped away. Step by step, year by year. We just need to look around us. Look at the Constitution. Us women are being carefully shepherded into the home and removed from being a part of things. I have to challenge these notions all the time in myself, quietly and strongly, so as not to surrender."

They had come to a bend in the river, a rocky outcrop, where its flow dropped ten feet over rapids. These reflections dominated their consciousness as they sat together on the rocks gazing into the current. Elm and Oak trees overhung the esplanade on the opposite bank in striking contrast; Elms with their tall confident arms reaching to the sky full of dreams for the future, like ancient heroes and heroines; Oaks, wizened and split, bending themselves to protect and cherish, their benign shapes for all the world like kindly 'Seanmháthreacha'. The river lived up to its name at this point. Its deep black mirrored surface, smooth as an oil slick as it approached the torrent of the rapids, echoed the shapes of the trees against the grey skies and provided an illuminating context for their reflections. Spring had come late, like the country itself, still mired in its long winter.

In their silence they were taken aback by a kingfisher exploiting the stillness of the water, flashes of aqua-blue, peacock green and rust exploding above the deep black of the river, sending spirals of glistening pearls into the air as it broke the surface. It was a numinous, intimate moment. The countryside and its beauty, the emerging spring screaming at them "Hope! Hope!"

Méabh was the first to break the silence.

"What's happened to us then, Eileen? Why aren't we up in arms about it all."

"Dear Méabh, It's 'up in arms' that has caused all this. The country has been traumatised. We can't underestimate the damage done by the civil war. Sure, there's people who have never spoken to one another since. Neighbours who will cross the street to avoid running into one another."

"I suppose you had to be alive then to realise the full brunt of it. I have an uncle, my dad's brother, a very qualified man, who couldn't get a job for years because he was a republican."

"There's many of them and the best disappeared to America." Eileen drew a deep breath at the thought of Micheál. But this was not a conversation for now and she quickly moved on.

"Everyone keeps their head down now. Sure, we're terrified the whole thing could erupt in minutes. I mean, look at the shame of us. The whole world giving everything to defend civilisation from fascism and here we were, us lot, neutral. Dev, to our eternal ignominy, sending his condolences to the German Embassy when he heard of Hitler's suicide. I cringe inside at the thought. But what's worse is that with us all in our corners, the Gombeens have come out and now rule the place."

"How do you keep going, Eileen, when you see all that?"

"I keep going because I have to, Méabh. For my Da, who believed in a different Ireland. Not this oppressive, pinched, priest-ridden state we have today."

"I suppose it's not only the effect of the civil war but the dominance of the church, telling us what to think, what to wear, how to behave. It all seems so false and hypocritical."

Their stroll had taken them to a bend in the river. They came across a vibrant meadow exposed to the open air. A thaw had taken hold weeks before at this spot and the riverbank was carpeted with late blooming snowdrops and early daffodils. The juxtaposition of their beauty against the dank earth, icy cold river and the snowcapped Knockmealdown mountains rising majestically

  The Drowning of Innocence

in the background was like an apparition.

Eileen took hold of Méabh and said,

"Do you know the Gerald Manley Hopkins poem 'God's Grandeur'?"

Méabh looked at her quizzically.

"The words of it haunt me with their transcendent, mysterious beauty. How does it go now, let me think."

Eileen composed herself and with a soft, enchanting voice recited it to Méabh and to the carpet of flowers arrayed before them,

> *"The world is charged with the grandeur of God.*
> *It will flame out, like shining from shook foil;*
> *It gathers to a greatness, like the ooze of oil*
> *Crushed. Why do men then now not reck his rod?*
> *Generations have trod, have trod, have trod;*
> *And all is seared with trade; bleared, smeared with toil;*
> *And wears man's smudge and shares man's smell: the soil*
> *Is bare now, nor can foot feel, being shod.*
>
> *And for all this, nature is never spent;*
> *There lives the dearest freshness deep down things;*
> *And though the last lights off the black West went*
> *Oh, morning, at the brown brink eastward, springs —*
> *Because the Holy Ghost over the bent*
> *World broods with warm breast and with ah! bright wings."*

"Gosh Eileen, That's beautiful."

"For years now, I've wanted to paint that poem. I set myself to begin continually and it always escapes me and shows me something new. I fail always. I think it has become my life's work to capture the extraordinary revelation it contains. Just coming on this meadow today reminds me of it again."

The walked on for a while absorbed in thought.

"What am I to do, Eileen? It all seems so overwhelming to me. I need work and the bargain I have to make seems that I must surrender my dreams. I need my own life to prosper, but all I'm told is that I have to find a man to prosper alongside. And, as you say, there's the Parish Priest standing over the town as judge and jury. None of it makes sense to me."

"Well you have to begin at the only place worth starting. And that's yourself. Your own make-up. What do your insides say about who you are. As likely as not, what lies there will be totally at odds with what is being demanded of you. I won't presume I know what drives the parish priest, or the government, or Dev, or 'JC' or even our families for that matter. But I don't have to accept what they come up with. They don't know me, like I know myself. I console myself all the time with the thought that I know more about me than they do about who I am. Why if it wasn't for the damage they are causing, I'd even feel sorry for the P.P., Dev and JC. They are so ignorant about what really matters. It's only me that can paint the picture of a life for myself. I'm not saying its easy and I suppose most people possibly give up and surrender to fit in. But, bless you, Méabh, that's never going to be a way for you to take."

"But all those dreams I had seem so fragile now, Eileen. Like a fantasy. I feel disconsolate even entertaining them."

"Well that's the crux right there, Méabh. You have to nurture them. You have to celebrate your difference. It's your very difference that is your precious gift to the world."

"But I'm really not anything like the others. I can't recognise myself in them. I used to love being with the girls. But they all seem a mystery to me now, so full of it all. Even if their jobs are boring, they can't wait to go dancing on Saturday night."

"But you like dancing."

"The truth is, Eileen, I don't have the same feelings they have for the boys and try and all as I have done, I don't seem to be able to manufacture them."

Eileen smiled at her.

"Well, dear Méabh, maybe that's because its girls you like and it's girls you are attracted to. You just haven't fallen in love yet."

Méabh blushed deeply, suddenly full of confusion, shocked by this outrageous comment from Eileen. At the same time, it conferred on her an inexorable peace, a sense of rightness, a safe landing, a comforting embrace. For the first time, she could see, could accept, that this was the cornerstone of all her misery. Her inability to give welcome to the essential difference in her

     The Drowning of Innocence

make-up was blocking her taking hold of her life. She felt an immense relief and tears welled up in her.

Eileen gave her a hug.

"Its something I have guessed about you. Your sensitivity and unique way of looking at things. And it's okay. There's a special place for unique standpoints. God knows, the country needs it."

"Thank you, Eileen. Gosh it makes me feel so different knowing someone else knows me, understands me and accepts me for who I am. Thank you."

"Ah sweet Méabh, it's nothing. Just don't let it circumscribe you and don't let people define you or categorise you. It's a precious thing for you to know and have for yourself and those who love you. Be careful where you share it. I fear the country is not ready for this yet."

The declaration and the now intimate vulnerability between them opened the day and their hearts to one another. They spoke about many things together, over their picnic lunch, during the rest of the walk. Eileen, in providing further reassurance and acceptance, also discovered a soul mate possessing the same burning vision for life passed on to her by her Da. The gap in years between them closed and they found themselves embarking on a rich companionship.

That day flowed into many hours they passed together, evenings and weekends, over the following year. Within six months Eileen had introduced Méabh to the curator of the Waterford Municipal Art Collection and Méabh was appointed as an assistant. Her world was transformed and magically, life and all its bounty opened up for her.

Mikey

3rd March 2012 at 21:05

To: Alannahmochroi@irl.ie   Cc: Mikey

Re: Hiya

Dear Alannah,

Siobhán gave me your email address when she sent me the postcard you found in the flea market addressed to my Dad. I was very touched that you made so much effort to find the rightful owner after all these years. There are very few people who would make that effort for a perfect stranger. Thank you so much.

To put your mind at rest, because Siobhán said you might be worried, I did know about Eileen but that's another story,

I am flying to Ireland this coming summer and wonder if we can meet up for a chat. I owe you a slap-up meal and I can come to you or you might be visiting Cork during that time. I am staying with Seanair.

Thank you again, Alannah and I hope we meet soon,

Kind regards, Mikey.

The Drowning of Innocence

Capuchin Monastery, Cork City

April 2012

As soon as she entered the hallway, Alannah was transported back in time. The highly polished, delicately patterned marble floor, the rich varnish of the elaborate, oakframed doorways, the sun lighting up the exquisite relief of the stained glass partitions was, on the one hand intimidating and on the other, warm, welcoming, guiding the heart to a place of peace, timelessness and tranquillity. She was enthralled. Her companion, Finbarr, as ever garrulous and witty, was endearing himself to the Friar assigned to help them in their quest.

Alannah had pursued the discovery of her birth grandparents with the Franciscans in Waterford.

"Yes," they had assured her, "the Friars had helped unmarried mothers at the Iveragh nursing home in the early part of the 20th century."

But they had no records that would assist her. It looked for all the world that she had once again drawn a blank. The Friar, himself, was helpful. He showed her a photograph of the twenty or so men who were part of the Order in Waterford at that time. There, in the midst of names listed underneath, 'Brother Paul' stood out, a gentle looking, older man with a rich beard.

"Oh, that's the man my Granny mentioned in a letter. What can you tell me about him?"

"Ah, Brother Paul. I think he's pretty famous, actually. A few years ago some research student at Trinity uncovered his story. He seems to have been a great networker and she gleaned a lot of detail of the social history of the time from his journals and letters. But he was only here a short time in 1923. He's part of the Cork Franciscans, really. We don't know much about him at all. I think you need to contact them if you want to find out more. I hope it all works out for you though and that you find your grandparents."

When she arrived in Cork she went to see Finbarr. As before, he came to her rescue.

"Era Alannah, that's no bother, like. The monks owe me a couple of favours. Sure, I'll ring them up now and we can make an appointment to see them. Does that sound good?"

They found themselves in the Friary and being led by a gentle monk to an office along a corridor of polished parquet; Statues of St Francis, The Christ Child of Prague and various dramatic religious paintings adding a secure foundation to the other-worldliness of the place. The office to which they were led was well furnished with a polished wooden table and comfortable chairs. Ranged around the walls were cabinets full of old, bound books and manuscripts. Their companion took some beautiful inlaid wooden boxes from a shelf and handed it to them.

"In here are all Brother Paul's papers and journals. You are very lucky. The student who unearthed his story a few years ago did a great job in ordering his heritage and the documents are beautifully kept."

Finbarr was already drawing folders carefully from a box as they both set to in anticipation and glee.

"Would you like a cup of tea while you are working?" "That would be grand."

It was a couple of hours later, when Finbarr raised his head. "What's your adoptive Granny's surname?" "Morley." "I thought so. Have a look at this."

He handed over a carefully scripted letter to Alannah. With a thrill of recognition, Alannah saw her Granny's handwriting.

Brother Paul,
Franciscan Friary,
Liberty Street,
Cork
6th December 1922

19, St. Otteran Place,
Waterford

Dear Brother Paul,

We received your letter yesterday. Oh how glad we are that you found us and grateful to Reverend Philpott for putting you in touch. He has sensitively known of our heartache for some years and our desire and failure in trying for a baby.

We would love to meet you. I think that's the best way for you and the girl to decide if we are the right people to adopt her child. It's hard for us to keep our emotions in check, so I hope we can meet soon. Thank you for thinking of us.

Elizabeth and Trevor Morley

                        The Drowning of Innocence

A rush of adrenalin coursed through Alannah. She felt nauseous with excitement. Here, definitive proof that they were on the right track in identifying Brother Paul. She looked at the documents still awaiting their perusal.

"Oh Finbarr, I feel sick with excitement. Thank you so much for helping me."

"Take it easy, girl, now. We don't need you passing out. Let's just keep it slow and steady. Maybe we'll take a break for lunch, get your strength back and we can continue in an hour. It'll give you a chance to absorb it all. Get your balance back, like. A slow discovery will be all the richer for it."

When they were outside, Alannah appreciated the wise counsel Finbarr had given. She realised she was worked up and the fresh air helped to calm her down.

"Shall we head over to Fellini's. Let's make them think we're an item. Sure, they've been feeling sorry for me for years and it will give them a great boost to see me with a gorgeous woman like yourself."

Finbarr's company, as always, lifted her spirits as they made the short distance to Patrick Street and onto Carey's Lane. Fellini's was full with a vibrant, animated crowd but they found a nice table near the window together. Alannah thought wistfully of the morning six months earlier when she had first met Finbarr.

"How ironic. That the route I took to return the postcard started in the same cafe that I hope to find my real grandmother. The world is really a small place."

"There's no doubt Cork is like a small village anyway. Sure that's why I love it and have never thought of leaving it."

"I didn't tell you, by the way, that Mikey wrote me an email. Micheál's son, from the postcard. He's coming to Cork in the summer and wants to meet up. He was delighted to receive the postcard and seemingly has a story to tell."

"That'll be grand, Alannah. I'm so glad that the fears you had of upsetting apple carts have been allayed. Sure its a lovely thing you did and I'm sure he's very grateful for it."

"I'll come over when he comes, anyway and maybe we can all meet up. The gang of Sherlocks!"

The hot tea and scones sent them back refreshed to their task. Alannah set about reading and reviewing, curbing the mounting excitement and apprehension building inside her. The late spring sunshine graced the room in the afternoon with a warm glow when her gaze was consumed by a letter taken from a small folder. Immediately, the handwriting seemed familiar. When she was halfway through the letter, she glanced down at the signature. "Eileen." Her heart began to ache at the coincidence.

Alannah could see the letter was sent from Sherkin island on Christmas Day 1922. The heartrending revelation it contained of Eileen's momentous decision to hand over her child sucked the air out of her and left her faint.

With enormous difficulty, she battled with her emotions. The quiet dawning realisation that the script was the same as that elegant hand that had written her treasured postcard. When she read *then there is the stone'*, she broke down completely. Great sobs of anguish exploded from deep inside her. The weight of a story buried deeply for nearly a century erupted in volcanic proportion through her frame. 'Eileen is my grandmother.' 'Eileen is my grandmother.' 'Her Ma's name Rosaleen.' She didn't know whether she was exclaiming it aloud or trying it out in her mind. She took the stone from her purse and held it fiercely, the final revelation of its ontology laid out before her on the page. Finbarr was startled into action by her manner and yet powerless in the face of this outpouring of grief. It was all he could do to move his chair closer and hold her hand.

"Oh Alannah, what is the matter?"

She pushed the letter towards him and he read it slowly, digesting its content.

"So this is your Granny. At long last, eh?"

"You don't see, Finbarr. Its Eileen. The Eileen who wrote the postcard. It's all too much for me to take in."

"Hold on, Alannah, mo chroí. That's a stretch. You can't know that for sure. There are many years between the two events."

"I can see the handwriting. It's the same. I know it."

"Bless you Alannah, Let's not get ahead of ourselves. We need to be sure

                          The Drowning of Innocence

about something like that."

Strangely, as if to emphasise this point, Finbarr's eyes were drawn to another letter peeping out of the top of the same folder. Astonishingly and with ultimate irony his eyes were captured by the first line which read *"I suppose this will come as a shock to you to see my handwriting on the envelope."*

"What's this, mo chroí?"

He reached over her and drew the second letter from the folder. Sitting close to one another, they read together with increasing trepidation and dread. Finbarr instinctively placed his arm around Alannah to hold her and give her comfort so that she did not have to bear the dawning realisation singularly and on her own.

As they scanned the letter together, a growing realisation transfixed them. The coincidence too great. The incongruous revelation that Eileen was her grandmother, Micheál her grandfather; Alannah related to Seanair and Siobhán; Mikey her mother's half-brother. And the staggering disclosure of Eileen's brother, Mattie's death; A painful mystery shrouded in time but lain as a cleaver at Micheál's door setting in train the years of unresolved passion she had first recognised in the postcard. Alannah found it hard to breathe.

After a time she stood up and paced about the room. Up and down, desperate to find a place to store, absorb this revelation. It was something for which she was completely unprepared. As indeed was Finbarr, who remained quietly rooted to the chair, his eyes anxiously trained on his friend.

After a long period of time, Alannah spoke.

"This is a lot for me to get used to, Finbarr. I hope you understand."

"Please Alannah. Its OK. I will do whatever you want."

"Well, I guess I need to be alone now. And I also need to find out as much as I can. I can't go to Seanair or Siobhán or indeed write to Mikey in this raw state. I need to see what more I can find out from the journals. It feels the right thing that I do this slowly over the next few days. Do you mind if I do that alone?"

"Not a bit of it, girl. I completely understand. I will speak to the Friar and help set it all up. But I think it's wise you take a break and start again tomorrow morning."

He stood and went over to her and gave her a reassuring hug.

They left the Friary soon after. Alannah returned to her hotel. She spent the evening and much of the night tossing thoughts around her head. There were moments of consolation. She was in awe at the coincidence that led her to find the postcard. But these were besieged by thoughts of her mother. How sweet her real name; Rosaleen. She repeated it over and over, almost meeting her Ma again for the first time. How Ma would love to know all this, no matter how painful. What assurance it would have given her that she was a desired and loved child. Then thoughts of Eileen, her wonderful dignity, humanness and courage. And what had happened to Micheál? The thoughts raged and trampled all over her consciousness, exhausting her and placing her in turmoil.

Over the next week, she returned each day to the Friary. The place itself gave her rest. She opened Brother Paul's journals tenderly. He became her companion as through his words she became aware of the dramatic events of the time; Eileen and Micheál's devotion to him particularly in the aftermath of the McSwiney funeral; The tragedies that had befallen Micheál in losing his mother, brother and father in so short a space of time; The deep love and romance of her grandparents cut short by the awful tragedy (she could barely absorb it) of Micheál slaying Mattie, his best friend, his childhood companion; The manhunt for Micheál on Collin's death and his forced emigration. Slowly Paul took her by the hand and gracefully, eloquently opened up the story of her origin.

There were moments when Paul's journal overwhelmed her. A particular conversation he had with her grandparents on which he reflected: *"I worry for Eileen and Micheál. They are full of ideals and I'm afraid for them. My life teaches me that they may come a cropper. I hope not."*

And then later on the day he bade Micheál farewell as he left for New York: *"I don't know how I made it back from Cobh today after seeing Micheál off. My heart is full of pain when I think of the three of them; Mattie now dead and Micheál fleeing for his life and no-one with any idea of where Eileen has disappeared to. The price a nation has to pay for its own intolerance is tragic and inevitable and this war of family against family, brother against brother has surely taken its full measure on these three childhood companions."*

Finally the passage she could barely read: *"Today is the saddest day of my life. Today I watched and tried to comfort young Eileen as she handed over her baby, just a few hours old, for adoption. Oh I am finding this so difficult to reconcile. All I can do is beseech God that both will survive it."*

                    The Drowning of Innocence

She had to be kind to herself those days. Wave after wave of emotion broke over her as a catharsis. She got to know the people of the story, her own flesh and blood and fell deeply in love with them, with their vision, passion, dignity and self sacrifice. Through all the emotional turbulence, a quiet gratitude and kindliness emerged.

At the end of the week, she felt strong enough to meet Seanair's family and talk to them about what she had discovered. They listened with avid attention, acknowledging the filling of gaps in their own understanding. When she had finished they, as one, reached across to her and embraced her as their own.

Lismore, County Waterford

Easter Monday, 1949

The demons which had haunted Eileen for years were in full sway. The deep pain of all her losses was cavernous. She had told herself for years that she must carry on, faithful to her Da's heritage and devote her life to building the Ireland they had both carried in their hearts. This conviction had enabled her to ride the tumultuous waves of grief that had overtaken her over the years when she thought about her child, gone from her, never forgotten, leaving behind a vacuum impossible to fill. And the moments when she had pined for Micheál, for the sweet, tender love they had shared, their togetherness in the vision they had for their lives.

The memory of her Da and the imperative he had passed on was now tenuous. The bulwark she had held fast to, embraced, now eroded as she witnessed the suffocation of her country now firmly in the grasp of a fundamentalist faith, its politicians firmly in its trawl. The pinched, oppressive ethos and mentality of the fledgling State trapping its citizens into conformity and silence. A long, long way from the place they had dreamed of years before.

She was overcome by a deep sadness and had entered a dark place. Over the previous week, she had painted an image of Guagán Barra on an ordinary plain, white postcard. Beckoning from memory, she sought to capture the serenity of the place and the context it had provided for the romance and love that had grown between her and Micheál. It took all the energy she had left to capture those moments on the simple, stark card. It was to be her gift to him, a last act providing completion to their blighted life.

Last night she had heard the corncrake call for the first time that year. Its incessant mournful croak of desperation for a mate to share its life. Memories flooded her being and she quietly sobbed to expiate them, her pillow wet through when she finally woke from a fitful sleep.

When she arose, she took the card from the drawer in which it had been placed and wrote carefully on the back the sentiments that had accompanied her in her odyssey over the previous twenty seven years. Tears flowed from her as she wrote ' *You are in my heart always. Not a day goes by when I don't think of you.*' Carefully she wrote his name and the Carey's Lane address. The evocation of the place, the memories of Cork and the halcyon days before the eruption of violence, submerged her deeper into the darkness into which she had been plunged. This Easter Monday, when Ireland became a republic

　　　　　The Drowning of Innocence

wholly at odds with what they had dreamed.

With supreme effort and will power, she made her way from her cottage into the town, like a ghost appearing among the living, and posted the card with no knowledge of its final resting place. She returned home with a fierce will to follow the course on which she was now determined.

In her cottage, she tidied her life, making everything neat and proper. Her clothes were all laundered and there was no food left to rot or decay. She took the rope which was to be her final intimate companion and wove a hangman's knot on one end. She did this with great care and attention making two loops, delicately winding the loose end of the rope around the smaller loop, securing its end by feeding through the bottom loop, pulling on the top loop to finish this aesthetic knot.

Then she took her small kitchen table and chair into the garden and positioned them under the mature apple tree which had provided her with fruit for years. Apples she had expertly converted into turnovers and tarts which had been offered to those who had called at her door.

She did not want to contaminate her house by her decision to end her life. She clambered up onto the table and now tied the rope expertly with a clove hitch around the most mature branch, carefully measuring the length of the drop. She placed the noose around her neck, feeling its smooth texture against her skin. Then, uttering a prayer for her lost daughter and all those she was leaving behind, she kicked the table away from her.

She fell the two feet until the rope seized about her neck, biting into her larynx and cutting her off from life.

A strangulated cry, deep and piercing, like that of a stuck pig, emanated from her throat, disturbing the garden and surrounding countryside. The nesting birds, occupied in preparing for their offspring, were shocked into flight and rose in a tumult into the skies, their trajectory and cries disturbing the tranquillity of this rural idyll.

Méabh woke with an indefinable sense of anxiety and apprehension. She couldn't explain it. Over the Easter weekend she had hosted a wonderful exhibition of the artists the Municipal collection had gathered, Jack Yeats, Maurice MacGonigal and extraordinary stained glass pieces by Evie Hone. The exhibition marking the momentous weekend that was in it. The reception and enthusiasm for the work was encouraging and she had gone to sleep on Sunday night exhausted and content.

This made her waking in disarray so unusual. Try as she did, she couldn't shake it off. She washed, dressed, ate her breakfast and set about writing her thoughts on the exhibition.

But her mind was utterly distracted, her spirit deeply disturbed. Eileen kept emerging in her thoughts, almost beckoning her. She hadn't seen her friend for a few days and this recurring anxiety about her was insistent. In the end and close to midday, she decided she must call on her, if only to eliminate this preoccupation.

She walked down the stairs and found her mother in the kitchen.

"I'm off out, Ma, to pop and see Eileen."

"Oh my God, you and Eileen. You're obsessed with her. Why don't you give it a rest. I've loads of things for you to do here."

"I'll come back later and help. I want to do this first."

"There you go. Always the same. Sure if that woman had let you alone, where would you be now instead of wasting your time in that Art world where nothing will come of you."

"Oh Ma, I can't get into that now. I'll see you later."

It was as if the conversation gave additional impulse to her quest to see her friend. The anxiety had increased and she found herself speeding down Main Street, turning into Ferry Lane and over the Blackwater to Eileen's. Once she had given into her apprehensive thoughts, her pace picked up and she was almost running when she reached the top of the boreen. All was quiet, eerily quiet, she would later recollect, when she reached Eileen's door.

Suddenly she heard this awful squealing from the back of the house, followed by birds taking flight in panic. She hadn't time to digest her alarm but raced into the back garden. Her legs almost gave way from underneath her

 The Drowning of Innocence

when she caught sight of Eileen hanging from the apple tree, her legs and arms given over to involuntary spasms.

Years later, when she would wake in terror in the middle of the night, she could never explain to herself what happened next.

With a strength and presence of mind borrowed from where she could not say, she rushed to Eileen and grabbed her around the thighs and lifted her. She held her like this for what appeared ages but was likely only seconds, before intuitively and with a skill and dexterity she could never replicate, hooked her foot under the overturned table and hoisted and flipped it onto its legs. Then she climbed onto it, all the time holding her beloved friend in her arms and found herself standing beside her on the table. The rope was now slack above Eileen's head as she adroitly removed it from around her neck.

She slumped to her knees in a pieta-like stance, embracing the lifeless body. It was only then that waves of pain and heartbreak overtook her.

"Oh Eileen, how could you leave me? How could you leave me?"

Surprisingly and unexpectedly, a great explosion of air was sucked into Eileen's chest, followed by a stark opening of her eyes.

"Oh Eileen." Méabh held her friend fast in an embrace and shook with great sobs of relief.

They stayed together in the same position on the table for a long time. Eventually, feeling the cold seep into her body, she, supporting her friend, took her into the house and bedroom and laid her tenderly on her bed. She brought some water and later made soup.

In the afternoon, she called the doctor who pronounced Eileen out of any danger and gave Méabh some ointment to apply to the almost imperceptible bruising on the skin of her friend's neck.

These moments of tender care became the progenitor of a deepening of their relationship. They became inseparable companions. During the months and years that followed, Eileen opened things that were hidden, locked away, kept in isolation. The fierce energy, with which she had held herself together, kept her pain from breaking lose and riding rough-shod over her life, dissolved. The telling as of the breaking of a dam of silence, washing over both of them as a life-affirming deluge.

There were days and nights when shock waves of grief overtook her in the telling, like the terror of flash flooding. Méabh for her part strong alongside her, holding her as Eileen broke against her. Sometimes she provoked Eileen with kind questions cutting into the cavernous darkness of her sorrow, like a skilled surgeon, removing the cancerous growths which had sought to devour her wholesome flesh and spirit.

Méabh was entranced by the beauty, grace, courage and generosity of her friend and told her so. In the letting go, Eileen transmuted her love, longing and dreams for her daughter Rosaleen, Micheál, Da, Mattie into rebuilding a life with Méabh which dug for beauty and creativity.

The telling recovered for Eileen the lyrical companionship she had shared with her Da, remembering for the first time in years the intimacy of their shared love of life, unencumbered by memories of his untimely murder.

And it gave back to her Micheál, her beautiful man and the days of their youth when she drank him in, thrived on his steady devotion, lived for his voice and touch. Their parting then reduced to an event which had taken him away and no more.

And lastly, in Méabh, she became reconciled to her decision, all those years ago, to let her daughter go free, away from the blight that her people had brought upon themselves. Méabh embodied hope, that somewhere, out there in her own beloved land, her daughter was forging her own life. If blessings and wishes were the substance of that life, Rosaleen, her dear Rosaleen would not be found wanting.

Some years later, they opened a gallery together in Waterford, gathering strength from their shared and complementary appreciation for the young artists who were finding their feet. Giving those artists a space in which to work and exhibit. What grew in their midst, under their kindly influence, became a thing of beauty which lasted until their final separation, in the early Nineties when Eileen passed away in her sleep, finally and gracefully at peace.

  The Drowning of Innocence

Waterford

10th June 2012

Alannah gazed at the two of them, Seanair and Siobhán, as they walked towards her across the car park and felt once again this newly-developed yet indefinable closeness and bond.

"It's so lovely to see you again," she said as she gave them warm, welcoming hugs.

Something had changed for her over the months since she had claimed her grandparents. As if she had been knitted back together, even though she had never noticed any unravelling. A kind of homecoming.

They fell in step with one another as they made their way to Gallways cafe. As they were seated, Seanair said, "Mikey is flying in next month and we know you are coming over to stay with us then. But I wanted to talk to you first. To prepare you."

"Oh really, why is that?"

"Well you'll never believe it, but after you came and told us all about your discoveries in April, I began to look through my Ma's old stuff again and I found this."

Seanair produced a battered-looking package from his bag. "I have no idea how I missed it before and maybe it's as well. Somehow I'm able to take it in now. Better than I could before anyway, that's for sure. I knew immediately it was something you should have. There's a letter in it sent by your Granddad to my Ma very late in his life."

"Gosh," said Alannah, "That floors me. It will be the very first time I come in direct contact with who he was. I hope I will be alright."

"Well, you have shown so much courage before now, Alannah, that I have no doubts for you. It's something you should have. It's yours really, girl, far more than it is ours."

"I'm not sure I want to read it here though, Seanair. I'm not sure I can trust myself. This whole thing has surprised me continuously and shook my emotions. I'm sure you understand."

"Indeed I do, mo chroí. Sure, I don't see any of this as an accident. It's almost like a vocation for you now. A calling, shall we say. To make sense out of our past. And find a way to bring it forward, I suppose too."

He handed the package to her.

Alannah could not contain herself and opened it. She drew out a well-thumbed letter and surprisingly an old music cassette fell out onto the table. She was shocked to the core to see it was The Pogues' album 'Rum, Sodomy and the Lash'.

"Gosh. Now that is something I never expected. The Pogues?"

"Us too. Your Granddad was not carved from a usual block. It's all explained in the letter."

"I love The Pogues. They carried me along for years. I can remember so well when this album came out. It was their second, I think. The title a reference to Churchill's description of life in the Navy. I think Shane McGowan was having a dig. Well, another mystery. I can't wait to find out more."

"Well, take it with you. Your Granddad talks in his letter about my two uncles, Charlie and Claude. Your grand-uncles. Claude died when I was a teenager, you know. A shell of a man he was at the end when I think of it. He just slipped away. A very young age to go really. I think he wasn't fifty. Very hard on Ma."

"I know a little bit about him from Brother Paul's journals."

"I think the letter will help you learn more and also prepare you for Mikey's visit next month. I'll say no more and leave it with you, anyway. I'll be thinking of you as you open it."

"Thanks Seanair, you're very kind."

"Not at all girl. Anyway now, let's see what kind of chocolates they have here then. See if they're up to scratch. Eh?"

They passed the rest of the morning catching up and in the afternoon, on that beautiful June day, explored the Viking quarter of the city and wandered around the old port of Waterford. It was early evening when Siobhán and Seanair took the car journey back to Cork.

Alannah waited until late evening when the house was quiet to open the

The Drowning of Innocence

parcel. She sat in her comfortable armchair, looking out on the back garden as the sun sank and a warm glow enveloped the fuchsia bushes covering its perimeter. She poured herself a whiskey for sustenance as she read,

East 36th Street,

Marine Park,

Brooklyn

12th September 1986

Dearest Joan,

I hope this letter finds you in good health although we are all getting near the end now and feeling the aches and pains of it. I'm sorry I haven't written much recently but I do think of you often. You know it has been so different for me here since Mikey has come back to himself. I'm only sorry that this didn't happen while his dear mother was alive. I blame myself a lot for his woes. It was never easy for me to talk about things when he was growing up and I think I wasn't the best father to him. But all that's forgotten now and the lovely thing is, he forgives me and we have been able to talk a lot over the past couple of years.

Something amazing happened to me a few weeks ago and that's why I'm writing to you now. You will also wonder about the enclosed music cassette by The Pogues. I know in Ireland you have heard a lot of their stuff on the radio and I hear they are not everbodys' cup of tea. Ah well.

So what am I doing sending you the cassette? Well, as I said, a few weeks ago, Johnny Maloney, you remember me telling you about him, asked me to a concert in Webster Hall. I know, me?! At my age?! He knew the band well and had talked to them about me and they were wanting me to play along with them on a few of their numbers. To honour the old days I think. When they brought me onto the stage, sure there were those in the crowd who remembered me from sessions in Celtic Hall years ago and they gave me a right welcome. It was a moment to remember, alright. Great fun.

The Pogues have so much energy about them and it's great to hear some of the old tunes get a new lease of life the way they play them. The young people certainly enjoy it anyway. Mikey, bless him, down there in the crowd hopping around like a hare.

They asked me to play the bodhrán on "An Maidrín Rua" and "The Kerry Polka". What craic it was. Sure I beat the ould thing with all the energy that was left in me. A last hurrah, so to speak. And bless them, those lads, they were so kind and respectful to

me. It was lovely up there on the stage again playing and the crowd of young people hopping away below us.

I left the stage after that and there was a cup of tea waiting for me in the wings. It was there that my real story begins. Very soon afterwards, the lads started to sing a song I had not heard before. It's called 'And the band played Waltzing Matilda'. It's on the tape. As you are reading this letter I'd like you to find it and put it on and share this moment with me. Do you know, I swear it was the energy of The Pogues, their raucous, almost irreverent interpretation of the old music that set the scene for what happened. With the greatest tenderness and sensitivity, the lead singer sang the song. It was an achingly beautiful moment that will live with me now till the end.

The song speaks for itself. It brought Gallipoli to me in a way that I have not experienced before. Charlie and Claude back in front of me, after all these years and as I listened great waves of memories swept up in me and I started to cry. You know I don't think I ever really cried for either of them and this was the moment. It was kind of a holy moment really. I felt so in touch with them.

Since then I have felt so much better, like I've been cleansed. It's like I made peace with what happened to our brothers after all these years. I came to understand the agony of Claude's life after Gallipoli and his sad, early death years ago. I know it must have been so hard for you and I am also writing to you to thank you for what you and Seán did for him. Providing him a home and safe place.

I hope it's alright sending this to you now after all this time. That it won't open up old wounds for you. We lived in such strange times, Joan and you have been our rock and strength through it and I am so so grateful to you.

I love you so much.

Your dear brother,

Micheál

Alannah read and re-read the letter. Her Granddad. Her flesh and blood. There on the page. She was touched by his honesty and humanity. And was amused at the idea of him playing on the stage with Shane MacGowan. That was something to recount down the pub or over the dinner table. She didn't remember the track he was talking about. She also didn't have a tape player in the house. This was the first time in the midst of all the turmoil and emotions that she had gone through in the previous two months, that she had thought about her two grand-uncles. And the pain her Grandpa must have gone through because of what happened to them.

     The Drowning of Innocence

She had never really given much thought to the First World War. Just remembered years ago seeing "Oh, What a Lovely War' in the cinema and being energised by it. That film had meant more in the context of protest movements, though - Vietnam and Ban the Bomb and all that, than to get her thinking on the toll the Great War had taken.

To honour both men now, her relatives, she knew she must take her time over this. To get some understanding of what they had been swept up into. She put the letter and package away and retired to bed, full of the extraordinary trauma that her family had lived through.

Over the next fortnight, she read and watched as much as she could about the Great War, absorbing its hopelessness and carnage. Her great-uncles in the midst of it, as so many of their countrymen, paying a huge price.

Then she felt ready, as her Granddad had done, to pay tribute to them. She found The Pogues version of 'And the band played Waltzing Matilda' on YouTube and carrying her family and her countrymen in her heart, she listened to the words,

> *"When I was a young man I carried my pack*
> *And I lived the free life of a rover*
> *From the Murray's green basin to the dusty outback*
> *I waltzed my Matilda all over*
> *Then in nineteen fifteen my country said Son*
> *It's time to stop rambling 'cause there's work to be done*
> *So they gave me a tin hat and they gave me a gun*
> *And they sent me away to the war*
>
> *And the band played Waltzing Matilda*
> *As we sailed away from the quay*
> *And amidst all the tears and the shouts and the cheers*
> *We sailed off to Gallipoli*

The sepia tinted images of the soldiers in tenches combined with Shane McGowan's rough voice gave a trenchant poignancy to the words.

> *How well I remember that terrible day*
> *When the blood stained the sand and the water*
> *And how in that hell that they called Suvla Bay*
> *We were butchered like lambs at the slaughter*
> *Johnny Turk he was ready, he primed himself well*

He showered us with bullets and he rained us with shells
And in five minutes flat he'd blown us all to hell
Nearly blew us right back to Australia

And the band played Waltzing Matilda
As we stopped to bury our slain
And we buried ours and the Turks buried theirs
And we started all over again

As the instruments sensitively joined McGowan's lonely voice, she imagined her Granddad sitting at the back of the stage, memory washing over him.

Now those who were living, did their best to survive
In a mad world of dust, blood and fire
And for seven long weeks I kept myself alive
While the corpses around me piled higher
Then a big Turkish shell knocked me arse over tit
And when I awoke in my hospital bed
And saw what it had done, Christ, I wished I was dead
Never knew there were worse things than dying

And no more I'll go waltzing Matilda
to the green bushes so far and near
For to hang tents and pegs, a man needs two legs
No more waltzing Matilda for me

So they collected the cripples, the wounded, the maimed
And they shipped us back home to Australia
The legless, the armless, the blind and insane
Those proud wounded heroes of Suvla
And as our ship pulled into Circular Quay
I looked at the place where me legs used to be
And thank Christ there was nobody waiting for me
To grieve and to mourn and to pity

Vividly the anguish of her great-uncle Claude inhabited the verses as she absorbed the pain he must have felt at seeing his brother and so many others taken in a futile battle. The irony of taking a simple joyous song as Waltzing Matilda and turning into this corruscating judgement on the futility of war was not lost on her.

 The Drowning of Innocence

Alannah played and re-played the track, trying to absorb its impact on her Granddad, across the miles, across the years. There was something extraordinary taking shape inside her. She began to imagine Micheál. He became someone to her, flesh and blood. She could feel his pain, and revel in his sensitivity and openness.

She loved the fact that he was active enough, he must have been in his eighties, to put himself on stage for a concert in New York. She also saw that he must have been a force in the city in his prime, keeping the old tunes alive. Of consequence even when they had fallen out of fashion. Bless him. He was some man.

She had a deep hunger to know him better. She was excited now to meet Mikey (his son after all) and to hear more about this man who had come into her life. Only another week's wait and she would be able to travel across to Cork to meet him.

Fitzgerald Park,Cork City

16th July 2012

The moment seemed magical to Alannah. All the more so because it could not have been more ordinary. Here sitting on a bench on the banks of the River Lee in Fitzgerald Park. Her Uncle Mikey beside her. They had escaped from everybody to be alone. The river glistened in the July sunshine. On its other bank they could see a heron, wading silently, his movements imperceptible as he fished in the shallow water. That bank rose up towards Sunday's Well, the stately homes conferring a sense of decorum on the city, while at their back in the park, children could be heard as they negotiated the swings and slides of the playground, their voices singing, rings of laughter, shouts of glee. Perfect. She drew a deep breath signifying contentment.

There was something extraordinarily familiar about Mikey when she was introduced to him as his niece. Peculiar, their respective ages made them more like siblings and that is how Alannah now saw him. As the brother she never had. He had deep lines on his handsome face, furrows which seemed to indicate a life lived the hard way. His striking blue eyes marked him immediately as a Hays.

"There are so many things I want to ask you, so many things I want to know." Her eagerness charmingly transparent.

"Fire away, Alannah. That's why I'm here."

"What was he like, your Da?"

"Oh gosh, how to describe him. Well, when I was growing up he always seemed a mystery to me. I would say I loved him of course. But now I understand I didn't really know him. He was a gentle man. Always kind. Considerate. But he was also very quiet. He kept everything inside. I know that now but didn't then of course. He met my mother very late really. He was in his mid-forties and I was the only child."

"You say you knew about Eileen of the post card. How did he tell you about her? Do you mind me asking? I was nervous, as you know, when I passed on the card to you."

"Well, he didn't tell me about her until very late. Until we really connected. At the end. By then mother had died and there was just the two of us. It took a lot for us to find one another."

          The Drowning of Innocence

"He mentions that in the letter. He says something like 'you had come back'. What does he mean by that? Had you gone away? Did you have a quarrel?

Mikey's face became sombre.

"Oh dear, sorry Mikey. I didn't want to touch on a raw nerve. We can skip it if you want."

"No, it's fine, Alannah. I want to tell you. It's very important for you if you want to get to know not only Dad but also me."

He sighed deeply, looked across the river and took in its restorative, soothing presence.

"I was lost for a long time. I don't talk about it any more now. The telling of it not helpful at all. It would just keep the destructive feelings alive. But I feel different talking to you about it. You see, my lostness was connected to not being able to know him, bond with him when I was growing up. I could see he was some kind of elevated figure among the Irish in New York. A war hero, I guess. He was a hero to me anyway."

He stopped for a moment. The memory of his Dad suddenly vibrant in the telling of their life together to his Granddaughter.

"I used to think he had some mysterious quality that I sought after. So in 1966 I enlisted in the Marines. I wasn't drafted. Mother and he were furious of course. They couldn't understand what I had done. They felt certain I could have escaped the draft."

There was edginess to him as he recounted his story, almost breathlessness. Alannah became conscious of the enormous effort it took for him to continue.

"You were self willed as a teenager then," she said in an effort to lighten the mood.

"Well it wasn't as simple as that. You have to remember Jack Kennedy. The influence he had on all of us. I was completely captivated. This young, dynamic, charismatic, handsome, Irish Catholic striding into our midst. Making us feel tall and proud for the very first time. He filled me to the brim. That speech, you remember it. 'Ask not what your country can do for you - ask what you can do for your country.' It reverberated through me. As an impressionable young teenager, I was won over. Gosh, Alannah, it was the age

of innocence. Camelot. A time when choices seemed so simple and
uncomplicated for a young, Irish, New York born and bred, Catholic boy.
When my time came in '66, I felt I could do nothing else but enlist."

"So that meant you went to Vietnam?"

"Yes, three tours. I thought that I was following Dad too of course, his
example. That he would be proud of me, serving my country and all. In truth,
I didn't know him at all. It broke his heart, but he couldn't say anything to
me."

He let out a deep sigh. The effort of remembering eating into his spirit.

"Of course, I realise now, that he had been traumatised by his own
experience in Ireland. In those days, nobody recognised PTSD and he had to
get on with it himself. Find a life for himself. Bottle it up, I guess."

"And you, what about you Mikey? Was that the breaking of your
relationship? It must have been terrible."

"No, they were good to me. They always were. I always knew I had a
loving home and two gracious parents. They were always there for me. But I
think what I did drained the life out of them. Mother, certainly. I don't blame
myself anymore. But it was tough."

Alannah reached across and grasped both his hands. The big man softened
as she held him. They sat there on the bench like this for a long time.

"Vietnam changed me completely. I went away when I was just nineteen, a
kid really. I came back and I felt fifty. It's hard to recover when the defining
moments of your life happen before you know what life is about. When there,
I was mostly on long range reconnaissance patrols, my senses on red alert the
whole time. It became impossible to relax. Indeed I hated relaxing. Made me
too vulnerable. You know, I used to volunteer to go on patrols because that
was one way of making sure I was always alert. I hated the coming down."

He hadn't thought or talked about this for years. His face changed in the
telling. Alannah noticed him as he twisted his hands, alternatively pressing a
thumb into the opposite palm and massaging the back of his hand with his
fingers, comforting himself.

"They gave us amphetamines to keep us awake. On night patrol, I felt I
could literally penetrate the dark. You see Alannah, when you hunt men,

                     The Drowning of Innocence

everything else pales into insignificance. I was addicted to the hunt."

"Did you see your family when you were home on leave?"

"In the beginning, yes. But then it became impossible. It became inconceivable to be sober in America. Everyone else was walking around doing ordinary things as if everything was normal, OK, Cool. Me I was walking around with my eyes out on stalks. I couldn't do it. So I took to alcohol and drugs to deal with it. After that, it became unthinkable to visit them. I didn't see them for years."

"Oh I'm so sorry to hear that, Mikey. That's so sad."

"It's the way it is, Alannah. I've come to terms with it now."

"Listen, do you think we've talked enough about it for today? I think I've put you through too much."

"No dear. I can only do this once. This is the one chance. If I don't tell you today, you'll never hear it and that's not fair on you."

"Thank you. But you must stop if it becomes too much."

She broke off, gazing at him to take in his response.

"I want to continue."

"OK. Thanks."

She drew a deep breath.

"How did you find your way back when you were that far gone? What happened to you?"

He had been used to people wanting to hear these tales. Voyeurs, those who wanted to hear a good yarn so that they could recount it themselves in a bar somewhere or around a dinner table, to impress. Indeed he had used it himself, elaborate versions of it, to get a woman into bed. He wasn't proud of that. Somehow with Alannah, his niece, it all seemed different. Cleansing, cathartic.

"Well after Vietnam, I disappeared for years. Living in Oregon. In the woods a lot of the time. Hiding from life, I guess. I was a drifter really. Taking short term jobs, my life consisted of getting wasted on drink and drugs and bar room brawls. Trying to escape the demons in my head, I guess. The dreaded flashbacks.

He broke off as two teenagers swept by them on skateboards, the suddenness of the action, the thunder of the wheels on the path emphasising the unpredictability of the events he was describing.

"The strange thing is that during that time, I looked back on 'Nam as the best time in my life, the time when I felt useful, alive even and I would have gone back there in a heartbeat. Return to the edge, I guess."

He looked at her and took in the quizzical expression on her face. Usual, he thought, no-one ever understands that sentiment.

"I did go to Mam's funeral, but I wasn't really there. She died a young woman comparatively. Sixty, she was. Couldn't face any of that. I think that must have been very difficult for Pop. He had lost the two of us then."

Alannah took in the unbearable sadness of this and placed her hand on his arm. A gesture of compassion.

"I had a good friend through it all though. That's the great thing about "Vets". He took me under his wing for years. It was a very slow and painful process for him but he eventually persuaded me to go to a veteran outreach centre. There, with help from some great people, I slowly put my life back together."

"When was this and were you able to see your Dad then?"

"It was 1984. Not in the beginning, I couldn't. That would have been too much. But in the end, I did develop enough confidence to go home. The man I found there was completely different to the man I left. He also had changed. We spent long hours with one another, talking deeply about things. There was a lot of tears. He had also come to realise the effect of his own involvement in war. He told me he hated all that adulation from the Irish exiles. And that was why he had been quiet. He was deeply sorry for the effect it all had on me. I guess you could say I was another casualty of that time. I forgave him of course and saw a huge weight lift off him. In truth we became great buddies."

He reached into his handbag and took out the postcard. It was framed in a decorative holder he had made. He looked at it seeking the comfort and reassurance necessary to continue.

     The Drowning of Innocence

"It was then he told me about Eileen. It was clear she was the love of his life, your Grandmother. He said that he had come to see her vision of freedom as the only one worthwhile and lived on conversations they had as young lovers and saw the picture she painted as a beacon of light and hope. He loved my mother, but there is no doubt that Eileen had been the greatest influence on his life."

"Oh that's so sweet. And the postcard shows that love was reciprocated."

"Indeed. But he was never able to come to terms with killing her brother. That was a wound that went deep. I think he felt that she would have forgiven him but of course he never met her again and so couldn't be sure."

"Oh, he talked to you about that?"

"Yes, with great difficulty. It was the thing that traumatised him. That and a battle he had been part of in West Cork. Where everything had turned barbaric."

"Bless him. The poor man. It's amazing that he retained his sense of humanity. I see beautiful qualities in the letter he sent to Seanair's Ma."

"Indeed. Of course, he also never knew they had a child together. I think, in hindsight, she did the correct thing not telling him, keeping it from him. It would have broken his heart completely knowing she had to give their daughter away because of this one, terrible act."

He placed the postcard in her hand.

"That's why this meant so much to me and why I am so grateful to you for following your instincts to find the owner and return it. It would have meant so much to him to receive it but also probably could have destabilised what he had built up in the meantime. Maybe it is meant for us, you and me. So we can lay all these things to rest now and begin afresh. For them. For everyone involved."

"Without doubt, Mikey. That's definitely what I feel. I know the both of them so well now. They live inside me. And I want to be faithful to their vision of us as a people. As a family, too. That's the thing I carry in my heart. Oh thank you so much for letting me hear what you and he have been through. It touches me deeply."

Slowly they lifted their eyes from the intensity of their conversation and found themselves once again looking at the river coursing below, its gentle smooth flow, comforting and exhilarating. Mikey was first to break the silence.

"Gosh this city is lovely. There is a wonderful spirit about the place. It feels alive and vibrant, yet at the same time, it's like a village. And so much beauty, the hills, the river, the buildings, the bridges. Some place to come home to."

"Indeed, I have thought about how much a wrench it must have been to your Dad to leave it and never return. The fate of so many."

"So is your quest over now, Alannah? Are you satisfied? Is this the end of the road?"

"In a way yes. I have discovered much more than I would have dreamed of when I started it all two years ago. So much more. And I have been blessed in knowing you and Seanair and all his family. It's truly wonderful. There's only the lack of knowledge of what happened to Grandma. I only have the postcard to tell me that she was still alive in 1949. But I have no idea how her life was before that, then or since. To find out about her would be like a dream. But I have to accept that it's unlikely and so am really grateful for all I've learnt. And thank you too for baring your soul to me. I found it so enriching."

"Not at all, dear. But you do see I am a different man now. Don't you? I am happy, content. All those ghosts are gone and I love my life."

"That's all we can wish for Mikey and I'm sure our parents would settle for that in us too."

"Indeed. But now, tell me about my sister. D'ya know I used to imagine I had an older sister when I was growing up. I never thought it was true. What was she like, your Ma?"

"One in a million, really. She was always herself. Growing up in a Protestant family in the new Ireland, I imagine was challenging. But she was a very sweet woman. She would say, 'if you don't have anything good to say about someone, say nothing at all.' She lived her life like that and I think it was so appreciated by everybody. But listen, I brought photos with me. I want to show them to you and I also want to go to Careys Lane with you. To see the original street. We can stop off at Fellini's, the tea house I told you about. I'll show you the photos and we can chat then. Are you up for that?"

"I'm your man, as they say in Cork." Mikey laughed as he tried out the sing-song accent.

     The Drowning of Innocence

They rose to leave then, a lightness in their step as they crossed the Shakey Bridge and made their way back to the city along Sundays Well road.

Waterford

20th May 2015

It was a cold day. The sun sneaking through the clouds brought little warmth. The occasional snow flurry, whisked to and fro in the wind, harked back to days of winter. This, despite the apple and cherry blossoms generating a hopeful, buoyant harbinger of days ahead. The blooms caught by the still-lateral light of the sun were resplendent and filled Alannah with confidence and determination. She was amused as she traipsed from door to door around the suburbs. Chuckling to herself, she recalled the brilliant advertisement on TV depicting a bright hopeful, determined young man travelling the cities and countryside of Ireland asking everyone for their permission to marry his beloved Sinéad. Brilliant she thought, underlying the reasonableness of the Marriage Equality referendum statement put before the nation; 'Marriage may be contracted in accordance with law by two persons without distinction as to their sex.'

It had galvanised her like nothing before. She had recognised it as an opportunity to fulfil an aspiration inherent in her grandparents' dream for the country. An equal place, where they could raise their children, a place of inclusion, without oppression. The words from Brother Paul's journal about her grandmother infused her every day with a quiet determination.

"I will never forget how Eileen looked out for me today. I was so broken over Terence's death (McSwiney). She held me in her arms and said such beautiful things to me. 'It's wrong,' she said, 'we never should have lost such a good man. And I worry about the future, all this violence. It won't achieve anything in the long run. That's why we need to be strong now. In our conviction. To get rid of hatred, division, rancour. And we are strong enough. My Da made sure of that. We will prevail. The meek will inherit the earth. I know this country will become a place where all of us will have our own place."

Bearing the mantle her Grandmother had passed on, Alannah had taken it upon herself to walk from door to door canvassing for a "Yes' vote, seeing it as a step to rid the country of the narrow, moralising, oppressive context of the past.

As she walked from door to door, her thoughts were occupied at how the country had changed and how she now had confidence to secure that change. In her early years she had often reflected at the darkness she felt coming from

   The Drowning of Innocence

closed doors. The government run by gombeens like Haughey, with their
secret deals, the uncertainty emanating from Artane and other institutions like
it, the fear and the unknown of the parish priest's house. All these things used
to disturb her, but had now evaporated. It had been a turbulent last few years
as the emerging state of the '30s, 40's and 50's had been exposed at how it had
treated its women and children. Where had been its watchmen? Where had
the fathers and brothers been hiding? At least now people were unlikely to
submit again to dominance and dogma. It had required a great deal of painful
soul searching. She knew not all had engaged in this reflection, but enough
had, to ring the bells of liberty.

She was also intrigued calling on each house. It had always amazed
Alannah how other people lived their lives, going about their humdrum,
mechanical routine, seemingly oblivious of the deeper meaning it beckoned. It
wasn't a judgement, just a mystery. How most seemed satisfied with their lot,
swinging between basic contentment and grumbles. What surprised her,
delighted her in fact, was the reception she was given as she walked from one
house to another. People of all shapes and sizes, old and young greeted her
warmly, innocently and with conviction.

"Sure, why wouldn't we. Its the right thing to do isn't it?"

She rarely had to dig deep to place her arguments in front of those she
encountered. On the days when she met the dissenters, she was respectful and
moved on.

On one occasion, the week before, a door had opened to reveal a man in his
late sixties. His kindly, soft face broke when he heard her request. "Will you
be voting yes on Thursday?" Tears began to well up in his eyes as he reached
forward to give her a hug.

"Oh my dear," he had said, "You bring joy to my heart. Come in, come in,
why don't you and have a cup of tea."

Inside, sitting at the coal fire, another man sat reading, the flames in the fire
reflecting his intent concentration. The introductions. Séamus and Aidan had
met in Dublin in 1966 and had been life partners since that moment. Living
quietly together, the tenderness they shared evident to her. It had confirmed to
her, even though she did not need it, the rightness of her commitment to
change.

This morning, she felt good. She had even been brave enough to call on the

Parish Priest and been surprised by his reaction. "It's the latest nail in the coffin of the old Catholic Ireland. We're all encouraged by Pope Francis and now is the time to include all our people and eliminate the authoritarianism that had brought continuity to our fear and servitude."

Now as she continued on her way, she felt a quiet confidence growing in her. In Newtown Park, she walked up the pathway of a sweet bungalow, its garden resplendent with spring flowers, their delicate colours fusing like an impressionist painting. Between the houses she could see the river Suir leaving the city behind, opening up its estuary to greet the Atlantic, with a huge sigh of relief, its journey over and work done at last.

She knocked on the bright red door and prepared herself to speak once again for a new Ireland.

The Drowning of Innocence

Méabh O'Connor was busy. With an energy that gave lie to her eighty eighth year, she was absorbed by her many projects. Her long living room, with its big picture window looking out on the river below, was replete with a cornucopia of colour, fabrics of all kinds, which were being stitched into delicate items of beauty. The wood-burning stove generating an atmosphere of quiet contentment.

She was developing a report of the recent Béaltaine festival. It was now the only festival for which she filed an artistic review for the Dungarvan Observer. She had kept her interest going in memory of Eileen. Together they had pioneered their own Béaltaine festival long before its adoption nationwide. For Eileen the festival had been a sweet memorial to her day with Micheál in Gougán Barra all those years before. Méabh had teased her as an incurable romantic. But now it had been a mission for Méabh herself, a moment to stop and recollect, to honour the beauty of their friendship, their long years together.

Deep in concentration, she almost missed the knock on her door.

"That'll be Mary," she thought, "Checking up on me."

Méabh was delighted to have such good neighbours. They had given her independence. Knowing they were always interested, vigilant even, she had relished the quiet, the reflective quality of her twilight years.

She moved towards the door.

Opening it, she was catapulted back thirty, forty years. There in front of her was a vision of Eileen. In a tumultuous flood of visual image and emotion, the pretty face before her, the high cheek bones and warm smile overwhelming her with a feeling of deja vu.

She was taken aback, speechless.

Alannah took in the frail woman in front of her and knew that something was wrong.

"Are you alright? she asked, fearful that in some way she had unnerved the woman. She guessed that in these days not many people knocked on her door and she was not ready for it.

Eventually Méabh gathered her senses.

"Sorry dear. It's such a shock seeing you, like I'm seeing a ghost. You are the spitting image of someone that I was very close to. My dear, dear friend, Eileen Barry."

Alannah was taken aback, bewildered, uncertain.

"You knew my grandmother?" she blurted out, unable to contain the surprise and stirring deep in her spirit.

"Mo Stóir, mo stóir," Méabh cried out the words and with an energy she did not know she possessed moved forward to embrace the woman in front of her with warmth and affection. She then stepped back and with tears welling in her eyes, said,

"My dear. She was my best friend. Come in, come in, please."

Alannah entered what seemed to her a sacred space, taking in, as she walked, the rich colour of the room with its vibrant materials and projects filling up the space with a sparkling, effervescent personality.

"We lived here together for many happy years."

They settled down in the warm, bright kitchen with a cup of tea. Alannah did not know where to start. The magical synchronicity of the event engulfing her thoughts and words.

Méabh led her in her recollections. Alannah peppering her eventually with questions, flowing our of her in a torrent. How had they met? What was she like? Did you know about Micheál? How had her life been?

All of her questions were answered as Méabh delved into the well of memories of her long-lost friend. There was wonder as she recounted their love story, their trysts in Gougán Barra, The terror of both wars, the tragedy of Mattie's death and Micheál's exile. She gazed in wonder as Méabh recounted the astonishing moment at the rapids near the mouth of Loughine.

Tears were shed, deep sobs emanating from both women, as Méabh recounted that fateful day in 1949 when she found her friend hanging from an apple tree in her garden. Méabh found it difficult to speak of that moment, the pain of which she had carried all her life.

"Oh, it was something she felt always. Her love and loss of her daughter. It was constantly with her through her life. She felt she had to carry it by herself. A lonely journey. She didn't think it would ever be right to seek out her

     The Drowning of Innocence

daughter and present herself as her birth mother. It would have been wrong.
It's what people thought then you know. But she would be thrilled to know
you turned up at my door out of the blue."

"What about Mattie's killing? How did she cope with that."

"Talking about that was always hard. She felt that Mattie was gone from
her long before that fateful day. The day her Da died was the day she lost her
brother. He was never the same after that. She felt terrible for Micheál but she
knew she could do nothing to change fate when it was assigned. Her one
regret about it all was that she could not hold Micheál and tell him it was OK,
that she understood. She knew he would suffer and carry it all his life."

They sat in silence for a long while, absorbing the memories that had been
recounted almost re-enacted before them.

"Tell me something, dear. I have a query for you. Do you have the stone?"

Alannah's face brightened. "You know about that?"

"Yes dear. Very precious to Eileen. She hoped it would be something that
would guarantee continual blessing on her family."

"Here it is." Alannah drew the stone from her bag.

Méabh was taken aback to see it, finally.

"You keep it with you all the time. How sweet. Oh Eileen would be
thrilled."

She then recounted the story of Eileen's dramatic rescue in Crosshaven and
how that day had always been enshrined as the happiest day of her childhood.
How she had found the stone. Its telling finally solving the mystery of its
origin for Alannah.

Later and with deep pride, she showed Alannah her grandmother's
painting. "'God's Grandeur' she named it after the Gerald Manley Hopkins
poem. It was a work to which she had devoted her lifetime. She was only
satisfied towards the end of her days with it."

Alannah gazed at her grandmother's painting for a long time, struck by the
earthy feel of it, the materials and colour she had used to capture hope in
adversity, spirit prevailing against the odds. She saw resonances with the

postcard she had found. Her eye could see the personality of the artist. The deep, sombre, earthy greens, effulgent, spirited mustards, bright orange-reds were present with the same extravagant exuberance, but in this painting complemented by ochre browns, rusty-red coppers and steely, muddy greys. The latter seem to symbolise the depth necessary to negotiate life, to plunder the fountain of hope and renewal. She was deeply, transcendently touched by it and wept in gratitude, recognition and awe at the opportunity life had afforded her to meet her grandmother and touch her compassionate soul and spirit.

They became firm friends. Méabh recounting the wonderful satisfaction and joy she had shared with Eileen as they worked together to curate art, to encourage and build up young artists. Alannah blessed that her grandmother had found such a true friend and shared such a full life.

They spent referendum day together, Alannah rejoicing with Méabh at her new status as a Gay Woman, her rights and position enshrined in the constitution.

It was for both of them a day of triumphant celebration.

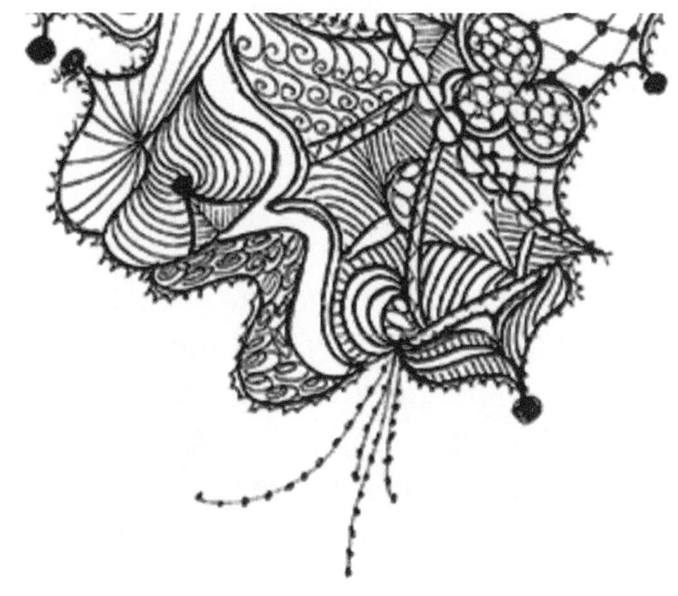

Pilgrimage

"Had I the heaven's embroidered cloths,
Enwrought with golden and silver light,
The blue and the dim and the dark cloths
Of night and light and the half-light;
I would spread the cloths under your feet:
But I, being poor, have only my dreams;
I have spread my dreams under your feet;
Tread softly because you tread on my dreams."

"The Cloths of Heaven" W. B. Yeats

"Yeats was the oddest, bravest, downright weirdest of revolutionaries – and he never killed a living soul. Yet it was his revolution that won in the end: the revolution of the Irish mind."
Bob Geldof, 2016

Rather than any false denial of the past, then, what can be achieved through ethical remembering is, I would suggest, a certain disposition, a way of relating to the past that does not serve to form exclusive judgments or reinforce grievances, but, rather, to embrace the stories, the memories and the pains of the other. I have described this particular disposition as "narrative hospitality", that is, an openness to the perspectives of the other carved out at the very heart of public commemorative discourse.
President Michael D. Higgins, 2016

As we reflect, in hindsight, on the contribution of the women of the Irish revolutionary movement, the irony of their subsequent marginalisation in the first five decades of our independence appears more starkly. Those restrictions placed on the participation of women in the public life of the state were all the more disappointing as the rights of women was a cause that a significant number of the women of 1916 had espoused with passion.
President Michael D. Higgins, 2016

Wild eyes, white hands, few words,
Not a female signature in sight, photos, names omitted,
Cumann na Mban an afterthought, Placenta to the male agenda.
Daughters of Ireland rise and be acknowledged for fighting with your minds, hands and hearts,
Rise and be acknowledged for modest multi-tasking, never seeking to bask in the limelight,
The twilight zone that is history
'Maude is Gone' by Julie Goo, 'Oestrogen Rising 2016

Guagán Barra National Park

Lá na Béaltaine, 1st May, 2016

The wind swept across the lake and the soft rain beat on her face as Alannah stood alone among the ruins of the old monastic settlement. The quietness struck her, the immensity of it, as the lake gently lapped at her feet. Men had come here centuries ago to contemplate life. In wild places, they sought to keep alive the integrity of belief. In a Europe then compromised by the "holy" Roman empire, monks and hermits sought peace and reflection at the edge of the known world and in so doing, saved civilisation. It was the perfect place to come and reflect on her grandparents and their contribution to the evolution of her people's identity. She gazed about her at the Spartan existence these pioneer monks had endured and understood that she, along with others, stood on the shoulders of giants.

The country had with some dignity been in the grip of memory this past month. Calling to mind the events that precipitated its birth, a full century previously. Ireland's 'Easter Rising'. For Alannah it had been enlightening. It helped to place the ever-growing appropriation of her family heritage in context. The ambiguities which erupted from the passionate idealism of the revolutionaries and the terrible violence and bloodshed acting as foundation stone for the country. The failures of the fledgling state to hold true to the idealism of that founding generation; Failures to its women and children, principally, the effects of which had dominated headlines in recent decades. The centenary both a time of reflection and repentance.

The wet day meant she had the place to herself. Perfect. She moved from the small monastic island to the great expanse of the national park. Its vista, however, very different from memory of her last visit years before. Bare now, stripped of thousands of trees which had given the hills and valley a lush texture on the previous occasion. Disease had struck in the meantime and much of the forest was lost. She couldn't help reflect on the symbolism; The cutting to the ground of those old trees lest their toxins spread and decimate everything. The planting of new growth. She saw it as a profound metaphor. The country itself needing to eliminate, to extirpate from its core, the violence of its origin which had blighted its growth for decades. To start again.

On the lower reaches near the lake, the park was luxuriant with spring growth. Up ahead, Alannah saw what she was searching for. A small pathway led away to the right, towards the lake. This was it. She was sure of it. Following Méabh's guidance and recollection, she knew this was Micheál's

     The Drowning of Innocence

pathway to his secret spot. Despite the rain and cold, she felt compelled to take off her shoes and feel the grass and moss beneath her feet. She was on holy ground.

As she walked the pathway of her grandparents, a raw excitement overtook her. This very ground the place of their tryst. The air felt still and pure. The birds were in the full voice of spring mating. After a few minutes, she came to a clearing, a mossy bank enshrining an impressive tree. It seemed like an old friend. Their tree. The branches reached down to greet her, beckoning her to climb.

"No, this is crazy," she thought, "how long is it since I climbed a tree. If I fall and hurt myself, I will be murdered by everyone for taking such a stupid, menopausal risk."

But the tree was insistent in its shape and beckoning. Micheál's retreat.

Eventually with beating heart, she could not spurn the invitation. She put on her shoes again and began to climb. It was exhilarating. Each moment, erupting with a soulful presence, she found her way easily to the top and emerged through its crown. She gazed out over the landscape and could see that, although unruly now, this gentle giant could at one time have provided the flat bed recalled by Méabh from Eileen's stories. She began to well up with tears of gratitude. She took in the vast sky with its dramatic cloud shapes, the hills and the lake and entered the magic of those first moments the lovers had spent together.

Eventually, the foolhardiness of her action invaded her consciousness and she made her way back down to Terra firma again, the coming down so much more precarious as she stepped gingerly from each branch to the one below. It was with a great sigh of relief that she reached the ground.

At that point she became overwhelmed. This was the spot where her grandparents had stood. Then it had been their present moment. In the same way as now was the present moment for her. It touched her deeply, the passing of time. The nowness of now ever changing. In some distant future, she will also be a memory, to Ezra and all who follow, her reality subsumed by future 'present moments'. The thought brought her in close proximity to her grandparents. She could almost hear their dialogue as they spoke about their hopes and aspirations. "Have we disappointed, those of us who followed." She reflected. *Tread softly because you tread on my dreams*" that glorious Yeats' line illuminating the moment for her. She hoped she had been gentle in her foot fall.

She spread her raincoat at the foot of the tree and sat to absorb the feelings, intimations which were overwhelming her. Out of the corner of her eye she saw it. There, hidden from sight. Micheál's water duct. She moved towards it and could see that it was redundant now. The spring it had carried dried up. The duct itself, however, was covered delicately, exquisitely by moss and lichen, delicate lines traced over its structure. Beneath Alannah could just make out Micheál's carvings, etched in the seasoned wood. It was a sacred hidden monument to him and Eileen. She gazed at it for a long while and saw the tracings of fungal growth. The fine, filigreed interweaving of lichen, vine and moss. They appeared as a metaphor for the changes that had occurred since Micheál had first placed it there. A century of laid-down lives and history. Providing a natural tapestry of his family. Rosaleen, her mother; Mikey; Alannah herself and now Ezra. The thought filled her with joy and hope.

She reached into her bag and drew out her stone. Here in this place the thing that connected her with her mother and grandmother. A profound peace subsumed her and as if on cue, the sun burst through the clouds on the other side of the lake, throwing out pearls of light over the water which, behind her, nestling in the hills, refracted through tiny droplets of a shower into the most picture perfect rainbow, mirroring the colours and contours of her stone.

She had completed her quest. She let out a deep sigh of contentment. She could rest now.

    The Drowning of Innocence

Acknowledgements

This story evolved as I took an online course run by Trinity College on the Irish war of independence. In an enjoyable way, the characters became real, directed me and have overtaken my life for the past two years.

The main inspiration for the story is to communicate to my grandson, Ezra (who, at the grand old age of two, became a naturalised Irish citizen), what being Irish means. I hope I have put him in touch with his heritage.

The story took me into the times of my father and mother and years after their death, I was able to ask them questions about what life was like then. I fell in love with them and their native city once again.

I needed help. My brother, Tony was always there to pass on encouragement and advice and to challenge me where necessary. It became his project too. Sue Kohler was an enthusiastic reader and helped immensely in providing texture to the story. I love the way her doodles lighten the page.

Emily Catherine created beautiful and original art work for the cover and postcard. What a great artist she is. Along the way she gave vital encouragement.

I hope you, the reader, enjoyed the story. I would love to know what you think. You can email me at padraigogorman@gmail.com

Padraig O'Gorman
Clonakilty 2024

www.ingramcontent.com/pod-product-compliance
Lightning Source LLC
Chambersburg PA
CBHW032002050726
47590CB00006B/2013